95

CITY IN SHADOW

A Hidden Manhattan Mystery

A frightened woman leaves a note reading 'HELP ME' outside Sanitation supervisor Anna Winthrop's apartment. A career-making story leads a journalist to a human-trafficking ring. A woman acts as bait in an effort to track down her missing sister, and Anna's visiting cousin Patti prowls New York's dark streets, but won't say why. All roads lead to the Kirkmore, a sinister apartment tower harboring a secret more horrifying than anyone could ever have imagined...

CITY IN SHADOW

A Hidden Manhattan Mystery

Evan Marshall

Severn House Large Print
London & New York

This first large print edition published 2011
in Great Britain and the USA by
SEVERN HOUSE PUBLISHERS LTD of
9-15 High Street, Sutton, Surrey, SM1 1DF.
First world regular print edition published 2010 by
Severn House Publishers Ltd., London and New York.

British Library Cataloguing in Publication Data

Marshall, Evan, 1956-
    City in shadow. -- (The hidden Manhattan mysteries)
    1. Winthrop, Anna (Fictitious character)--Fiction.
    2. Sanitation workers--New York (State)--New York--
    Fiction. 3. Human trafficking victims--Fiction.
    4. Detective and mystery stories. 5. Large type books.
    I. Title II. Series
    813.6-dc22

ISBN-13: 978-0-7278-7972-1

Severn House Publishers support The Forest Stewardship Council
[FSC], the leading international forest certification organisation. All
our titles that are printed on Greenpeace-approved FSC-certified paper
carry the FSC logo.

Printed and bound in Great Britain by the
MPG Books Group, Bodmin, Cornwall.

*To Lennie Alickman and
Lisa Gates with love.*

ACKNOWLEDGMENTS

My thanks, as always, to my wife, Martha Jewett, and our sons, Justin and Warren, for their loving support. A thank you also to my dear friends, especially Belinda Plutz for very thoughtfully supplying me with a steady stream of hidden-Manhattan clippings.

I am grateful to my agent, Maureen Walters at Curtis Brown, and to Edwin Buckhalter, Amanda Stewart, Rachel Simpson Hutchens, Piers Tilbury and the rest of the staff at Severn House. I am extremely fortunate to work with such talented and dedicated people.

ONE

Anna Winthrop arranged throw pillows on the twin bed, then stepped back to admire her handiwork. The touches of cocoa and pale green were a perfect complement to the freshly painted cream-colored walls. She looked around the room, taking in the lamp on the nightstand, her grandmother's crocheted lace runner on the dresser, the area rug in rich earth tones. A very pleasing guest room, she decided. The only reminder that this space had previously served as her home office was the oak roll-top desk in the corner. With any luck, that would be gone within the hour if the man coming in response to her Craigslist ad decided to buy. She was fond of the old desk – it had once belonged to her father – but her cousin Patti needed a guest room more than Anna needed the desk.

Patti Fairchild was actually Anna's second cousin: Anna's mother and Patti's mother, Mary Jean, were first cousins. Three weeks earlier, Mary Jean had called Anna from Cincinnati and asked if Patti could come for a visit. She had graduated from high school seven months earlier, wasn't interested in college yet had no idea what she wanted to do with her life. In New York Mary Jean thought Patti might get some ideas. Mary Jean also felt Anna would be a good role model for Patti, who would spend some time with Anna at the sanitation garage where she was a supervisor. Long interested in art, Patti could also visit museums and maybe even take a class. She would arrive in two days and stay for a month.

Gazing at the nightstand, Anna remembered a spare alarm clock she'd put away somewhere and went to look for it.

In the apartment directly above Anna's, Nettie Clouchet tackled another box. She'd forgotten how much work it was to move. She'd also forgotten how much stuff she had. Two months earlier, when she'd left Eddie and moved into the Webster Apartments, a women's residence, she had put her things into storage. Now, a week after retrieving them, she was still unpacking.

Of course, she'd been doing other things as well, mainly grinding out the articles she produced for dozens of bloggers on the Web. Not that anyone would ever know Nettie wrote them. She was a ghost blogger, by her calculation the most prolific ghost blogger on the Internet. No matter what the subject, if someone needed a blog, Nettie Clouchet could deliver quality work fast.

Thinking about her blogs made her step over to her laptop, open on the dining table. She'd been working on a piece called *The $2,000-a-Month One-Bedroom New York Apartment: Fact or Fantasy?* So far she'd written:

Contrary to popular belief, it is possible to find that elusive $2,000-a-month one-bedroom apartment in New York City, but you'll need to look in neighborhoods like Harlem, Washington Heights and Morningside Heights, in non-doorman buildings. If you've got your heart set on more desirable areas such as the East Village, the Lower East Side and neighborhoods north of Midtown, $2,000 a month will only get you a studio.

Dull but serviceable. These pieces paid the bills and Nettie was grateful for that, but once her book deal came through she would never write another blog as long as she lived. She closed the file she'd been working on and opened the book proposal being shopped to publishers by her literary agent, Jane Stuart. *New York SuperWomen: Fifty Fabulous Females Who Have Made a Difference.*

She scrolled down. *Chapter One: Anna Winthrop – From Deb to Debris.* Nettie smiled. She'd been very clever to come up with that, she decided. Even cleverer to nab this apartment when Uncle Allen mentioned it was available. What better way to learn about Anna than to live right above her? Not that Anna could know yet that Nettie was delving into her life. Over the course of her career Nettie had formed the firm opinion that you learned more about people when they didn't know you were writing about them.

Nettie wanted to know everything about Anna Winthrop. She already knew a lot. For example, that Anna was a debutante from a wealthy Greenwich family who had broken with tradition and become not a lawyer or a doctor but a sanitation worker, then worked her way up to section supervisor in a garage off Times Square. That Anna had a talent for solving murders. That she had once killed a murderer in self-defense.

But Nettie needed to know more, a lot more. She was sure there was a lot more to know. Ever since Uncle Allen had first talked about Anna, well before Nettie had had the idea for *New York SuperWomen*, she had considered Anna one of the most interesting women in New York City.

Nettie continued scrolling through her book proposal, smiling at her own talent. Yes, this book would make her wealthy, and when she was wealthy she wouldn't have to hide from Eddie in this third-floor walkup apartment near Times Square. She could live where she liked, hire security like movie stars and Wall Street executives.

12

In the meantime, her ghost blogs were all she had, a grim necessity. She reopened the apartment article and wrote:

Of course, you'll find many more apartments within your reach if you opt to take on a roommate, a strategy favored by many new and not-so-new New York City renters...

Directly under Nettie, Anna heard her intercom buzz and hurried out to the living room. 'Yes?' she called down.

'I am here about the desk,' came a man's deep voice, heavily accented – Russian, it sounded like. She let him in, then went out to the landing as he came into view on the stairs. He was tall and gangling, with dark curly hair and extreme features that were ugly yet attractive. He wore a brown leather jacket over jeans and a hooded black sweatshirt. He looked at her, his face expressionless.

'Anna Winthrop,' she said, putting out her hand.

'Grigori,' he said, taking it.

'Russian?' she asked pleasantly.

'Ukrainian.'

'Ah,' she said, smiling, and led him to the new guest room. He studied the desk for a moment, moved the roll-top up and down. Then he gave one nod. 'She will like it,' he said and counted out two hundred dollars into Anna's hand.

She thanked him. 'Did you bring someone to help you get it out of here?'

'Of course.' He took out his cell phone, punched in a number and muttered something in Ukrainian.

A moment later the intercom sounded. Anna went to the living room. 'Yes?' she called down.

'Desk,' came a man's voice.

She buzzed him in, then waited in the doorway as he mounted the stairs. He was Grigori's exact opposite: short and fat, with thinning blond hair cut very short, smooth pink skin and angelic features. 'I am Yuri,' he said.

She introduced herself, then led him back to Grigori and the desk. The two men spoke briefly in Ukrainian, then picked up the desk and carried it out to the living room. Anna opened the door for them and stood out on the landing to one side. Yuri went first through the doorway, backing out. As Grigori squeezed through he suddenly cried out in pain. He quickly lowered his end of the desk and shook his hand. *'Durnyj!'* he barked at Yuri, who mumbled what sounded like an apology.

'Are you all right?' Anna asked Grigori.

'I am fine,' he replied, then turned back to Yuri and said something else to him in a heated tone. Then they began carrying the desk down the stairs.

* * *

14

Nettie looked up sharply from her laptop, brows lowered. From the hallway outside her apartment had come the sound of a man's voice speaking – could it be? – Ukrainian. Specifically, the word *durnyj* – 'stupid.' Eddie was Ukrainian and during the two years she had lived with him her Ukrainian had become quite serviceable. Curious, she hurried out to the landing and peered over the railing to the floor below, careful not to be seen.

Two men, one tall and thin, the other short and fat, were carrying a roll-top desk through the doorway of Anna's apartment.

'Are you all right?' came Anna's voice, surprisingly close – she must be on the landing.

'I am fine,' the tall man replied, then spoke angrily in Ukrainian to the short man. Nettie understood it immediately: *Hurry up! If she gets away I'll kill you.*

Wide-eyed she watched the two men start down the stairs.

Another opinion Nettie had formed over the course of her writing career was that she produced her best work when she followed her instincts. Those instincts were now telling her a man who threatened to kill another man was worth following, especially if he was connected to Anna Winthrop, the subject of chapter one.

Without another thought Nettie ran back into her apartment, threw on her coat, grabbed her keys and dashed back out, locking the door. The men were still on the stairs, negotiating the turn at the bottom. She would wait until they were outside to make her move. As she watched, Anna came into view below, peering over the railing to watch the men's progress with the desk.

As Anna watched Grigori and Yuri near the bottom of the stairs, the front door opened and her boyfriend Santos entered. He looked handsome in his police uniform, dark jacket and glossy-brimmed cap. His face was red from the cold. Looking up he saw Anna and gave her a big grin. He stood aside to let Grigori and Yuri carry the desk out to the sidewalk.

Anna ran down the stairs and gave Santos a kiss.

'Way to go,' he said. 'Finally getting rid of that old thing.'

They followed Grigori and Yuri out to the street and watched them lift the desk on to an olive-green pickup truck parked at the curb. Anna crossed her arms against the bitter cold. Gusts of wind played with her shoulder-length ash-blond hair. Santos put his arm around her and pulled her close against him.

Once the desk was on the truck, Grigori and Yuri got in. As Yuri opened the passenger door Anna caught a glimpse of a young woman sitting on the front seat. She was extraordinarily beautiful, with creamy skin and full, sensuous features. Rich chestnut hair cascaded to her shoulders.

As the truck's engine roared to life the brownstone's door opened and a woman hurried out. Anna guessed her to be in her mid-thirties. A voluminous black coat flapped open on her bony frame. Her brown hair was tied into a pineapple-like spray on top of her head. She dashed past Anna and Santos and grabbed a passing cab. The pickup truck pulled into traffic and the taxi followed.

'Who was that?' Santos asked.

'She may be my new upstairs neighbor. Moved in last week.'

'Whoever she is, she sure is in a hurry.'

As Anna turned to go inside, something in the gutter where the truck had been parked caught her eye. She walked over and picked it up. It was a sheet of yellow lined paper, folded in quarters.

'Someone dropped that out of the truck as I was walking up to the building,' Santos said with a laugh. 'I should have ticketed them for littering.'

As they headed back inside, Anna stopped in the open doorway and unfolded the paper. In its center, printed in crude block letters, were two words:

HELP ME

She looked up at Santos. 'You're sure you saw this fall out of the truck?'

'Absolutely.'

'It was that young woman in the truck who dropped it out,' Anna said, meeting Santos's

17

gaze.

'Shut that door!'

They spun around. Iris Dovner, who lived directly below Anna and with whom Anna was in nearly constant conflict, stood in her doorway with her hands on her hips. She wore an over-large purple velour track suit that made her look like a clown. Her fluffy white hair was pulled back in an incongruously youthful ponytail.

'I guess since you live upstairs you don't care about the cold air that blows in here like the Arctic.'

'We're sorry,' Anna said, shutting the door. She and Santos started up the stairs.

'Letting questionable people into the building again, I see,' Mrs Dovner called up after them. 'Criminals, from the look of them.'

Anna stopped, turned. 'I hardly think you can know that just by looking at them.'

'I did more than just look at them. I saw how they treated that girl.'

Anna met Santos's gaze.

'The girl in the pickup truck?' Anna asked as she and Santos came back down the stairs. Mrs Dovner nodded. 'How did they treat her?'

'When the tall one got out of the truck she reached out to him, like she was pleading with him. He shoved her back and slammed the door. Then the fat one got out and the girl did the same thing. He took her face in his hand and said something to her in Ukrainian before he

18

shut the door. I know Ukrainian because my parents were from there,' she explained.

'How were you able to see and hear all this?' Anna asked.

'I was coming back from shopping when the truck pulled up. I was suspicious so I watched from a couple of yards away. Once you'd let them both in, I came in, too.'

'I wish I'd taken down their license plate number,' Anna said, 'but why would I have?'

'I took it down,' Mrs Dovner said easily. 'I always do when I see a suspicious car.'

'May we have it, please?' Santos asked.

Mrs Dovner narrowed her eyes. 'Why?'

Anna handed her the paper. Mrs Dovner glanced down at it and her white brows rose. She looked up, eyes wide. Then she disappeared into her apartment and returned a moment later with a slip of paper which she handed to Santos.

'I told you those two were bad news,' Mrs Dovner said and turned to Anna. 'And you let them into the building. With a neighbor like you it's a wonder we're all still alive.'

Her door slammed.

Santos held up the slip Mrs Dovner had given him. 'I'll see what I can find out,' he said, gave Anna a kiss and hurried out.

Nettie tapped on the Plexiglas separating her from the cab driver. 'Go faster. You'll lose them.'

The driver shook his head but sped up slightly.

It had been a surprise to see Anna standing outside on the sidewalk. The handsome dark-haired cop with his arm around her must be her boyfriend. Later Nettie would knock on Anna's door and introduce herself, apologize for rushing by without a word, make up some excuse, stay on her good side.

A vacant cab had been passing and Nettie had grabbed it. 'See that green pickup truck?' she said to the driver as she hopped in and slammed the door. 'Follow it.'

'Lady, this ain't a movie.'

'It's leaving. Go!'

Now, as the pickup reached the end of the block and turned north on Tenth Avenue, she leaned forward excitedly, at the same time finding her cell phone and calling Jane Stuart's office.

'Stuart and Willoughby,' came the voice of Adena, assistant to Jane and her partner, Daniel Willoughby.

'It's Nettie Clouchet. Is Jane there?'

'Let me check.'

After a moment Jane's strong voice came on the line. 'No news.'

'That's some greeting,' Nettie said with a laugh.

'You called five times last week to see if we'd gotten an offer. It seemed pretty likely that was why you were calling this time.'

'Well I'm not,' Nettie said, 'though what I have to tell you may help you get an offer.'

'Go on.'

'Two Ukrainian men just came out of Anna Winthrop's apartment and one of them threatened to kill the other.'

'Really?'

'Really. To be exact, he said – in Ukrainian – "If she gets away I'll kill you."'

'If who gets away?'

'I think a young woman in their pickup truck. I'm trying to find out who these people are.'

'How?'

'I'm in a cab following them. Stay tuned.' Nettie snapped her phone shut.

The pickup had gone only a block up Tenth Avenue before turning east on West 44th Street. Then it had gone seven blocks, turned south on Park Avenue, gone two blocks and turned west on 42nd Street. The cab followed the truck across Madison and Fifth avenues, at which point the truck pulled up in front of a Crazy Ice Cream shop.

'They're getting ice cream?' the driver said.

Nettie ignored him. The two men got out of the truck. While the tall one came around, the short one reached into the truck and helped the young woman out.

'Holy...' The driver let out a low whistle. 'She's gorgeous.'

The two men each took one of the young woman's arms and escorted her not to the ice cream parlor but to a plain glass door next to it. Above the door hung a brown awning. Nettie couldn't tell what this door led to. Maybe an apartment building.

She shoved some bills through the money tray and got out. The two men and the young woman were in front of the glass door, where a uniformed doorman let them in.

Nettie decided to use a technique that often worked for her. Affecting a nonchalant air, she walked briskly toward the glass door, as if she had every right in the world to go through it.

It didn't work.

The doorman's arm shot out, barring the way. 'May I help you?'

'I'm visiting someone here.' She was careful not to say *someone who lives here*, since she didn't know if this was an apartment building.

'The name, please?' the doorman asked.

'Those three people who just went in.'

He frowned skeptically. 'And their names?'

'Look, are you going to let me in, or do I have to make trouble?'

'You're going to have to make trouble, because I'm not going to let you in.'

She decided to try another technique that often worked: outright bluntness.

'What is this building?' she asked.

'It's private.'

'I know it's private, but what is it?'

He made no reply, simply glared at her.

She turned and walked away, wondering how she could get in.

Dressed in her favorite sweats and slippers, Anna carried her tea to the sofa, where she covered herself with an afghan and picked up a mystery she'd just bought. As she opened it there was a knock on her door.

Through the peep hole she saw the woman who had hurried out of the building and past her and Santos to grab a cab. She opened the door.

'Hi.' The woman's smile was warm. 'I'm Nettie Clouchet.' She pronounced it *clue-shay.* 'I'm your new upstairs neighbor.'

Anna returned her smile and put out her hand. 'Very nice to meet you. Please, come in.'

Nettie saw the tea, afghan and open book. 'I'm sorry, you were relaxing.'

'I can do that anytime,' Anna said graciously. 'Where are my manners? I'm Anna Winthrop.'

'I know. By the way, I'm sorry I rushed past you before without saying anything. I was late for an appointment.'

'No problem. Please, sit. Can I get you some tea?'

'No, thanks. I just wanted to introduce myself.'

Anna sat down beside her on the sofa. 'I think it's important to know your neighbors in a place like New York.'

'Actually, I knew about you before I moved here. Thanks to Uncle Allen.'

'Uncle Allen?'

'Allen Schiff, your district supervisor. He's my late mother's brother. He happened to mention the apartment above you was vacant, I needed a place, so here I am.'

'Small world. Allen's a great guy.'

'He says the same about you. Not that you're a guy, of course.' Nettie laughed. 'He says it's remarkable how you've worked your way up from sanitation worker to section supervisor, especially with your, um, background.'

Anna smiled politely. It was something she would never escape. Years earlier her father, Jeffrey Winthrop, had helped found Winthrop & Carnes Medical Products, which he and his partner later sold to Johnson & Johnson. For some time now Jeff Winthrop had been a billionaire.

'I'm sorry,' Nettie said, 'I've made you uncomfortable. I have such a big mouth. Anyway, I think you're terrific and it's an honor to be your neighbor.'

Anna smiled. 'And it's an honor to be yours. So tell me, what is it *you* do?'

'I'm a ghost blogger,' Nettie answered simply.

'I ... don't understand.'

Nettie laughed. 'I write blogs for other people under their names. Women's blogs, men's blogs, cooking blogs, TV blogs, movie blogs, gossip blogs, medical blogs, fitness blogs, celebrity blogs, you name it. From what I can tell, I'm the Internet's most prolific ghost blogger.'

Anna shook her head in wonder. 'I can't wait to tell my friends.'

'Don't do that.'

Anna blinked in surprise.

'What I mean is, don't tell anyone I'm living here.'

'Why not?'

Nettie lowered her voice to a near-whisper. 'The reason I moved was to get away from my ex-boyfriend, Eddie.'

'I see. Was he ... abusive?'

'That's putting it mildly. He wants to kill me.'

'Kill you!'

Nettie nodded. 'I came home late from a meeting with a man I blog for and Eddie accused me of having an affair. I got out of there fast.'

'Why didn't you have him arrested?'

'I couldn't call the cops. Eddie *is* a cop.'

'So?'

'You know what they say about cops protecting one another? The thin blue line? It's true. And Eddie's not just a cop; he's got connections to some very-high-ups in this city. The first and only time I filed a complaint it was made clear to me that it wouldn't do me any good. In fact, it would do me harm.'

'But that's outrageous! You need to complain elsewhere. There are agencies—'

'Don't you think I know all that?' Nettie

interrupted. 'I've blogged about it. The truth is I should have left this city a long time ago, but I can't. New York is my livelihood, it's in my blood. I live it and I write about it. It's what makes me so good at what I do. If I leave, I'm dead. Not literally, of course.'

'Sounds more like if you stay, you're dead. Literally.'

'Not if Eddie doesn't know where I am. And he's not going to find out, because people like you and Uncle Allen are going to keep my secret.'

'What if you happen to run into Eddie on the street?'

'He still wouldn't know where I live, unless he followed me, which I wouldn't let happen.' Nettie wiggled her shoulders as if to shake off the subject. 'So, how do you like living in this building?'

'Mostly it's fine. Mrs Dovner is always a challenge.'

'Yeah, I figured that when I met her. The constant complainer.' Nettie let her gaze travel around the room. 'The apartments are a good size, don't you think?'

Anna nodded. 'That was one of the things that attracted me to this building in the first place.'

'Though an apartment still never seems big enough, you know? For instance, I saw you getting rid of that desk this afternoon...'

Anna nodded. 'I'm turning my office into a guest room. My cousin Patti is coming for a

26

visit in two days. I hope you'll let me introduce you. I'm sure she'd find your work interesting.'

'Of course, as long as she keeps my secret,' Nettie said with a smile. 'Give me a call.' She found a scrap of paper in her purse, jotted down her number and handed it to Anna. Then she stood. 'Now I'll let you get back to that book.'

Anna walked her to the door. 'Getting to know you is far more important. Welcome to the neighborhood.'

TWO

Anna's apartment was on West 43rd Street between Ninth and Tenth avenues. The New York Sanitation Department's Manhattan Central District 13 garage was also on West 43rd but a block east, between Seventh and Eighth avenues, so Anna almost always walked to work. Early Tuesday morning she walked with her hands shoved deep in her coat pockets, her scarf wrapped snugly around her neck. The sun was bright but the wind was bitterly cold, making her eyes water. She passed a fenced-in elementary school playground and then came to the garage, a nondescript two-story building of tan brick.

She passed through the garage's chain-link gate into the cavernous building. Ahead of her, against the far opposite wall, stood some of the 150 vehicles and pieces of equipment parked or stored here.

Directly to her right was a door to stairs leading up to the break room, locker rooms and showers. Beyond this door was the beginning of a corridor formed by widely spaced cinder-block columns. It was on the right side of this corridor that the garage's offices were located, their large rectangular Plexiglas windows darkened by closed venetian blinds. Anna's office was at the end. She unlocked her door and flicked on the light. In the sudden garish fluorescence she looked around the tiny room and smiled. It was shabby but it was her space, her job she'd attained through her own efforts, and she was proud of it.

As one of the garage's three supervisors, Anna oversaw her section's garbage and recycling collection, street sweeping and snow removal. She had the use of a Department car but the garage was her center of operations.

She loved her job – the amazing variety of people she dealt with ... the ever-changing demands, from trash to recycling collection, from snow removal to cleaning up Times Square after New Year's Eve ... and simply the challenge of getting it all done, day after day, in a city that never stopped demanding.

She hung her coat and hat on the back of her door, placed her handbag in a bottom drawer of her desk, fired up her computer and got to work on a report she'd begun the previous day detailing complaints from the public.

The relationship between the garage and its neighbors was always tenuous. Complaints were constant and involved everything from loud radio playing inside the garage to noisy trucks, improperly parked trucks trapping residents' vehicles and trucks blocking the entrance to the school next door. Once the garage had had a rat infestation, which of course had spread to neighboring buildings. The Department had never heard the end of that.

Allen Schiff passed Anna's doorway and she called to him. He leaned in.

'I met your niece Nettie yesterday,' she said.

A dark cloud seemed to pass across his face. 'She told me she was looking for a new apartment and before I knew it I'd mentioned the one above you was available. I'm sorry.'

'There's nothing to be sorry about. She's delightful.'

'I'm not sure that's a word I would use to describe Annette.'

'What word *would* you use?' she asked, but he was already on his way again, tapping a quick good-bye on her door.

Half an hour later Santos called. 'I looked up that license plate. It's registered to a Grigori Sidorov in Brooklyn. Brighton Sixth Street, to be exact.'

'That's Brighton Beach.'

'Right. A-k-a Little Odessa.'

'Maybe Russian mafia?'

'If he is, that young woman in his truck could have good reason to want help. These people make the Italian mafia look like the Rotary Club. I'm going to Grigori's house to check him out.'

'I'm going with you.'

He laughed. 'Since when is the Sanitation

Department part of the New York Police Department?'

'This isn't funny, Santos. That woman could be in real trouble.'

'I'll be serious, then. You're not coming with me.'

'Let's not play this game. You know how it always ends.'

'True,' he said, resignation in his voice. 'I'll pick you up when you finish at two.'

Irena Lebedev hurried along Kreshchatyk, Kiev's main street, dodging people who talked and laughed. When would she laugh again? she wondered. Maybe never.

She entered the massive Central Department Store, whose ground floor was decorated with oversize blue and silver snowflakes for Christmas. The escalator took her to women's fashions, where an older woman in a tight turtleneck sweater asked if she needed help.

'Yes, please. I am looking for something dressy.'

The saleswoman nodded and went to a rack displaying beautiful watered silk jackets in jewel colors. 'Something like this, perhaps?'

'Dressier,' Irena said.

The saleswoman thought a moment and then crossed to a display of low-cut tops covered in ice-blue sequins. 'Too revealing perhaps?' she ventured.

'No, it is just right.'

Irena tried one on and looked at herself appraisingly in the mirror. Yes, this would do.

'It fits you perfectly,' the saleswoman said. 'If you'll forgive my saying so, you have a perfect figure.'

'Thank you,' said Irena, who not only knew she had a perfect figure but was also banking on it.

At the register the saleswoman discreetly showed Irena the price tag, just to make sure. It was a lot but Irena had expected that. In her purse was the money she had been able to save from her secretarial job at the real estate office. It just covered the price of the top. Irena nodded that the price was fine.

She left the store by a different door and passed a Salvation Army Santa Claus ringing a bell beside a large red pot full of coins. She ignored him but he wished her a merry Christmas anyway.

She wondered where she would be when Christmas came.

'May I help the next person in line, please?' said the acne-faced young man behind the ice cream counter at Crazy Ice Cream on 42nd Street. His name tag said Conan.

Nettie stepped up.

'What can I get you?' Conan asked her.

Nettie felt she needed to buy something – she couldn't very well expect these people to help her if she didn't – though she had no intention of eating anything. She rarely ate because the thought of food almost always made her feel queasy. When she did eat it was nearly always a Charleston Chew candy bar or a Suzy Q cream-filled chocolate cake, her favorites.

She scanned the menu for something expensive. 'Give me a ChocoNut Lunacy.'

'What size? Enjoy It, Want It, or Need It Bad?'

'Need It Bad.' She felt silly but it was the most expensive size at $4.59. She watched as Conan slapped a blob of coffee ice cream on to a granite slab, then used metal spatulas to mix in peanut butter, fudge and roasted almonds. She had to look away.

'Here you are.' Conan slid the dripping mess toward her. 'Please step over to the register.'

She moved down, gingerly carrying her ChocoNut Lunacy, careful not to look at it. She got ice cream on the base of her thumb and had to put down the dish in order to grab some napkins. The cashier, a young woman with red pig tails whose name tag said Sondra, smiled at Nettie as she rang up the Lunacy.

Nettie smiled back. 'Tell me,' she said, digging in her handbag, intentionally drawing out the search for her wallet. 'That building next door. What is it?'

'The gift shop?'

'No, on the other side.'

'I don't know.'

'Any way you could find out?'

'Excuse me,' came a man's voice to Nettie's right. He was the next person in line, a middle-aged man in a ski parka carrying an ice cream creation even more disgusting-looking than hers.

'Yes?' she replied patiently.

'We're all waiting to pay here. Can you please hurry up?'

'No, I can't,' she told him simply.

The man shook his head. 'Crazy New Yorkers.'

'You don't like it, go back to Idaho.'

'We do need to move the line along,' Sondra said.

'Of course.' Nettie fished some more in her bag. 'I really need to find out what that building is.' She brought out a twenty-dollar bill. 'This is all yours if you can find out for me.'

A young man in a purple Crazy Ice Cream polo shirt came over. His name tag said Arnold, Manager. 'Is there a problem?'

'Not at all,' Nettie replied brightly. 'I'm just paying for my ice cream.'

'More like trying to bribe the cashier,' said the man Nettie was sure must be from Idaho.

'Bribe?' Arnold turned to Sondra, who shrugged helplessly and widened her eyes in an expression Nettie knew meant Sondra thought Nettie was crazy.

'Here you are,' Nettie said, handing Sondra the twenty. She took her change and left the line with her ChocoNut Lunacy, which she dropped into the nearest trash receptacle.

'All that and you're not even going to eat it?' the Idaho man said.

Nettie spun on him. 'Listen, potato boy, why don't you mind your own business?'

'Ma'am. Ma'am.' It was Arnold, speaking softly. 'Is there a problem?'

Was that all he knew how to say? Nettie lowered her voice to match his. 'No. I was simply asking your cashier about the building next door.' She reached into her handbag and this time came up with a whole wad of bills which she moved enticingly. 'I'm a reporter, you see.'

Arnold did see. 'Why don't you come with me? I'll see what I can do.'

He led the way to a tiny office in back and closed the door. 'My fiancée works as a maid there.'

'What is it, exactly?'

'How bad do you want to know?' Arnold asked, gaze fixed on the wad of cash.

'Fifty.'

'A hundred and I'll get her to come over and talk to you. She's working there now.'

'Deal.'

Nettie counted out a hundred and handed it to him. He stuffed it into his pocket, then grabbed the phone and punched out a number. After a moment he said, 'Can you come over here for a few minutes? ... I know you're busy. It's just for a minute ... I'll explain when you get here ...

Yes, now.' He hung up and turned back to Nettie. 'It's called the Kirkmore. It's a residence club.'

'What's that?'

'People pay a membership fee to use an apartment for a certain amount of time. Like a time share. It's very expensive. Exclusive, you know?'

Nettie nodded. They stood silently for a couple of minutes, waiting. Then the office door opened and a young blond woman in a pale-blue maid's uniform entered. 'What is it?' she asked Arnold peevishly.

'Lucy, this is...'

'That doesn't matter,' Nettie said. 'The Kirkmore,' she said to Lucy. 'Who lives there?'

'Lots of people. I don't know.'

'You don't know?' Nettie turned to Arnold. 'What was my hundred for?'

Lucy glared at him. 'She's *paying* you?'

'Just answer her questions.'

'I don't know, people. They're not, like, movie stars or anything.'

Nettie said, 'Yesterday I saw two Ukrainian men in a pickup truck take a young woman into that building. A woman who looked as if she didn't want to be there. Any idea who these people were?'

'No idea. Can I go?' Lucy asked Arnold. 'Mr Eckart will be angry.'

'Who's Mr Eckart?' Nettie asked.

'The manager.'

'How can you help me?' Nettie said to Lucy. 'I promise I'll make it worth your while.'

Lucy looked puzzled. 'I've already told you everything I know. What do you want from me?'

Nettie gave her a patient smile. 'I want you to get me in.'

'Have you heard from Dasha?' Irena's father asked lightly as he shook salt on his roast beef.

Irena shook her head.

'I can only imagine how busy she is,' her mother said, joining them at the table.

Silently they ate, each knowing what the others were thinking: that Dasha was not busy at her new job as assistant to a fashion-magazine photographer in New York, she was in trouble. But as long as they pretended, hoped, the possibility remained that the phone would ring and it would be Irena's younger sister, full of apologies for not calling sooner.

'I tried her cell phone again,' Irena said matter-of-factly, 'but no luck.'

'That's not surprising,' her mother said. 'We don't know if Dasha's phone plan works in the States. Or maybe the magazine gave her a new cell phone. Who knows?'

'Yes, who knows?' her father said, his mouth full. 'A month is a long time to us but for someone starting a new job, setting up an apartment, it flies.'

It wasn't as if Irena hadn't tried. When two

weeks had passed with no word she had called the offices of *Attraction*, the magazine where Dasha was supposedly working. When she asked for Dasha she was told there was no one there by that name. Irena told her parents and implored them to call the police. Everyone knew the stories of girls who disappeared, tricked by promises of acting, modeling, glamorous jobs. But her parents would hear none of it. Of course she was at the magazine, they said. She had been there such a short time her name wasn't in the corporate directory yet. Ridiculous melodramatic talk, they said. Remember, the man Dasha is working for is a friend of her boyfriend, Alex. Irena had already asked Alex if he'd heard from Dasha. He hadn't. What was the name of his friend, the man Dasha was working for? Irena asked him. Grigori, Alex said. He didn't know Grigori's last name.

All dead ends.

'I'm tired,' Irena said, kissed her parents and trudged upstairs to her room.

THREE

Santos pulled up in front of the garage on the dot of two. Anna jumped into the cruiser and slammed the door against the cold. He had the heat turned up. She warmed her gloved hands against the vent.

'I knew you'd be freezing,' he said.

'Thanks. So thoughtful.' She fastened her seat belt as he pulled into traffic. 'Now, let's see what we can find out about this Grigori character.'

He turned down Broadway. 'We've got to establish some ground rules.'

'What kind of ground rules?'

'This is police business. You're with me not as my girlfriend but as a fellow witness to the woman in the pickup truck. I'll do all the talking unless I indicate otherwise.'

'Check,' she said, people-watching out her window.

He took 42nd Street to the West Side Highway and went through the Brooklyn Battery Tunnel. Then the Belt Parkway carried them south along the shorefront. Looking out at the bleak, deserted beach, the water that looked icy cold, Anna shivered.

Santos got off the Parkway at Coney Island Avenue, then took Neptune Avenue to Brighton 6th Street. 'It's number 3032,' he said. He found a parking spot not far from the house, which was one in a long line of dreary two-family homes, each with two front doors and two sets of front steps side by side.

'If he's in the Russian mafia,' Anna said in a low voice as they approached the house, 'he can't be very high up. This place is a dump.'

They climbed the staircase on the right and Santos raised his hand to ring the bell.

'Wait,' Anna whispered suddenly. 'How are you going to explain why we're here?'

'Easy.' He rang the bell. 'I'm going to tell the truth.'

At first there was no sound. Then they heard footsteps thumping on carpeted stairs and the door was opened by a young woman Anna guessed was in her late twenties, with fresh, pretty features and abundant light-brown hair that fell in curls to her shoulders. She wore black corduroy trousers and a white hooded sweatshirt. She blinked once in surprise at the sight of Santos in his uniform, but the smile she'd brought to the door didn't falter. 'Hi. Can I help you?'

Anna realized she'd expected a Ukrainian accent like Grigori's. This young woman was one hundred percent American.

'I'm Officer Reyes, NYPD, Manhattan

Midtown North Precinct.' Santos held out his badge, which she studied carefully before returning her gaze to his face. 'And this is Anna Winthrop.'

'Also police?' the woman asked.

'No. I'll explain why she's here. May we come in?'

'Of course.' Standing in the middle of the foyer was a beautiful fluffy collie. It panted eagerly, its tongue hanging out.

'Hey, boy,' Anna said, unable to refrain from bending down and giving him a big hug. He smelled clean and fresh. Eagerly he licked her face. For an instant she thought how nice it would be to have a pet like this at home.

'Now you've done it,' the woman said with a laugh. 'Bruno won't leave you alone.'

'That's fine with me,' Anna said and she and Santos followed the woman into a small, neat living room containing a few pieces of inexpensive contemporary furniture in blond wood. Ikea, Anna thought. She and Santos sat on a sofa facing the woman, who had taken an armchair. Bruno plopped down at Anna's feet.

'Now,' Santos said, bringing out a small pad of paper and a pen, 'I take it you are Mrs Sidorov.'

She nodded. 'Vicky. Now can you please tell me what this is about?'

'Your husband,' Santos said.

'Grigori? What about him?'

'Last night, he and another man came to Ms.

Winthrop's apartment to pick up a desk she was selling.'

'A desk?' Vicky shrugged to indicate she knew nothing about it. 'He's a contractor. Maybe it was for one of his jobs. Did something happen?'

'Yes,' Santos replied. 'Your husband and a man named Yuri—'

'He works for Grigori,' Vicky interjected.

'—had a young woman in their pickup truck. Do you have any idea who she was?'

'A young woman?' Vicky gave her head a little shake. 'What did she look like?'

'She was extraordinarily beautiful...' Anna piped up but a warning look from Santos silenced her.

'That's true,' he said to Vicky, 'she was beautiful. In her early to mid-twenties, I'd say. Lot of brown hair.'

Vicky shrugged. 'I suppose she could have been an interior designer he was working with.' Vicky frowned uncomprehendingly. 'What difference does it make? It's not against the law to have someone in your truck.'

'True,' Santos said, 'but we think this woman was being held against her will. When she was alone she dropped out a note that said "Help Me."'

'"Help Me"? Help her what?'

'That's what we're trying to find out.'

'How could Grigori and Yuri have been holding her against her will? You said she was alone

42

in the truck. She could have just opened the door, right?'

'Not if she was afraid of what they might do to her if they caught her. They definitely threatened her.'

Abruptly Vicky rose. 'This is ridiculous. I'm sure whoever this woman was, she had a good reason to be in the truck. As for the note, it must have been some kind of prank.'

From the front hall came the sound of the door being unlocked. Unaccountably, Anna felt a nervous flutter in the pit of her stomach.

Vicky gave a falsely bright smile. 'We don't need to wonder anymore, do we? Here's Grigori. He'll explain everything.'

Grigori appeared in the doorway, his face its customary blank. When he saw Anna and Santos his eyes widened in surprise. 'What are you doing here?'

Anna and Santos stood. Bruno got up and shook himself.

Santos led the way to the foyer. 'We weren't introduced yesterday,' he said to Grigori. 'I'm officer Reyes, NYPD, Midtown Manhattan North Precinct. Ms. Winthrop you know, of course.'

'Why are you here?'

Vicky said to Grigori, 'You bought a desk from her?'

'Yes.'

'What for?'

'As a favor to someone I am doing a job for.'

43

'See?' Vicky said to Santos.

'You had a young woman in your truck,' Santos said.

'A young woman?' To Anna's surprise, Grigori had to think for a moment. 'Of course. She was visiting someone at a hotel where we are doing a renovation. Yuri and I were in the lobby and this girl heard me say I was going to Brooklyn. She asked if I would give her a ride home.'

'What's her name?' Santos asked.

'She never said.'

'She accepted a ride with you but you never found out her name?'

'I did not ask. I was just giving her a ride home.'

'If you were giving her a ride home, why was she in your truck when you picked up the desk?' Santos asked.

'I told her I had to pick up the desk on the way home and she said she did not mind.'

'She looked frightened. Can you tell me why?'

'I have no idea.'

'You and Yuri were seen threatening her. Could that have had anything to do with it?'

'There was no threatening. Who saw this?'

Neither Santos nor Anna replied.

'She dropped a note out of the truck,' Vicky said.

'A note? What kind of note?'

'It said "Help Me,"' Santos said.

44

Grigori made no response.

'Where did you drop her in Brooklyn?' Santos asked.

'Park Slope.'

'At her home?'

'No, she wanted to get out a few blocks from her apartment and walk, get some fresh air.'

'Did she say where she lived?'

Grigori shook his head.

'You said she was visiting someone at the hotel. Who?'

'How should I know?'

'You didn't see her with whoever it was?'

'No.'

'What hotel was this?'

'The Taylor Hotel, on East Twenty-Eighth Street between Madison and Fifth.'

Santos jotted this down. 'What is Yuri's last name?'

'Morozov.'

'Why was he with you?'

'To help with the desk.'

'Where did he go after he helped you?'

'I drove him to his apartment on the Upper West Side.'

'Can you give me his address, please?'

Grigori stared at Santos for a moment, then said, 'I have it upstairs. I will get it.'

While he was upstairs Anna took the opportunity to pat Bruno. Grigori returned a few moments later and handed Santos a sheet of paper.

Santos gave Grigori his card. 'If you see this

young woman again, call me immediately.'

Grigori nodded.

As Anna and Santos went down the front stairs, Anna turned and saw Bruno's long snout disappear in the closing door.

'Grigori's lying,' Anna said as she and Santos drove north on the Belt Parkway. 'It was written all over his face.' She had a thought and her face turned troubled. 'What if he punishes the girl for leaving that note? I should have thought of that.'

For a few moments they rode in silence.

'How 'bout we grab a bite,' Santos said, 'then pay Yuri a visit? He's up on West 113th Street, near Morningside Park.'

'Unfortunately, I can't. I'm having dinner with my sister Beth.'

Beth, the younger of Anna's two sisters, had until recently worked as an attorney at a leading Manhattan immigration law firm called Schutz Fine Kovner. Six days earlier she had been fired.

'I still don't understand how that could happen,' Santos said. 'Beth is one of the best.'

'She explained it to me. When the economy is growing, companies need more employees. Some of them will be foreigners who need the services of immigration attorneys.'

'And when the economy is shrinking,' he said, nodding, 'companies don't need more employees.'

'Which means less business for firms like Beth's, which means they don't need as many attorneys.'

'What's she going to do?'

'I don't know.'

'I guess it's early yet.'

'No, I know my sister. She knows what she's going to do. She would have seen this coming and made a contingency plan. She just hasn't told me what it is yet. I'll bet that's what she wants to tell me tonight.'

Two hours later Anna walked east on 43rd Street, her face huddled into her scarf. The air was still but the cold was the wet kind that penetrated deeply. She passed the Algonquin Hotel, then the Iroquois and its restaurant Triomphe, then came to Victoire, the restaurant where she was meeting Beth. Anna spotted her at the back, sitting on the banquette. Seeing Anna she stood and waved. She looked pretty in charcoal trousers and a silk blouse in deep maroon. The two sisters embraced warmly.

As they sat, Beth took in the restaurant's elegant décor. 'I won't be able to come here much in the future,' she said wistfully. 'It's pizza for me.'

'Listen to you,' Anna said. 'Making believe you don't have all the money you'll ever need.'

'I could say the same thing about you ... yet you work for the Sanitation Department.'

'Touché. Now that we've established that

neither of us needs to work if she doesn't want to, what *are* you going to do with yourself?'

Before she could answer, their waiter appeared to take their order. After he had departed Beth leaned forward excitedly. 'It's a brilliant idea, if I do say so myself. I can't believe no one has thought of it. I'm going to open a Cheap Shop.'

'A what?'

'A Cheap Shop. I thought up the name. I'm going to trademark it.'

'Ever the lawyer. But what is it?'

'A store that sells things that help people save money,' Beth said simply. 'Used items of all kinds. Refilled printer cartridges. Cloth diapers and napkins. Bulk and low-cost foods. Thermostat timers. Get it?'

Anna nodded. 'It's very clever, actually.'

'Of course it is. I've already rented space on Third Avenue in the Sixties, not far from my apartment.'

'Isn't that neighborhood a bit tony for a Cheap Shop?'

'Are you kidding? The Upper East Side is full of people who suddenly have to watch their money.'

'How far along are you?'

'I'm opening this Sunday. I figure it's a day most people are around.'

Anna's eyes widened in surprise. 'You *have* moved fast.'

Beth nodded. 'What do you think?'

'I told you, I think it's very clever.'

'Want to join me?'

Anna blinked. 'Excuse me?'

'Do you want to be my partner? It would be such fun. You're perfect for this – practical, great with people, tough when you need to be.'

Anna placed her hand over her sister's. 'I'm touched. Flattered. But you know how I feel about my job.'

'Right, working with garbage,' Beth said dryly.

'Now don't *you* start. You sound like Gloria,' Anna said, referring to their sister who was always trying to steer Anna into a more 'suitable' occupation.

'Sorry,' Beth said. 'I kinda figured you'd say no but it couldn't hurt to ask, right?'

'You'll be dynamite on your own.'

'I've decided at the last minute to have a grand opening party. It's this Saturday night. The least you can do is come,' Beth said good-naturedly.

'I wouldn't miss it. I'll bring Patti. And I'll see if Santos is free.'

Anna excused herself to go to the ladies' room. A few minutes later on her way back to their table her gaze rested on a couple in the corner, an older man with a very pretty young woman.

Anna froze. Stared.

It was the young woman from the pickup truck.

FOUR

There was no mistaking her – the magnificent mane of chestnut hair, the porcelain skin, the full red lips, the large smoky eyes. She wore a simple blue silk dress and cream-colored heels. She sat very still in her chair, gaze lowered, while the man leaned toward her, a beseeching expression on his face. He was large and stocky and wore a dark suit. His white hair was combed back from his heavy red face. Anna guessed him to be in his late sixties, maybe early seventies, old enough to be the woman's grandfather.

Without even needing to think about it Anna headed straight for their table, passing Beth.

'Anna?' Beth called after her, but Anna kept walking.

As she approached the man and woman's table they looked up at her – puzzlement in his eyes, fear in hers.

'Do I know you?' the man asked, his voice a deep baritone.

Ignoring him, Anna fixed her gaze on the young woman, who looked up timidly at Anna. Close up like this, Anna noticed a tiny tattoo of a daisy on her left ankle.

50

'I saw you in the truck yesterday,' Anna said to her, moving even closer. 'I found your note.'

As Anna spoke these last words the woman's eyes grew immense.

The man shot up. 'What is this? What are you talking about? Who are you?'

Still Anna ignored him. 'Are you in trouble?' she asked the young woman, who only continued staring.

The manager hurried over. 'Is something the matter?'

'Yes,' the older man said, 'this woman is harassing us.'

'Do you know her?' the manager asked him.

'I've never seen her before.'

The manager turned to Anna. 'Is something wrong?'

'Yes,' Anna replied defiantly. 'I believe this young woman is being held against her will and is too frightened to say so.'

The manager drew back in surprise. 'Is this true?' he asked the young woman.

She gave her head a quick little shake.

The manager turned back to Anna. 'I must ask that you return to your table.'

'No. She's clearly afraid to tell us what's going on.'

Suddenly Beth was at Anna's side. 'Anna,' she said through gritted teeth, 'what are you doing?'

'Stay out of this.' Anna turned to the manager. 'I want you to call the police.'

51

'Yes,' the older man said, 'by all means, call the police.'

But the police had already been called. A uniformed officer was striding purposefully toward them. 'What seems to be the problem?' he asked the group of five.

'This young woman is being held against her will,' Anna told him. 'She's too frightened of this man to say so.'

'Is this true?' the officer asked the young woman.

'She doesn't speak English,' the older man said. 'She's my niece, visiting from Ukraine.'

The officer turned to Anna with an expression that said *There you have it*. 'You need to return to your table or you'll have to leave.'

Beth took Anna's arm but Anna shook her off.

'What is going on?' Beth demanded.

Anna turned to her. 'Last night two men came for that desk of Daddy's I was selling. This young woman was waiting for them in their truck. Santos saw her drop out a note that said "Help Me."'

They all turned to the young woman.

'Is that true?' the officer asked her.

'No,' the young woman said softly, finally finding her voice.

'You see.' The older man turned to the officer. 'I demand that you get her out of here.'

The manager gave a little nod and the officer took Anna by the arm. 'Come with me, please.'

Anna knew better than to fight any further.

She'd already made a scene. If she didn't stop now she'd end up in a cell overnight.

The officer began guiding her away. With as much dignity as she could muster she took back her arm. 'All right. I'm going.' She retrieved her coat from the check room and left the restaurant. Beth was close behind her.

'Have you lost your mind?' Beth said when they were outside. 'What just happened in there?'

'I told you. That young woman dropped a note asking for help. She's being held prisoner, I'm sure of it. You know about human trafficking; you're an immigration lawyer.'

'You have an overactive imagination. Let it go.'

'No,' Anna said, furious. 'That's why things like this happen – because people "let it go."'

She turned and headed west. When she reached Sixth Avenue she looked back. Beth was gone.

Anna had walked a block when the idea hit her. She hurried back to Victoire but went to the opposite side of the street, hiding in the shadow of a tailor shop.

She didn't have to wait long. The older man and the young woman emerged from the restaurant holding hands. The man looked upset. They were heading toward Fifth Avenue. At one point the young woman lagged a little behind. 'Eva, hurry up,' he snapped angrily and yanked her hand.

Anna followed them, keeping a safe distance. At Fifth Avenue they turned south. At 42nd Street they went west again, stopping at an unmarked glass door beneath a brown awning, between a movie theater and an ice cream parlor. A uniformed doorman emerged and held the door for them, then followed them inside.

Anna waited a few minutes, then walked up to the glass door. Just inside, the doorman sat on a stool. Behind him was a small lobby with dark sofas and a chandelier. He saw Anna and came out.

'May I help you?'

'Hi,' she said cheerfully. 'This is the Hilton, right?'

'No, it's not.'

'You wouldn't believe how many times I've gotten lost trying to find it. I'm from out of town, obviously,' she said with a dopey grin. 'Is this a hotel?'

'It's not the Hilton.' He lowered his cap in a slight nod. 'Good night,' he said and went back inside.

Anna hurried away, at the same time calling Santos.

'I thought you were having dinner with Beth,' he said.

'I did.'

'That was fast. I was about to call you. I ran background checks on Grigori and Yuri. Nothing on either of them. I also went to see Yuri.'

'What did he say?'

'Exactly what Grigori said. That he had no idea who the young woman was, that they were just giving her a ride. Then I went to the Taylor Hotel. It's one of those room-by-the-hour dumps. The lobby is being renovated and the manager confirmed that Grigori is doing it. But she never saw him with a young woman.'

'Interesting. Now are you ready for my news? I've just seen the woman from the pickup truck.'

'Where?'

'In the restaurant. She was with an older man who claimed he was her uncle and that she was visiting from Ukraine. She may be "visiting" from Ukraine, but no way is he her uncle.'

'How do you know?'

'I just know.'

'So what happened? Did you speak to her?'

'I tried, got close enough to see a little daisy tattoo on her ankle. But she was too terrified to say a word. Then they kicked me out. I followed the man and the woman. He called her Eva. They went to a building on Forty-Second Street between Fifth and Sixth. Plain unmarked door with a doorman.'

'Hotel? Apartment building?'

'I don't know, he wouldn't tell me.'

'I'll check it out in the morning.'

'Does it have to wait till morning?'

She heard him slowly expel his breath. 'I guess I didn't want to watch that *Law and*

Order marathon anyway.'

'You're an angel. It's a plain glass door under a brown awning, between an AMC Loew's movie theater and a Crazy Ice Cream.'

'I'll see what I can find out and drop by later tonight.'

Anna had been home for nearly an hour when Beth called.

'I'm sorry I embarrassed you,' Anna said.

'I don't know what to say. What were you doing?'

'I already explained it to you.'

'You really believe that man was holding that young woman against her will?'

'Yes. That's why she wrote that note.'

'Isn't it possible Santos only *thought* he saw that note fall out of the truck? Maybe it's someone's idea of a joke. Maybe the woman in the restaurant wasn't the woman you saw in the truck. Maybe that man really was her uncle.'

With a great sigh of exasperation Anna bade her sister good night and ended the conversation.

Two hours later Anna's buzzer sounded. It was Santos. As he climbed the stairs his face was red from the cold.

'I've got coffee,' Anna said and went to the kitchen.

Santos flopped on to the sofa. 'I checked out your doorway,' he said as she carried in the steaming mugs. 'The building is called the Kirkmore. It's a "private residence club," built ten years ago by a Japanese real estate conglomerate.'

'What's a residence club?'

'Members – there are about three hundred of them – buy a share entitling them to use a suite anywhere from two to thirteen weeks a year and other times if and when space is available. It's called fractional ownership.'

'Like a time share.'

'An extremely lavish one. I spoke to the manager, who happened to be working late. Man named Karl Eckart. He was quite friendly and showed me around. There are twenty floors. The penthouse is the most exclusive, costs extra to use one of the suites. Private key access on the elevator. Eckart showed me a couple of the lower suites. They're all fully furnished, luxury all the way. Members also get the use of the "amenities" – fully equipped fitness center, pool, Jacuzzi. There's also a private chef and childcare whenever you need it. Eckart also serves as a concierge, taking care of anything a resident needs that hasn't already been thought of.'

'Interesting. So this man Eva was with is probably a member.'

'And Eva may simply be a prostitute with whom he's spending the evening. If she's a prostitute, that would explain why Grigori made up that story in front of his wife about giving the young woman a ride.'

'Even if she's a prostitute, that doesn't mean she's not being held against her will, that she's not a victim of human trafficking.'

'It's highly possible,' he said thoughtfully. 'We see a lot of it. Girls lured with promises of jobs wind up drugged and smuggled into a strange country. When they ask about the job they're told a lot of money has been spent on them for visas, passports, transportation and so on – money they have to pay back. In Eva's case, she may be paying it back by working as a prostitute. Usually the girls are told if they try to run away, their families back home will be killed. But the traffickers don't want running away to be a possibility, so they keep the girls imprisoned or on a very tight rein.'

'You hear about these horrible things,' Anna said, 'but you never think you'll meet anyone involved in them.'

'*You* might never think that but I'm a New York City cop, remember? I never told you this, but early this year I was on Central Park South and heard screams coming out of a fancy apartment building. I ran upstairs and found a seventeen-year-old girl standing over the body of a man who'd trafficked her from Nigeria. He'd nodded off and she'd cut his throat. She used such force his head was nearly severed.'

Anna grimaced.

'These things *are* happening, all around us and in places you'd never think they could happen.'

'Like the Kirkmore.'

'Very possibly.'

'Did you ask Eckart if he knew Grigori, Yuri or Eva?'

'Of course. He had no idea who I was talking about.'

'We've got to get in there, look for her.'

'That's where we hit a problem. We'd have to get a warrant and unfortunately we don't have enough to convince a judge to issue one.'

'Don't have enough! We've got a young woman who leaves a note that says "Help Me." What more do you need?'

'More than that. What I can do is speak to my chief. He can put everyone on notice that this Kirkmore is to be watched.'

'*I* can watch.'

'But you're not going to, are you?' It was a statement more than a question.

'I intend to do far more than that.'

'Be careful, Anna.' He pronounced it *Ah-na*, the Spanish way. 'People like Grigori and Yuri, if they are Russian mafia—'

'I know, they make the Italian mob look like the Rotary Club.'

He pulled her gently back against him and put his arms tight around her. 'Don't you get it? I love you. I don't want to lose you.'

She gazed up at him, smiled. 'You won't lose me. I promise.'

He lowered his head to kiss her.

FIVE

In her cubicle at Arrow Realty, Irena kept one eye on her typing and one eye on the corridor. It was nearly ten o'clock and still Alex had not come in. But she knew his services would be needed soon because she had just finished preparing a contract that would need to be sent by messenger.

She was halfway into another contract when she heard the office door open, then his voice: 'How's my favorite girl today?' Zoya at the reception desk giggled.

Irena knew she must be careful. Alex had been working as a messenger for Arrow for six months and during that time she had all but ignored him. She must make her sudden attention believable.

She heard Alex speak again to Zoya: 'So what've you got for me?'

'I think Irena has something,' Zoya replied.

Irena grabbed the envelope containing the completed contract and, careful not to let Alex see her, hurried across the corridor to the break room. When he came in looking for her she was seated at the small table, sipping a coffee from the pot on the counter.

'Zoya says you got something for me,' he said.

She gave him her sweetest smile. Looking surprised, he grabbed a chair, spun it around and straddled it, leaning his chin on the back with a bemused smile. 'So ... you got something for me?'

She looked at him from under her long lashes. 'Maybe,' she teased, then, 'Yes, I do.' She handed him the envelope.

'Thanks ... Irena,' he said, gaze trained on her, and gave her a little wink before striding out.

'How come you're so friendly all of a sudden?' Alex asked Irena when he returned at one o'clock that afternoon. He rested one arm on the top of her cubicle partition.

'I don't know,' she said with a shrug and a pout. 'I guess I'm lonely.'

'What about your boyfriend?'

'We broke up.' In reality Irena hadn't had a boyfriend in over a year, but she had invented one with which to repel Alex.

'Ah,' he said, his smile broadening. After a long pause he said, 'Listen, you wanna go dancing with me sometime? I know some unreal places.'

'Sure, why not? When?'

He looked surprised. 'How about tomorrow night?'

'Sounds good. Are we going to Cloud Ten?'

His brows lowered. 'I guess we could. Why?'

'I don't know,' she said lightly. 'Dasha used to tell me how much she liked it there. Speaking of Dasha,' she said, not looking up from a contract she was folding, 'have you heard from her? We sure haven't. But my parents keep reminding me how busy she must be getting settled in a new city and starting a new job at the same time.'

'Matter of fact,' he said, 'I did hear from her.'

She looked up sharply. *Keep it light.* 'You did?'

'About a week ago. She said she's doing fine. Loves the job and everything. But she's real busy, like you said.'

'Do me a favor,' she said. 'Next time she calls you, tell her to give us a call, too.'

'Will do. You want me to come by your house tomorrow night?'

'No need,' she said with a smile. 'I'll meet you outside the club. Say, ten?'

'Ten it is.'

With narrowed eyes she watched him saunter off down the corridor.

In the service area behind the Kirkmore, Nettie pulled her coat tighter around her and shivered as she waited for Lucy to arrive. They had agreed to meet at 5:45 a.m. The previous afternoon, while Nettie waited at Crazy Ice Cream, Lucy had returned to the Kirkmore and found a uniform for her. 'This is the smallest one I could find. You're so skinny, I hope it's not too big,' Lucy had said, which Nettie hadn't appreciated.

As it turned out, the uniform fit fine. Nettie actually thought she looked quite sexy in it. She heard footsteps and turned to see Lucy coming down the alley. She wore a puffy down jacket over her uniform.

She cast a nervous glance at the service entrance. 'Go through that door, turn right and go all the way to the end. On the left you'll see a little room with lockers for your stuff. At the end of the hall is a supply room. There should be a woman there named Carmela – heavy with black hair. She's head of housekeeping. Tell her the Kemp Agency sent you. If she says she didn't request anybody, tell her Mr Eckart did.'

'Who's Mr Eckart?'

'The manager. Where's my money?'

Nettie handed her two hundred dollars. Right now it was a lot of money for Nettie, especially after having already shelled out a hundred to Arnold, but she told herself she'd get more than a thousand times that when Jane Stuart sold *New York SuperWomen*.

'I'll go in first,' Lucy said, pocketing the money. 'Wait five minutes and then come in. Remember, don't try anything funny. If you get caught and tell them I had anything to do with it, I'll deny it. Just do your work.'

'Just my work,' repeated Nettie, who considered her work anything she had to do to learn about the two Ukrainian men, the beautiful young woman and their connection to Anna Winthrop.

When five minutes had passed she strode confidently toward the door.

Brianna Devlin dunked her tea bag a few more times, looked into her cup, frowned and continued dunking.

Brianna's collection partner, pretty Kelly Moore, made a face. 'You make your tea so dark one of these days you're going to end up with a solid.'

Brianna gave her husky shoulders a shrug. 'Fine by me,' she said in her deep voice. 'In fact, that gives me an idea. A tea-sicle! I'll be rich.'

'Sorry, it's been done.' Anna finished spreading cream cheese on her toasted poppy seed bagel and took a big bite. 'My mother made them all the time when we were growing up,' she said with her mouth full.

'Yeah, right,' Brianna said with a laugh, still dunking. 'Like your mother ever set foot in the kitchen.'

'You're right,' Anna admitted. 'It was the maid. But she did it on my mother's instructions!'

For several moments the three women sat in companionable silence – Anna munching her bagel, Brianna dunking her tea bag, Kelly sipping her coffee. It was a little before six o'clock

64

and they were seated around Anna's desk, a longstanding tradition that had begun when Kelly and Brianna were the only female sanitation workers on Anna's crew. Other women had come and gone since, but now Kelly and Brianna were once again the only females. The three women had become friends, something Anna knew Allen Schiff frowned upon, but she wasn't breaking any rules and was careful never to show favoritism.

Brianna sipped her tea and set down the cup. 'So what's the scoop with this cousin of yours?' she asked Anna. 'When's she coming?'

'She's flying in from Cincinnati tonight. I'm picking her up at the airport. I'll be bringing her to work tomorrow.' She checked her watch. Six o'clock. 'Better do roll call.'

Out in the garage the rest of Anna's crew had already congregated. Anna stood before them.

To the extreme left, small, wiry Fred Fox, with his piercing blue eyes and face like a ferret, was glancing about uncomfortably. Beside him his partner, tall Bill Hogan, grinned as if looking forward to starting his day. More than two years ago Anna had sent Bill to the Sanitation Department's Medical Division for alcohol counseling. He had joined Alcoholics Anonymous and, as far as Anna could tell, stayed sober since.

To Fred and Bill's right stood two rookie members of Anna's crew: young Glenn Carmon, who always seemed to have a smile on his

65

good-looking dark-skinned face, and Tony Hsu, with his dark hair that fell over his eyes.

The next two men in line, though both in their twenties, were Sanitation veterans. Handsome Tommy Mulligan, married less than a year and a half ago, stood with his hazel eyes unfocused, as if lost in thought. That was like Tommy, who seemed able to do his job without thinking much about it. Not surprising, since he was third-generation Sanitation.

Tommy's partner, Pierre Bontecou, hadn't looked his happy self lately. His father, with whom Pierre lived, was in the final stages of terminal cancer. Relatives had been flying in from Jamaica to say goodbye.

Next came Pablo Rodriguez, in his mid-thirties, always quiet and withdrawn, and his partner, little Wei Ma, as quiet as Pablo, a good match.

And at the right end of the line stood Kelly and Brianna.

Back at the other end, Fred Fox fidgeted during roll call. 'Anna,' he said when she was through, 'we had a little problem early this morning.'

'What kind of problem?'

'A lady slipped on some ice out front.'

'How did the ice get there?'

Fred looked down. 'I was hosing mud off our truck near the entrance and the water flowed out to the sidewalk.'

'And you neglected to put down sand.'

Mutely Fred nodded.

'Is the woman all right?'

'Her hands were bleeding from trying to stop her fall, but otherwise she seemed fine. We took her to the hospital just in case, since she was older.'

'How much "older"?'

Fred winced. 'Eighty-three.'

'Come to my office, please. We're done,' Anna told the rest of the crew.

In her office, Fred was still staring at the floor.

'That's not like you,' Anna said.

'It was a mistake.'

'A mistake we can't afford to make. That poor woman could have been killed.' She dismissed him. He gave her a sullen look before departing.

Anna sat down at her desk and started work on her time book, but her mind wandered. Numbers blurred. She saw Eva being dragged along by the older man.

Maybe if Anna found out who he was, she could find Eva...

Nettie finished dusting the end table with a surface like a blotchy mirror and replaced the lamp with the X-shaped base. She'd never done so much cleaning in her life.

She wasn't sure what she had expected. Of course she would be allowed to clean only unoccupied suites, but it was no way to find out anything. She threw her dust cloth on to her supply cart and surveyed the room.

It was one of the most beautiful rooms she had ever seen. The floor was of polished gray granite with an S-shaped rust-colored inlay. A double window draped in taupe-and-bronze damask looked down sixteen floors on to 42nd Street. Large modern armchairs with matching ottomans flanked the window and faced a granite fireplace in which a fire crackled cozily. There were countless other details – giant wooden candlesticks to each side of the fireplace, a basket of orchids below the window, a Chinese statue of a horse on the windowsill – yet the room was so large it gave the impression of being minimalist.

And there were lots more rooms. A spacious foyer opened on to a dining room and four bedrooms. There was a state-of-the-art kitchen the size of Nettie's living room and bedroom combined. Five bathrooms. In the master bath was a kind of bathtub Nettie had once blogged about, an infinity tub, which when full gave the impression of overflowing when in reality the water ran into a channel below. The effect was that the water appeared to flow into nothingness, into infinity.

Finally finished with her cleaning, Nettie wheeled her supply cart out to the quiet corridor and locked the door.

It was nearly four o'clock. She had cleaned three apartments so far. That had kept her busy all day except for her lunch hour, which she had taken in the break room with two maids from whom she gleaned no information because they spoke no English.

Carmela had told Nettie to return to the supply closet for instructions when she was finished cleaning the third suite. Nettie had no intention of doing so. She had gathered no information, had only an hour left and intended to make the most of it. She had decided to seek out Mr Eckart, the manager Lucy had mentioned, and see what she could learn from him.

She glanced up and down the corridor. No one in sight. She summoned the elevator and when the doors slid open got on with her cart. There were twenty floors, the twentieth accessible only with a key. Randomly she pressed Nineteen. Emerging into the corridor she saw the door of a suite propped open with a supply cart, a woman vacuuming inside. Nettie knocked hard on the door. The woman spun around, switching off the machine.

'What is it?' she asked impatiently.

Nettie was grateful she spoke English. 'What are you doing here?' she asked the woman.

The woman scowled. 'What does it look like I'm doing? I'm cleaning.'

'But Mr Eckart told *me* to clean this suite.'

The woman wrinkled her nose. 'Mr *Eckart*?'

'Maybe I got it wrong,' Nettie said. 'I'd better ask him. Do you know where his office is?' She laughed. 'It's my first day.'

'Second floor, left out of the elevator, all the

way to the end. His name's on the door.'

Nettie found it easily. She knocked and a man's voice called, 'Come in.'

She entered a large office in which a man in a dark suit sat behind a plain wooden desk. He was small in stature with pale features and black hair slicked back. Intelligent eyes took her in. 'Yes?'

'Mr Eckart, my name is N–Noreen,' she caught herself, using the name she'd given Carmela. 'There's something I felt you should know.'

'Yes?' he asked impatiently.

'It happened two days ago, on Monday.'

'You're sure it was Monday?'

'Absolutely.' She figured he had no way of knowing she'd really only started today.

She was wrong. His brows lowered ominously. 'You weren't here on Monday. You've never worked her before. The agency sent you today.'

Her heartbeat quickened. 'I'm afraid that's not correct, sir. The agency did send me, but Monday was my first day.'

'What is it you feel I should know?'

'Two Ukrainian men came in the front entrance with a young woman, and one of the men said something to the other in Ukrainian about not letting her get away,' she said, changing the story a bit. 'I speak a little Ukrainian,' she explained.

'I find it odd that you could have overheard

anything, since as I said, you weren't here on Monday.' He got up and came around his desk to face her. 'Who are you?'

Her heart began to pound painfully. Without answering she turned and hurried out. Instead of waiting for the elevator she flew down the service stairs, out the back door and along the alley to 42nd Street, where she lost herself among the crowds.

She'd gone two blocks when she realized with a draining of blood from her face that she had left her coat and handbag at the Kirkmore.

SIX

Anna worked late on Wednesday, not finishing until four thirty. From the garage she walked to Victoire, where she knocked on the rear service door. When there was no response she tried the knob and found it locked. She knocked harder and this time heard hurried footsteps. The door was thrown open by a man in checkered chef pants. Behind him the kitchen bustled with activity. Before Anna could think of what to say, a woman appeared behind him. Tall and elegant, she appeared to be in her early thirties. She had straight brown hair to her shoulders, parted in the middle, and refined, aloof features. 'What is it?' she asked Anna coolly. She had a faint French accent.

'My name is Anna Winthrop. May I please speak with you for a moment?'

The young woman stepped forward, dismissing the man with a flip of her hand. 'About what?' she asked Anna.

'About something that happened here last night.'

The woman frowned, not understanding.

'I was here for dinner and something

72

happened that I'm following up on.'

'Yes?'

Anna explained what had occurred.

'Ah,' the woman said, 'that was you.'

'You were here?'

'No. I didn't feel well last night so I didn't come to work. My father told me about it. He said you were a nut.'

'I assure you I'm not.'

'I don't think you are,' the woman said, to Anna's surprise. 'I am Peggy Bernard. My father and I own the restaurant. I would like to talk to you but not here. Can I meet you?'

'Of course. Where and when?'

'There's a coffee shop called Olympia on Tenth Avenue between Thirty-Fourth and Thirty-Fifth streets. I'll meet you there at five.'

Nettie hung up the phone and drummed her fingers on the table, trying to remember if there were any more credit cards in her purse she needed to cancel. She couldn't think of any. She'd alerted her bank that she'd lost her ATM card. She thought that covered everything.

She glanced at her laptop surrounded by research materials. She owed pieces on winter gardening, natural cosmetics and gift-scrapbooking. She should get them done – she needed the money – but she was too nervous to think about them now.

Not with what had happened with Mr Eckart. And not with having spotted Eddie.

It had happened on her way home from the Kirkmore. At Ninth and 43rd she'd stopped at Mr and Mrs Carlucci's grocery store, ostensibly to buy some Charleston Chews and Suzy Q's but in fact to warm up, since she had no coat. Her maid's uniform drew stares as she filled her basket with candy bars and cakes.

As she approached the register she happened to glance out the window on to Ninth, and that's when she saw Eddie go past. He was walking very fast and wasn't wearing his police uniform but she was certain it was him. It was the first time she'd seen him since fleeing their apartment and it took her breath away. Dropping the cakes and the candy bars on to the counter she rushed out to the street and looked in both directions. He was gone. But that was just like Eddie, to let her see him and then hide.

When she reached the brownstone, sour Mrs Dovner happened to be on the sidewalk, leaving something for the trash. Bundled in coat, hat and gloves for her fifteen seconds outside, she looked at Nettie in horror. 'Where is your coat?'

'I ... lost it.'

'Lost it?' Mrs Dovner shook her head. 'Shame. That was a nice coat.'

'My keys were in the pocket. Can I use your phone to call Mr Vickery?' Nettie asked, referring to their landlord.

'I suppose,' Mrs Dovner said and they went inside.

Nettie had tea with Mrs Dovner while they waited for Mr Vickery. Nettie found herself telling the older woman about her ghost-blogging career, then about her breakup with Eddie. She made no mention of having just seen him.

It took about forty-five minutes for Mr Vickery to come over from his apartment on 46th with a key to Nettie's apartment. He agreed it was necessary to have the lock changed but said Nettie would have to pay for it. The locksmith Nettie called arrived within the hour and was finished in twenty minutes.

On top of the lock-changing expense, Nettie realized she'd need to buy a new coat. She had no other. What with bribing Arnold and Lucy, money was tight until Jane Stuart nailed down her multi-million-dollar deal. Nettie would go to the consignment shop and see if she could find something affordable.

The phone rang. She grabbed it, said hello.

'Yes, may I speak with Nettie Clouchet, please?' A man's voice, refined.

'May I ask who's calling?'

'I believe I'm speaking to Ms. Clouchet, is that right?'

Frowning in puzzlement, she made no response.

'This is Mr Eckart at the Kirkmore.'

Nettie's heart began to thud. Still she said nothing.

'I see you're shy so I'll do the talking,' he said, still in a polite tone. 'I would like to know why you came here today impersonating a maid.'

'I–I wasn't impersonating a maid,' she finally got out. 'It's one of my jobs ... to make extra money.'

'I'm sorry but I don't believe you. You see, I've been through the contents of your handbag quite carefully. You're a journalist of sorts, aren't you? You write blog pieces, articles. You also have a book project in the works, something about super women in New York. I ask you again, what were you doing here?'

As Nettie listened to him, her fear turned to a nervous excitement. This man was threatened by her visit. He wouldn't be talking like this unless he was hiding something, something worth finding out about. She had the upper hand. She felt empowered. She must be smart here.

'What do you think I was doing there?' she said coyly.

'I'm sure I have no idea.'

'I'm sure you do have an idea. Because I saw what it is you're hiding,' she bluffed, 'and I intend to go public with it.'

There was a very long silence on the phone. She waited.

At last he spoke. 'I'm sure we can work something out, something advantageous to both of us. Can you come and see me?'

'Ha! I don't think so. You wanna meet, it's gotta be somewhere public.'

'That will be fine. Just say where and when.'

'The atrium at Madison and Fifty-Seventh Street. Old IBM building. You know it?'

'Of course. What time?'

'One hour from now.'

'Excellent. I will see you there.'

'Oh, and Mr Eckart? Don't forget to bring my coat and bag.'

As Nettie hung up she broke into a grin, eyes gleaming.

Peggy Bernard slid into the booth Anna had taken at Olympia. 'I can't stay long,' she said. 'It is our busy time.'

The waitress came and they ordered coffee.

'I'll tell you what I know,' Peggy said.

Anna nodded, waiting.

'The man is Dr Jeremiah Renser. He comes in from time to time but my father says he has never seen this particular young woman before.'

'How do you know his name?

'From his credit card. Dr Jeremiah Renser.'

'You said "this particular young woman." Has he come in with others?'

'Yes, several. Always young and beautiful.'

'Who do you think they are?'

Peggy gave a little shrug. 'At first my father and I thought they were high-priced call girls. Now we're not sure. They don't act like call girls. They're all terrified of him.'

'Where does Renser live, do you know?'

'Not far from the restaurant, on Forty-Second Street between Fifth and Sixth avenues. I know because one of our waiters once forgot to give him back his credit card. I called the credit card company and got Renser's address. When I realized how close it was I took it over myself, left it with the doorman. What do you intend to do? Call the police?'

'My boyfriend is a police officer. He says there's not much we *can* do without actual proof that Eva needs help. I intend to get that proof.'

Nettie entered the atrium and swept her gaze over the soaring glass-enclosed space full of café tables among trees and sculpture. She spotted Eckart at a table way in the back. At the same time he saw her and waved, smiling, as if they were two old friends meeting to chat.

She made her way over. He stood as she approached, put out his hand.

'Save it,' she said. 'You're not my friend and I'm not yours. This is business.'

'As you wish,' he said with a deferential nod, and they both sat.

'You said you wanted to work out something advantageous to both of us. So what are we talkin' here?'

He smiled, amused. 'Surely you can't expect me to make a deal without knowing exactly what you know.'

She threw back her head and laughed. It

echoed through the atrium and caused several people to look in their direction. 'Nice try. But I'll give you a clue.' She had decided to take another chance here – risky, she knew, but she needed to convince him she held dangerous information. 'I know all about the two Ukrainian men and the woman they had with them, all about ... what's going on.'

His eyes narrowed. 'You asked me about those two men and the woman. I told you I had no idea who you were talking about.'

'And you were lying.'

She watched him, could practically see the gears of his brain turning.

'I suppose that by posing as one of our maids you were able to see quite a lot, go virtually anywhere.'

'Whoa, yeah.'

'How long were you in the building, exactly?'

'From six this morning till I left your office at four. You can see an awful lot in ten hours.'

'Indeed. What floors did you visit, exactly?'

'"Visit"? That's cute. All of them.'

'Including the twentieth?'

'Yep.'

He gave a little nod. 'All right. What do you want?'

'What do you think I want?'

'I need a figure.'

What to say? What was too much, what was too little, for what he thought she knew? 'Fifty thousand dollars,' she heard herself saying.

He moved his head from side to side as if weighing the amount. 'Let me think this over and get back to you.'

'Think fast, because if you keep me waiting too long I go public, get money elsewhere.'

'I understand. I will call you. Thank you,' he said, rising.

'Hold it. Where are my coat and bag?'

'In my office. I will return them to you once we've reached an agreement.'

He turned and walked away. She watched him go, strolling casually in his trim dark suit, his expression composed and inscrutable.

Irena walked along Basseynaya Street toward Cloud Ten. She was cold because she had worn only a light jacket over her new sequined top. But being cold was nothing compared to what Dasha might be going through. Tears sprang to Irena's eyes and she wiped them and walked stoically on.

Up to the time she disappeared, Dasha had worked for five months as a secretary at another real estate agency called Criterion, owned by the same man who owned Arrow. Alex, who worked as a messenger for both agencies, had systematically employed his handsome smile on the flirty Dasha, who had quickly succumbed. They began dating.

Late one night Dasha came home filled with excitement. She and Alex had gone to a club called Cloud Ten, and there Dasha had met a friend of Alex's named Grigori. Grigori was a good bit older, Dasha said, not at all attractive with his tall gaunt body and craggy features, but he was a lot of fun. Most significantly he lived and worked in New York, where he was a photographer for a women's fashion magazine called *Attraction*. He was in Kiev shooting a spread with a Ukrainian winter theme.

Dasha lived and breathed fashion and had always fantasized about a glamorous job in the field. 'He's a big deal and doesn't want to be bothered with me,' she told Irena. 'But maybe he can give me some advice on breaking in here in Kiev.'

Two weeks later Dasha returned home from another date with Alex bursting with news. They had been to Cloud Ten again and Grigori had been there. He was back in Kiev to do some reshooting on the spread. He was in a bad mood but Dasha had managed to get him to talk to her a little. She told him about her dream of working in fashion and he told her to keep hitting the magazines, applying for entry-level positions. Some girls did this for over a year before hitting on something, he said. Why, for the new opening as his assistant he had already received more than three dozen résumés.

Dasha couldn't believe it hadn't occurred to Grigori to tell her about this job, when she had just finished telling him how badly she wanted something like that. Very tentatively she suggested that maybe she could apply. Grigori was extremely doubtful. She was not even eighteen. She lived in Kiev. Moving to a place like New York was difficult even for experienced adults.

But Dasha gently persisted. She promised not to bother him with any of her personal matters like moving or finding an apartment. She would simply report for work like any local Manhattan girl, and she would work harder for him than anyone had ever worked.

By the end of the evening Grigori had agreed to give Dasha the job. She could start as soon as she was ready. The magazine would even pay Dasha's airfare.

One week later Irena and her parents had seen Dasha off outside the airport.

That was the last they had seen or heard from her.

As Irena approached the club she slipped off her jacket and threw it over her shoulder. A man passing her let out a low whistle, exactly the response she was after. The sequined top actually had two purposes: first, to make sure she and Alex got into the club (Dasha used to say Alex always got in because he was a friend of the bouncer, but Irena wasn't taking any chances), and second, to appeal to Grigori if he was there. Irena was pretty sure he would be.

She was right. Grigori and Alex embraced, then Alex brought Grigori over to meet Irena.

'Irena is the sister of your new assistant, Dasha,' Alex said, looking into Grigori's eyes.

Grigori looked puzzled for a fraction of a

second. Then understanding dawned. 'Right, right.' He turned back to her with his ugly-handsome smile. 'I cannot decide which of you is more beautiful.'

She gave him an appreciative smile.

'Would you like to dance?' he asked.

They danced two dances, one fast and one slow. When he asked her to dance again she said, 'I would rather chat, get to know you.'

He smiled and they sat down with Alex at a table in a quiet corner of the club.

'So,' Grigori said, 'you and Alex work together.'

'That's right,' Alex said. 'Irena works at one of the real estate agencies I messenger for.'

'How do you like the real estate business?' Grigori asked Irena.

'Don't make me laugh,' Irena said. 'I'm only a secretary. I prepare contracts all day.'

She caught a look between Grigori and Alex but they didn't know she'd seen it. 'What would you rather be doing?' Grigori asked lightly.

'Something glamorous like my sister. How is she doing, by the way?'

'She loves it.'

'She is a good assistant to you?'

'The best.'

Alex said to Grigori, 'I told Irena that Dasha called me and told me how much she loves New York, loves working for the magazine.'

Grigori nodded and returned his attention to

Irena.

'Got any more openings like that?' she asked, making a show of being facetious.

'Actually,' Grigori said, 'we may.'

She looked up in excited surprise. 'Really?'

'Mm-hm. The assistant to one of our top editors just left on maternity leave.'

Irena feigned disappointment. 'You'd need someone with experience to replace her.'

Grigori laughed. 'Not necessarily. Daphne – that's the editor's name – she says she gets the best work from people who are new to the industry, who see through fresh eyes.'

Irena pointed to her eyes. 'Very fresh.'

They all laughed.

'But seriously,' Grigori said to Irena, 'if you would like Daphne to consider you for the job I could put in a good word for you.'

'Yes, please!'

'There goes another girlfriend,' Alex said dejectedly.

'Not so fast,' Grigori said. 'She hasn't been offered the job yet.'

'*Yet*,' Alex said and raised his glass. 'To New York!'

'To New York!' Irena and Grigori said in unison, smiling as they clinked glasses.

Anna hadn't seen Patti in years. The chubby, homely middle-schooler had become the tall, thin, attractive young woman with the black Cleopatra haircut who strode confidently down the ramp. She wore a tight mini skirt, fishnet stockings and impossibly high zebra-patterned pumps. When she saw Anna she broke into a pretty smile. The two women embraced. Then they retrieved Patti's suitcase and were soon on Grand Central Parkway heading toward Manhattan.

'I suppose Mom's told you all kinds of awful things about me,' Patti said.

'Not at all. Just that you're looking for a direction.'

'Fair enough. I can't thank you enough for having me.'

'It's my pleasure. We're going to have a lot of fun.'

Santos was waiting for them when they got home.

'This is a pleasant surprise,' Anna said. 'I thought you couldn't join us until after ten.'

'Change of schedule.' He turned to Patti and took her hand. 'So good to meet you.'

Patti turned to Anna. 'He's gorgeous.'

Santos blushed a deep red.

'And he's a sweetheart, too,' Anna said. 'Let's order some food. I'm starving. Do you like Chinese food?' she asked Patti.

'Love it. But would you mind eating without me? I'd like to just walk for a while, see the neighborhood, get my thoughts together.'

Anna and Santos looked at each other in surprise.

'I guess it's all right,' Anna said.

Patti laughed. 'I'm nearly eighteen. You don't need to worry about me.'

Three hours later, Patti had not returned. When the buzzer finally sounded, Anna hurried to the intercom. 'Patti, is that you?'

'It's me,' came Patti's cheerful reply. 'Sorry,' she said as she breezed in. 'Lost track of time.'

'Lost track of time!' Anna said. 'You were gone three hours. Where were you?'

'I told you, walking around, learning the neighborhood.'

'Learning the neighborhood! By now you could draw a map.'

'Chill out,' Patti said kindly. 'You don't need to worry about me. I'm your guest, not your responsibility.'

Anna gave her a tight smile. Suddenly a month seemed like a very long time.

Later, sitting on her bed with her laptop, Anna googled 'Dr Jeremiah Renser' and 'Jeremiah Renser, M.D.' Several Web pages came up indicating that he was a neurosurgeon with offices on Fifth Avenue. According to the listings, he was affiliated with NewYork-Presbyterian Hospital. That was where Anna's sister Gloria had done her medical residency. Anna called her.

'What do you want to know about him?' Gloria asked.

'Everything you can find. So far I've got that he's a neurosurgeon, has offices on Fifth

Avenue and is affiliated with New York-Presbyterian.'

'Odd that I've never heard of him,' Gloria said thoughtfully. 'I'll see what I can find out.'

At 5:00 a.m. Thursday, Nettie woke up hungry. Her refrigerator contained a nearly full bottle of peach Snapple and a can of whipped cream (to put on her Suzy Q's). With a pang of regret she remembered the Charleston Chews and Suzy Q's she'd left on the counter at Carlucci's. How she wished she had them now. Carlucci's wouldn't be open yet but the twenty-four-hour QuikMart on Tenth Avenue would be.

In lieu of a coat she put on a flannel shirt, a thick wool sweater and her favorite hoodie, but they didn't keep out the cold, a cold so deep her nose hairs froze. She wouldn't be out long.

She giggled as she hurried down Tenth. Eddie would no doubt come looking for her again today, but he didn't know where she lived and he would never expect her to be out this early. She felt like the Little Pig who tricked the Big Bad Wolf by going to the fair early and then rolling at him in a butter churn. She smiled at the image of herself in a butter churn, rolling up Tenth Avenue after Eddie.

Irena did not tell her parents she was leaving. The morning of her flight she hid her suitcase in a recess under the front steps. When she left she said good-bye to her parents exactly as if she were going to work at Arrow Realty, except that her heart was breaking and she wondered if she would ever see them again. She thought it unlikely.

Alex drove her to the airport. Grigori, who coincidentally was returning to New York and would be on the same flight, met them inside the terminal. He had already purchased Irena's ticket for her. He held it up with a smile. 'Now I will check your bags for you,' he said, picked up her two suitcases and went inside. He re-appeared ten minutes later. 'We must hurry,' he said, pointing to the long line of people waiting to pass through security.

She hugged Alex good-bye. 'Come and see me in New York,' she said with an excited giggle.

'I'll come and see you and Dasha *both*,' he said, gave her a kiss and handed her over to Grigori.

They passed through security quickly, Irena showing the passport she'd obtained long ago for family vacations on the Black Sea in Romania.

'I will hold this for you,' Grigori said, taking the passport from her hand. When she looked surprised he gave her a reassuring smile. 'For safekeeping.'

She nodded, dread building inside her. *This is for Dasha. This is for Dasha.*

Despite Grigori's eagerness to pass quickly through security, as soon as they had done so he announced he was hungry and would buy them lunch. They ate hamburgers and fries at a café near the entrance to the boarding gates. After about twenty minutes Grigori suddenly looked at his watch and said, 'We must go now or we'll miss our flight.'

He hustled them down the long corridor to a gate on the right. People were already boarding, waiting in line to show their tickets, passports and ID to the flight attendant. As Irena and Grigori got in line Irena happened to glance at the screen behind the service desk. It said Aeroflot Russian Airlines 186, Departing 8:25 a.m., Mexico City.

Irena turned to Grigori. 'We're at the wrong gate.'

'It's a mistake,' he said and urged her along in front of him.

On the plane they took their seats and settled in, Irena by the window, Grigori beside her. A woman's voice came over the loudspeaker. 'Good morning, ladies and gentlemen, and welcome aboard Aeroflot's flight 186 service to Mexico City...'

Irena turned wide-eyed to Grigori. He looked back at her coldly.

She had made a terrible mistake. Frantically she unfastened her seat belt and began to rise. At the same time Grigori had fished something out of a tiny side pocket in the lining of his briefcase. It was a hypodermic syringe. Swiftly his hand moved toward her and he

89

jabbed the needle through her jeans into her thigh. Instantly she felt hot, a dizzy darkness overtaking her...

SEVEN

'Ready to roll?' Anna asked Patti.

'Ready,' Patti replied and they left the apartment and descended to the foyer. Mrs Dovner was at her door, speaking to a young dark-haired man. 'I have no idea where she is,' she was saying.

'All right, thank you,' said the man, who looked somehow familiar to Anna, and he went out.

'Morning, Mrs Dovner,' Anna said.

Mrs Dovner gave her one curt nod.

'Who was that?' Anna asked.

'Nettie's boyfriend, Eddie. Nettie told me they broke up, but I guess he wants to get back together. He knocked on Nettie's door but she didn't answer, so he asked me if I knew where she was.'

'What did you tell him?'

'You heard what I told him – I have no idea where she is.'

Mrs Dovner slammed her door before Anna could introduce Patti.

Anna wondered if perhaps Nettie was home but hadn't answered the door when she saw it was Eddie. If not, Anna would have to tell Nettie that Eddie had found out where she lived, a deeply troubling development.

Anna wondered why Eddie had looked familiar to her. Nettie had said he was a police officer. Anna decided she must have seen him at some police function she'd attended with Santos.

They ran into Nettie at the end of the block. She was carrying a white plastic QuikMart bag through which could be seen Charleston Chews and Suzy Q's. Anna introduced Patti and the two women shook hands.

'Nettie,' Anna said, 'I have something disturbing to tell you.'

'What is it?'

'Eddie was just at our building looking for you. He spoke to Mrs Dovner.'

Nettie's eyes were huge. 'What did she tell him?'

'That she didn't know where you were.'

'Oh no, oh no,' Nettie said, wildly twirling the bag. 'Now what am I going to do?'

But she scurried away before Anna could reply.

'Wake up. Wake up.' Someone was pushing Irena's arm. She struggled to come up from the warm darkness, lifted her heavy eyelids. People were standing in the aisle, leaving the plane. 'Come on,' Grigori said.

'Where are we?' she asked groggily.

Without answering he took her roughly by the upper arm to shore her up and guided her off the plane. In a half-conscious fog she was dragged across the terminal toward the exit.

'Wait, my bag,' she said. He ignored her. She hit him on the upper arm. 'My suitcase, we have to get it.'

He spun on her, cold fury in his eyes. 'Don't you ever touch me again. Forget the bag. You won't be needing it.'

This is what you wanted, she told herself as they passed through the sliding glass doors.

Waves of heat. Palm trees and flowers. Bright colors. Music playing somewhere. Taxis of all colors lined the curb but Grigori guided Irena past them, across the drive to a parking deck. There a man stood waiting for them. He was short and heavy, with closely trimmed, thinning blond hair and pink childlike features. Neither man spoke. Each took one of Irena's arms and they led her to a beat-up old sedan. The blond man opened the back door and threw her in. Before she could even right herself she felt a stab of pain as a needle was jabbed into her buttocks. Darkness overtook her once more.

'Eat this.'

Irena opened her eyes. The blond man was seated beside her. He pushed a sandwich at her.

'Take it.'

She took the sandwich, bit into it hungrily. They were on another plane, this one much

93

smaller than the first, with two seats on the right and one on the left. Across the aisle Grigori dozed, head thrown back, mouth open.

'Who are you?' Irena asked the blond man.

'My name is Yuri.'

'Where are we going?'

'Tijuana.'

'*Why?* I thought we were going to New York.'

He chuckled. 'In time.' His face grew serious. 'Now here's what's going to happen. We are taking you to a hotel in Tijuana. You have a choice – we can keep drugging you or you will do everything we say.'

'I'll do what you say.'

'Good, because if you don't we will send someone to 229 Lyuteranska Street to cut off the heads of Gennadiy and Yana Lebedev.'

Her parents.

'Because you owe us, you know.'

She had to laugh. 'I owe you? For kidnapping me?'

'Getting you a visa took time and money. Your plane ticket was expensive.'

'My plane ticket to Mexico.'

'You will end up in New York.'

'Working for a fashion magazine? I don't think so.'

He shrugged. 'At any rate you will do as we say.'

'What do you want me to do?'

'You will see.'

* * *

Anna was gratified by the warm welcome her crew gave Patti. After roll call Anna asked Kelly and Brianna if they would mind if Patti rode with them on their route.

'Of course we wouldn't mind,' Brianna boomed. 'Glad to have another pair of hands.' And she winked at Anna.

When Anna reached her office her phone was ringing. It was Gloria.

'I looked into that Dr Renser for you. The reason his name wasn't familiar to me is that he's been retired for ten years. The information you found on the Internet is out of date. The hospital has none of his records after all this time, but I spoke to a friend of mine who's been there forever and hears everything. She said Renser retired after a patient of his died. Girl named Heather Montgomery, from Hoboken, New Jersey. Malpractice may have been involved.'

'Did the Montgomerys sue Renser?'

'You'll need to ask Beth, our lawyer in the family. She knows where to look for that kind of information.'

Anna thanked Gloria and called Beth.

'Still mad at me for embarrassing you at Victoire?' Anna asked.

'No. I've been thinking about it. Your heart was in the right place.'

'I appreciate that. Especially because I need your help with something relating to that night.'

'What kind of help?' Beth asked warily.

'The man at Victoire is named Dr Jeremiah Renser.' Anna told Beth everything she had learned about him so far. 'Can you find out if the Montgomerys sued him? If they did, the records could prove helpful.'

'I'll try.'

Anna walked along Washington Street, Hoboken's main thoroughfare, and checked the piece of paper in her hand. Number 680. That was the address she'd found on the Internet for Cyrus and Edwina Montgomery. She looked up at the building and frowned. A sign said Fine Chinese Cleaning.

'This can't be right,' she said to herself and went in.

The woman behind the counter was not Chinese but African American. She gave Anna a warm smile as she entered. 'Picking up?'

'No,' Anna said, returning her smile. 'I'm looking for Cyrus and Edwina Montgomery.'

The woman frowned. 'Looking for them where?'

Anna shook her head helplessly. 'This is the address I have for them.'

Suddenly the woman shrieked over her shoulder, 'Mr Park!'

Mr Park was not Chinese either, but Korean. He looked at the address, thought a moment and said, 'Go through door next to us and up stairs. Ask there.'

She thanked them and went out, finding a

door she hadn't noticed before, also marked 680. At the top of a stairway that smelled of garlic and cabbage was a dingy, linoleum-floored corridor with several doors. Anna knocked on the nearest one. There was no sound at first, then slow footsteps and the door was slowly opened by a woman who looked to be in her seventies wearing a cotton housecoat not unlike the ones Mrs Dovner wore. 'Yeah?'

'Good afternoon,' Anna said. 'Mrs Montgomery?'

The woman looked as if she'd just eaten something bad. 'Whah?'

'Are you Mrs Montgomery?'

'Nah, I'm Mrs Adams. What do you want?'

'I'm looking for Cyrus and Edwina Montgomery. This is the address I have for them. Perhaps they once lived here?'

Mrs Adams looked back over her shoulder, much like the woman in the dry cleaner's, and yelled, 'Tom, you know anybody Montgomery?'

There was no answer but eventually Anna heard shuffling footsteps, and a white-haired man appeared, walking slowly with a cane. 'Who?' he asked in a high voice.

'Montgomery.'

'Montgomery...' Mr Adams repeated, thinking. 'You know, I think that was the name of the people who lived in this apartment before us.'

'When did you move here?' Anna asked him.

'About ten years ago.'

'Do you know where the Montgomerys live now?'

'No, but Barbara might.'

'Who's Barbara?' Anna asked.

'Lives next door,' Mrs Adams said in a tone that implied Anna should have known that. 'Been in this building over thirty years.'

''Course I knew them,' said Barbara, whose last name was Curtis. She was an elegant lady who Anna guessed was in her late eighties, with fluffy white hair and a sweet face. 'Miss 'em like crazy.'

'When did they move out?' Anna asked.

'Mm ... spring of 2000, so ten years ago now. Hard to believe.'

'Where did they go?'

'New Jersey.'

'Did you know their daughter Heather?'

''Course I did. A handful, that one.'

'How so?'

'You know how kids are. Gave her parents a terrible time.'

'How did she die?'

'Cancer. Cy and Edwina were devastated. I didn't blame them for wanting to move, leave all those memories behind. And living here was hard for Cy.'

'What do you mean?'

'He had Parkinson's. All these stairs were too much for him.' Barbara shook her head sadly. 'Poor man. Had some kind of procedure for the

Parkinson's, but it did no good.'

'Do you know if the Montgomerys sued the doctor who treated Heather?'

Barbara shrugged, shook her head.

'Have you seen the Montgomerys since they moved away?'

'No, but I send them a Christmas card every year.'

'Do you ever hear from them?'

'Can't say I have, but I suppose they're busy.'

'Do you have their address? I guess you must if you send them a Christmas card every year.'

''Course I do. And the cards don't come back, either.' Barbara walked into the kitchen and returned with a slip of paper that she handed to Anna. On it was written: Mr & Mrs Cyrus Montgomery, 1070 Upper Mountain Avenue, Upper Montclair, NJ 07043.

'Pretty fancy address,' Anna remarked. 'What do Mr and Mrs Montgomery do for a living, do you know?'

'Cy was an electrician, but he couldn't do much once the Parkinson's kicked in. Edwina had no job outside the home.'

'You wouldn't happen to have a phone number for the Montgomerys, would you?'

She shook her head. 'Like I said, Christmas cards only.'

Anna followed Valley Road through Upper Montclair Center, an upscale shopping street whose faux Tudor buildings gave it the look of an English village. As she turned on to Bellevue Avenue her cell phone rang. She pulled over, nabbed a parking spot. It was Patti.

'Everything all right?' Anna asked.

Patti laughed. 'You saw me an hour ago. You sound like my mother.'

'A lot can happen in an hour. What's up?'

'When will you be home tonight?'

'Not sure. Why?'

'No particular reason. I was wondering if I should grab a slice at that great pizza place I found, or wait to eat with you.'

'Go ahead and grab a slice – no, wait, I just remembered, Libby's reception is tonight.'

'Who's Libby?'

'Santos's niece. She's got an art installation at the Jonas Museum. There's a reception at seven. I hope you'll come.'

'Sure,' Patti said, though there was something in her voice that made Anna think she wasn't happy about it.

Anna didn't pursue it. 'I'll be home by five thirty and we can get ready and grab a cab. Deal?'

'Deal.'

Anna pulled back on to the road and climbed a hill before turning on to Upper Mountain Avenue, where some of the town's most magnificent mansions were located. She passed a Georgian manor, an enormous Tudor, an ivy-covered fieldstone number that reminded her of her parents' house in Greenwich, then came to

100

number 1070, a sprawling stone castle complete with a crenellated wall above the garage. Parked in the driveway was a black late-model BMW.

Majestic waist-high stone greyhounds guarded the double front doors. Anna rang the bell and heard it chime inside. After several moments the door was opened by a man on a motorized scooter. Neat and trim, he had a long face and expensively cut dark hair threaded with gray. He wore rust-colored wide-wale corduroy slacks, an oatmeal chamois shirt and over it an open black cardigan sweater. The country squire. 'Yes?' he said, giving Anna a small polite smile.

'Mr Montgomery?'

'Yes.'

'My name is Anna Winthrop. I'm sorry to disturb you, but I wonder if I could have a moment of your time.'

'What about?'

Without preamble she said, 'Dr Jeremiah Renser.'

She watched him carefully. At the mention of Renser's name Cyrus's eyes grew wide and he quickly drew in his breath. Then just as quickly he regained his composure, but made no reply.

'He's the doctor who treated your daughter Heather, isn't that correct?' Anna asked.

Still no answer. She decided to take a chance. 'I believe you and your wife had a grievance against Dr Renser. My firm represents a couple

101

who are suing him for malpractice. Like you, they lost their daughter because of his negligence.'

'I think you'd better come in,' he said, reversing the scooter a little and opening the door wider. Anna stepped into a large foyer with a stone floor.

'Cy, who is it?'

A petite blonde woman was descending a wide stairway. She wore a navy blue pant suit with a white cardigan draped on her shoulders.

Cyrus turned to her. 'This woman is here about Heather.'

The woman stopped short. 'Heather?'

He nodded. 'She works for a law firm, representing a couple whose daughter died.'

Edwina's gaze snapped from her husband to Anna and back again. 'What's that got to do with us?'

Anna replied, 'As I told your husband, these people are suing Dr Renser ... as you did.'

They both looked at her sharply. 'We didn't sue him,' Edwina said, eyes wide with emphasis.

'I'm so sorry,' Anna said, pretending to be flustered. 'I'm afraid I've been given inaccurate information. Would you mind telling me what did happen in your daughter's case? It could still prove helpful.'

'We would mind,' Cyrus said, rolling toward Anna. 'I don't know where you got our name, but we can't help you.'

Suddenly Edwina stepped forward. 'Dr Renser couldn't have done more than he did for Heather,' she said earnestly. 'We bear him no ill will.'

'That's enough,' Cyrus said to her and turned back to Anna. 'You'd better leave. Don't come back.' He began using the scooter to push Anna toward the door.

'If I could ask you one more question,' Anna said as she was hustled out. 'How exactly did your daughter die?'

Neither of them answered. Cyrus pushed Anna the rest of the way out and slammed the door, leaving her alone between the greyhounds. She walked back down the path. As she reached her car someone called, 'Excuse me! Hello!'

She turned around. Edwina was hurrying down the path. 'Please wait,' she said. 'I'm sorry my husband was so rude to you,' she said when she reached Anna. 'The Parkinson's has changed him, made him not always ... socially acceptable.'

'I understand,' Anna said. 'Not a problem.' What did Edwina want?

'Who did you say you work for?' the older woman asked, pulling her sweater tighter around her.

'Schutz Fine Kovner,' Anna said, using the name of Beth's erstwhile law firm.

'And you say your clients are suing Dr Renser?'

'Yes. As I told your husband, his negligence caused their daughter's death.'

'But Dr Renser has been retired for ten years.'

'This case has been pending for a very long time.'

Edwina nodded. 'I want you to understand we do not believe Dr Renser caused Heather's death. Quite the contrary. He did everything he could think of to try to save her, but sometimes...' She shrugged sadly.

'How did she die, if you'll forgive my asking?'

'She had inoperable brain cancer. Dr Renser tried some new drugs on her that had done well in clinical trials. He warned us they might do no good or even hasten Heather's death, but we were desperate and had nothing to lose.'

'I'm very sorry for your loss.'

'Thank you.' Edwina looked into Anna's eyes. 'Dr Renser is a wonderful man. Please don't ever say we sued him or have any grievances against him, because it's not true.'

'Thank you for talking to me,' Anna said.

Edwina nodded, turned and started up the path. The front door opened and Cyrus appeared on his scooter. He glared at Edwina as she approached the house.

Anna watched as Edwina entered the house and slowly closed the door.

The hotel in Tijuana was like no hotel Irena had ever seen. It was a long, two-story wooden structure with a balcony along the top floor. In places the railing had rotted away. Grigori and Yuri threw Irena into a filthy room that reeked of sweat. One small window at the back had been nailed shut so that the room was airless, stifling. The only furniture was a mattress on the floor, so dirty it was nearly black. Several blankets lay tangled nearby.

There were three other girls in the room, all of them Mexican. They spoke only Spanish, a language Irena didn't know, but no words were necessary to convey their fear at having become the personal property of an international slave trader.

For that was what Grigori was. This was what had happened to Dasha. Irena's only chance of finding her was to hope he did the same things to Irena that he had done to Dasha. In the meantime she was trapped, helpless.

Two of the Mexican women dozed on the mattress. The other sat on the floor, nervously fingering one of the blankets and staring at Irena. Nothing happened for what seemed like hours. Then the door opened and Grigori strode in. He grabbed one of the Mexican women and dragged her out. Later he brought her back, crying and shaking, and took another of the Mexican women, later bringing her back for the third. Irena braced herself to be next, but after Grigori threw the third woman on to the floor he simply walked out. The three women looked at Irena in resentful amazement.

Later Grigori took the three Mexican women again, but not Irena. Yuri came with food – sandwiches and cans of soda. Irena went up to him. 'What are your plans for me?' she asked him.

At first he made a face that suggested she was impertinent to ask. Then he seemed to think better of it and gave her a slow smile. 'Actually we have rather big plans. You are a virgin, yes?'

She nodded. 'What has that got to do with it?'

'It has a lot to do with it. You are a virgin and you are also exceptionally beautiful, like an angel.' He said it not as a compliment but as a simple fact, as if he were describing a car. 'Girls like you we keep for special treatment.'

Dasha was a virgin and even more beautiful than Irena. 'Is that what happened to my sister? Your special treatment?'

He did not answer, only went out and locked the door behind him.

Moving, of course, was impossible. It took money to move, money Nettie didn't have. When Eckart paid up and Jane Stuart nailed down Nettie's mega book deal she would be able to move anywhere she liked, hire security. But for now she would simply have to be careful, keep an eye out for Eddie at all times. He would be back. Her building had no rear entrance through which she could sneak out. She would have to use the front door, but fortunately her apartment looked out on the street so that when she went out she could first make sure the coast was clear. She went to the window now, carefully lifted the blind and looked out with one eye.

With a gasp she drew back, dropping the blind.

Eddie was out there, standing on the opposite side of the street in a long overcoat, a hat hiding his face, but there was no mistaking him. He'd been looking straight up at her window and the second she'd looked out he'd stepped back into the shadow of a doorway.

That settled it. The coast would never be clear. She must avoid going out, period.

There were too many shadows in which Eddie could hide. New York was an entire city in shadow.

The Jonas Museum's stone-and-glass façade glowed cheerily in the frigid night. The lobby was already full of people and more streamed in. Anna, Santos and Patti joined the crowd and were soon inside.

'All this is for Libby?' Patti asked Anna above the din as they handed their coats to the check room attendant.

'Absolutely,' Anna replied. 'She beat out hundreds of other high school seniors. It's a big honor.'

'You bet it is,' came a man's voice behind them and the three of them turned. Santos's brother Hector was a few inches taller than

Santos but in Anna's opinion not nearly as handsome, though he had wonderfully warm brown eyes and a winningly sweet smile. He and Santos embraced, then Hector and Anna kissed each other on the cheek. Santos introduced Patti to Hector. 'Always happy to meet members of Anna's family,' Hector said.

He was beaming. Libby had come a long way in a short time. Two years earlier she had gone through an impossibly rebellious phase. It was at Anna's encouragement that Libby had allowed herself to explore her love of art, and from the moment she touched brush to canvas she was a different person.

'Congratulations,' Anna said to Hector. 'It's a wonderful night.'

Hector nodded in agreement but suddenly looked sad. He didn't have to say what he was thinking. His wife, Carla, had died two and a half years earlier of breast cancer. She would have given anything to see this day.

'So where is the woman of the hour?' Anna asked.

'I'm right here.' Libby had grown from a pretty girl into a beautiful woman, model material if she'd been interested. Her creamy complexion was flawless, her transparent gold eyes were fringed with long lashes and her lips were naturally red and full. Lately she had cut her back-length brown hair. It hung shiny and smooth to her collar bone in a stylish blunt cut.

Patti and Libby were introduced to each other

and were instantly chattering excitedly, moving off into the crowd.

'There's something missing,' Anna said to Hector. When he raised his brows inquiringly she said, 'The art!'

'Right this way.' He led Anna and Santos to the back of the lobby where Libby's piece had been installed. Anna and Santos stared at it blankly.

From a ten-foot-square piece of plywood rose hundreds of thin, closely spaced spikes. Atop each spike sat a bald plastic doll head. All the heads had been positioned so that they stared in the same direction. In the very center, a single doll head was painted black.

Santos turned to Hector. 'OK, what is it?'

Hector laughed. 'It's called *Apathy*.'

Anna studied the piece again. 'I give up. Why is it called that?'

'That's for you to figure out,' said Libby, who had reappeared with Patti.

'I think it's bangin',' Patti said in an awe-struck voice.

On the other side of the piece Santos's mother appeared, a stout woman of medium height in a flowered dress with a long wool coat over it. Her dark-blond hair was brushed back attractively from her kind, open face. She walked over to Libby and pinched her cheeks hard.

'Ouch! Grandma!' Libby whined.

'I could eat you up,' said Dolores, known to one and all as Lola, and pressed Libby's face deep into her huge bosom.

'Grandma, I'm suffocating,' came Libby's muffled voice and everyone laughed as Lola released her.

Lola spotted Anna and Santos and hurried over. Warmly she kissed and hugged Anna, then her son. 'I told Hector his daughter is a genius, the new Andy Warwick.'

'Warhol, Mama,' he corrected her.

She waved it away. 'It is the start of her great success story.'

Anna considered Lola an unqualified success story. When Santos was six, living with his parents and five brothers and sisters in the projects in Washington Heights, Lola discovered her husband was having an affair. 'Make your choice,' she'd told him. 'Her or me. And if it's her,' the legend went, 'you can leave right now and don't ever bother coming back.' To Lola's surprise he had walked out the door. No one in the family had ever seen or heard from him again. Proud Lola never mentioned his name again as she raised her six children alone.

'What do you think?' Lola asked Anna, indicating Libby's art.

Anna opened her mouth, stopped, then said, 'It's ... interesting.'

Lola, no fool, gave her a knowing smile. 'It could be clothes drying on a line and it would be genius. *Anything* my granddaughter does is genius.'

A few feet away, Libby smiled and rolled

110

her eyes.

'Where's my other brother and my sisters?' Santos asked Lola.

'Coming,' she replied. 'They wouldn't miss this.'

Across the room, Anna spotted her sister Gloria and her husband, Donald, walking in from outside. Anna waved to get their attention. Gloria saw her and started across the room, dragging Donald behind her.

'Very exciting!' Gloria squealed amid kissing and hand-shaking.

Anna thought Gloria looked especially pretty tonight. Taller than Anna, she had an elegant slim figure and long straight blond hair she was especially proud of. Not long ago Donald, one of New York City's leading plastic surgeons, had done some work on Gloria's face. Gloria was only now thirty and Anna had given her a terrible time, but Anna had to admit that Gloria, already pretty, was now a knockout. 'You look fabulous,' Anna told Gloria, who burst into a thrilled smile.

'Thanks to my guy,' she said and squeezed Donald's arm.

'How are you, Anna?' Donald said.

'I'm fine, thank you,' she replied with a smile and let her gaze wander over his face, perhaps the most beautiful face she had ever seen on a man. Naturally blond hair with exactly the right amount of crisp wave, emerald green eyes ... he was like a movie star. Better. Unfortunately he had absolutely no personality. Zip. Gloria had never seemed to notice, however, or if she had she didn't care. 'Come on,' she said to him, 'I want to see Libby's masterpiece.' She gave Anna a happy wink and she and Donald headed off.

'Anna!'

She turned and saw her parents walking toward her. Tildy, in her early sixties, had had her brown hair cut in a pretty soft bob. She wore an attractive black pant suit and no jewelry. Tildy never wore jewelry. Anna's father Jeff, in his early seventies, looked hale and handsome in khakis, a crisp light-blue shirt and a blue blazer. 'Darling,' Tildy said to Anna during the greetings, 'where's Patti? I'm dying to see her.'

Anna shrugged. 'In there somewhere.' She indicated the ever-growing crowd.

'Come on,' Tildy said to Jeff, 'let's look for her. I can't very well tell my cousin Mary Jean I was here and didn't see her daughter.' They wandered away.

'It's a family reunion,' Santos joked.

'Not quite,' Anna said. 'My brother Will and his wife Lisa couldn't make it. They're in Aruba.'

'Lucky devils.'

'Who's a lucky devil?' came a voice behind Anna and she turned to face her sister Beth, who kissed Anna and Santos hello.

'Will and Lisa,' Anna replied. 'They're in

Aruba.'

'I'd rather be here celebrating Libby,' Beth said brightly, then stepped closer to Anna. 'Can we talk for a minute?'

'Sure,' Anna said and followed Beth to the hallway where it was quiet.

'I did that research you wanted,' Beth said. 'About Heather Montgomery.'

'And?'

'You know I'm pretty good at this, right?'

'I thought we'd established that.'

'I did everything short of hiring a private detective. The Social Security Death Index. Public records. Obituaries. Databases. You name it.'

'And?' Anna repeated, growing impatient.

'And,' Beth said, shifting her weight to one hip and looking her sister in the eye, 'from what I can tell, Heather Montgomery is still alive.'

EIGHT

'Still alive?' Anna said. 'That can't be.'

'Who told you she was dead?' Beth asked.

'Her own mother. Heather died of brain cancer.'

'Maybe she's lying.'

'Why would she lie about that? Besides, she wasn't the only one who told me Heather is dead. Renser was affiliated with New York-Presbyterian, where Gloria did her residency, so she did some research for me. According to the person she spoke to, Heather is dead.'

'All right. Let's ask Gloria who she spoke to.'

Anna went in search of Gloria and brought her back.

'What is it?' Gloria asked peevishly. 'I'm missing all the fun.'

'You mean all the wine,' Beth said dryly, gaze fixed on Gloria's nearly empty wineglass.

Anna said, 'Where did you get the information you gave me about Heather Montgomery?'

Gloria frowned. 'Who's Heather Montgomery?'

'Come on, you can't be that drunk yet. She's the girl you said was a patient of Dr Renser's.

114

You said she died. How do you know that?'

'From my friend Toby in Admitting.'

'Did she say who told her?'

'No.'

'I'd like to speak to Toby. Can you set it up for me?'

Gloria groaned. 'Don't start this detective stuff again.'

'Are you going to help me or not?'

'She won't be able to tell you any more than I have, but sure, I'll call her. When do you want to see her?'

'As soon as possible. Let me know.'

The three sisters rejoined the festivities.

As Anna and Patti approached the garage the following morning they chatted happily about Libby's art installation. Patti preceded Anna through the entrance and down the corridor to Anna's office.

'Ew, gross!' came Patti's voice from around the corner.

Anna caught up with her. Patti was pointing to the floor in front of Anna's office door. Anna looked. It was a dead mouse, its fur bloodied.

Anna laughed. 'Haven't you ever seen a mouse before?'

'Not a bloody one. Who put it in front of your door?'

'No one *put* it in front of my door. It ... died there.'

Patti gave Anna a dubious look. 'It walked up

115

to your door and dropped dead.'

'It didn't know it was my door. It ... happened to die here. Animals do die.'

Patti stared down at it again. 'This one looks like it had some help.'

It was true. The mouse's gray fur was quite bloody. When Anna looked closer she saw that its head was crushed. Patti went into Anna's office and lounged on the love seat while Anna fetched a dustpan and brush and disposed of the poor animal.

'I know who put the mouse there,' Patti said when Anna returned.

'Who?'

Patti lowered her voice. 'That funny little guy who looks like a weasel, Fred Fox.' She giggled. 'Weasel ... fox.'

In Anna's opinion, Fred looked more like a ferret. But she said to Patti, 'That's not nice.'

'Ugh, you sound like my mother.'

Anna closed the door. 'OK, why do you think Fred put the mouse there?'

'Because of what I heard yesterday in the break room.'

Anna waited.

'It was right after roll call,' Patti said. 'I went up there to eat my bagel. Fred and his partner—'

'Bill Hogan.'

'Yeah. They came in and sat at another table. Bill was teasing Fred about how you reamed him out about a lady who slipped on the ice.

Bill said something like, "She really told you where it's at." And Fred said, "Yeah, and I'm gettin' real tired of it." Bill said, "Tired of what?" And Fred said, "Takin' orders from a broad."'

Anna smiled. 'So that's why you think Fred left the mouse at my door? Because he's mad at me?'

'Sure. Makes sense, right?'

'In a childish sort of way.'

'I'll take my tuna sandwich up there at lunchtime and see what else I can find out.'

'Thanks, but we're going out to lunch today.'

Patti brightened. 'We are?'

Anna nodded. 'To celebrate your arrival in New York.'

'No arguments from me. Where're we going?'

'The Oyster Bar in Grand Central Station. You can't get more New York than that.'

Irena and the other three women looked up fearfully as the door was unlocked and Grigori and Yuri entered the room. Grigori ordered them to stand, then Yuri tied the Mexican women's hands behind their backs and led them out.

'You come with me,' Grigori said to Irena.

'Where are we going?'

He gave her a disingenuous smile. 'Why, New York, like I promised.'

She didn't ask whether this was part of the

'special treatment.' Her instincts told her perhaps Yuri shouldn't have told her what he had. If so, getting him in trouble with Grigori could only be bad for her.

'Aren't you going to tie my hands?' she asked as he led her out by the arm.

'Do you want me to?' He shook his head. 'Would damage the goods. We need you perfect in every way.'

'Where are the other girls going?'

'Strip clubs in Tijuana ... now that they've been broken in.'

The sun was blindingly bright, its heat brutal. Grigori guided Irena across a yard of dirt and scrub where two chickens strutted and scratched. Across the way a man Irena hadn't seen before was helping the three Mexican women into a van.

Grigori led Irena to the car and put her in the back. As Grigori got behind the wheel, Yuri reappeared and hopped into the front passenger seat. With a growl of the old car's engine and a burst of black smoke they were off again.

'Now listen carefully,' Grigori said as he drove along the highway. 'We are going now to Tijuana. It is a busy place, busiest land border in the world, but the Americans are still careful. If they decide to stop us at the checkpoint they will speak to you, and you are to say the following – nothing more, nothing less. "Yes. US." Say it.'

'Yes. US,' she repeated.

'Good. Keep saying it until you are sure.'

Yuri twisted around to speak to her. 'Do not think this is your chance to escape. If you try, the Americans will put you in jail or deport you and your parents will die, so everyone will lose.'

Soon they were driving through the city of Tijuana and eventually came to the border, where many lanes of cars waited to go through the checkpoint, above which a sign said United States Border Inspection.

Irena hoped their car would be stopped. She had no intention of saying 'Yes. US' and every intention of screaming for help.

But in the end they sailed through and Grigori began following signs that said San Diego.

'What do you mean, it wasn't believable?' Nettie snapped into the phone, the spray of hair on top of her head wobbling like a quail's plume.

'Just what I said,' replied Ginny Armstrong, who owned a blog called EatUpNewYork.com. 'I don't get the feeling you really ate the eel.'

Nettie's assignment had been to visit a new Japanese restaurant in midtown called Dazaifu, one of whose specialties was barbecued eel layered with spinach and shiitake mushrooms.

Of course Nettie hadn't eaten the eel. She would have had to actually go to the restaurant to do so, and she couldn't very well do that because she was now leaving her apartment only when absolutely necessary. But that was beside the point. Even if she'd gone to Dazaifu she wouldn't have dreamed of eating such a disgusting thing. She'd written about lots of restaurants for Ginny, and though Nettie had never really eaten the foods she wrote about, she had always gone to the restaurants. How could Ginny tell?

'Words like *succulent* and *exquisite* don't mean anything,' Ginny was saying. 'I could say that without ever setting foot in the place. My readers want to know what that dish really tastes like. They count on me for that.'

Nettie rolled her eyes. 'Then you know what, Ginny? Go to the restaurant and eat the eel yourself.' And she slammed down the phone.

She regretted it immediately. That piece would have paid fifty dollars, a sum she sorely needed. Not to mention there would be no more assignments from Ginny. Nettie always had lots of work but it didn't pay well – fifty dollars here, fifty dollars there. She was able to pay her rent and that was about it. She couldn't buy clothes, couldn't go to movies, couldn't even buy the vitamins the doctor told her to take. She needed that fifty dollars from Ginny. Nettie considered calling back and delivering a groveling apology but just as quickly dismissed the idea. There was such a thing as pride.

But pride didn't pay the bills or buy Charleston Chews and Suzy Q's. Her stomach growled painfully. That Eddie – this was his fault. Why couldn't he leave her alone, accept that they were through?

She began to cry. She must be strong. She had other pieces to write. Fortunately she was still on board with so many other blog sites that sometimes she couldn't remember them all. She took up a steno pad in which she recorded her assignments with their deadlines and saw that a piece on eyebrow threading was due to Tori Spencer at CityGorgeous.com the following day. *That* she could do with her hands behind her back. She certainly didn't need to go anywhere. Yes, that and plenty of other assignments would see her through until Mr Eckart paid her to keep quiet and Jane Stuart called with news of her humongous deal.

Grigori turned off the busy New York City street and drove through an alley to the rear of a building. He grabbed Irena from the back and took her inside. It was a hotel, seedy and old. Grigori took her down a long corridor with closed doors on each side to an elevator which they took to the seventh floor. There Grigori knocked on a door and a man's deep voice inside called, 'Come in.'

The man sitting on the bed was big and stocky. His white hair was combed back from his red, bloated face. Irena guessed he was around seventy. He wore a navy blue polo shirt and a blue blazer.

'Come in,' he said and gave Irena a grandfatherly smile. 'Close the door,' he ordered Grigori. 'Don't be afraid, my dear,' he said to Irena and rose from the bed. 'My name is Dr Renser. I want you to take off your clothes.'

She knew better than to disobey. Silently she stripped, letting her clothes drop to the floor, until she stood naked and shaking before the two men.

Dr Renser drew in his breath through his nose. 'Exquisite.' He looked at Grigori. 'You have done well.'

'She's Dasha's sister,' Grigori said. 'Irena.'

'Ah.' Dr Renser nodded. 'And just as lovely. No one has touched her?' he asked Grigori.

'No one.'

'Very good. I will verify that for myself, of course.' Dr Renser stepped nearer to Irena and ran his finger across one creamy breast. 'Don't be afraid,' he repeated. 'No one is going to hurt you.'

'What do you want with me?' she asked in Ukrainian.

Grigori translated.

'Nothing that will cause you any pain, I promise,' Dr Renser said. 'Now, Grigori is going to leave the room so I can examine you. Then some things will happen that I think you will find rather nice.' He turned again to Grigori. 'Get over to the Kirkmore and check on Eva. She's been alone for some time.'

At noon Anna and Patti walked over to Grand

Central Terminal and took the stairs down to the Dining Concourse. The Oyster Bar was situated in a tunnel just off this bustling food court. In front of the restaurant was a hallway of sweeping terracotta tiled arches, with the tunnel leading upward on the left and downward on the right.

'There's something fun I want to show you out here,' Anna said, 'but after lunch. I'm starving.'

As they were led through the busy restaurant to a table, Anna pointed out the low vaulted ceiling made of the same tiles as the hallway. They took their seats and Patti glanced around wide-eyed. 'I love this place.'

'Me, too. It's the oldest business in Grand Central. Dates back to 1913 when the terminal first opened.'

It took a long time for Patti to make a selection from the huge menu, but at last she settled on the fried Ipswich whole clams with tartar sauce and French fries.

'Make that two,' Anna told the waiter. 'So...' she said when he had gone, 'how do you like New York so far?'

'I love it,' Patti replied without hesitation.

'How about the sanitation garage?'

'That,' Patti said with a sorry smile, 'not so much.'

'Really?'

'Don't be hurt, but sanitation's not for everybody.'

123

'Does that mean you'd rather not come to the garage anymore?'

Patti leaned forward earnestly. 'Would you be terribly hurt?'

'Of course not. What would you do instead?'

'What I'd most like to do is walk around. Explore.'

'You can't do that all day, every day.'

'Why not? As far as I can tell, a person could explore this city for years and still not see it all.'

'I don't think your mother would be very pleased. It's not what she had in mind.'

Patti cocked her head to one side. 'Just what *did* my mother have in mind? Do you know?'

'Of course. She wanted you to spend some time with me to get an idea of what a career would be like.'

'In the Sanitation Department?'

'Not specifically. She thought, well, that I would be a good role model for you.'

Patti leaned forward again. 'You *are* a good role model for me. But I don't need to be in the garage to see that. My mother also thought New York would give me career ideas.'

'Fair enough, but I don't like the idea of you wandering around Manhattan all day.'

'I won't be wandering around, I'll be exploring. I've already got some things I want to do.'

'Such as?'

'The museums, for one thing. The Met, Natural History, Guggenheim, MoMA, City of New York ... Mom must have told you I'm interested in art.'

'Yes,' Anna conceded, 'she did.'

'I'm dying to see these places. I'm an adult. I'm OK on my own. Please.'

Their lunches arrived.

'Let me think about it,' Anna said. 'In the meantime, please pass the ketchup.'

After lunch as they were leaving the restaurant Patti said, 'What did you want to show me?'

Out in the vaulted hallway, Anna walked over to one of the corners where the tiled arches met. 'Stand here,' she said and Patti obeyed, frowning in puzzlement.

Anna walked over to the corner diagonally opposite Patti, turned around so that she was facing the wall and whispered very softly, 'Can you hear me, Patti?'

From across the hall came Patti's gasp of delight. 'I heard you perfectly! It was like you were standing next to me. What *is* this?'

'It's the Whispering Gallery.' Anna returned to where Patti stood. 'It's a New York secret. No sign, no markings, no explanation of how it works. Only insiders know about it.'

'How *does* it work?'

'It's the acoustics of the arches. The sound actually follows the curvature of the wall and ceiling. It's a favorite spot for marriage proposals, especially on Valentine's Day.'

Patti looked up, marveling. 'It's all in the arches.'

'They say the same thing happens inside the restaurant, since it's got the same kind of vaulting. Apparently there are secret spots, some quite far from each other, where conversation carries across the room.'

'Good thing we didn't say anything we would not want anyone to hear,' Patti said and laughed.

But Anna didn't laugh. Her gaze was fixed on someone who had just walked down the ramp to their left and was now crossing in front of them.

'What's the matter?' Patti asked.

There was no mistaking her. A beautiful young woman in jeans and a navy blue sweatshirt.

It was Eva.

NINE

Eva was walking quickly, eyes straight ahead.

Patti came up beside Anna. 'Who are you looking at?'

'It's her,' Anna said in a low voice.

'Who?'

'Eva ... the girl in the pickup truck.'

Anna ran up to her, touched her shoulder. 'Eva!'

Eva spun around, saw Anna and froze, eyes wide.

Anna placed her hand on Eva's arm. 'I know you're in trouble. I want to help you.'

But now Eva was looking past Anna. Anna turned and followed her gaze. A short, fat man with blond hair was hurrying down the ramp. Yuri Morozov.

'Hey!' he shouted at Anna, whose hand was still on Eva's arm. He ran up to them and threw off Anna's hand. 'Mind your own business,' he barked and grabbed Eva roughly. He mumbled something under his breath to Eva. For a moment they struggled. There was a ripping sound and then Yuri's sleeve gaped from his jacket. He spoke to Eva again, then began dragging her back up the ramp. As Anna watched in horror Grigori appeared behind them and ran up to them. The two men spoke rapidly in Ukrainian.

'Don't try that again!' Yuri said loudly to Eva. Then the three of them hurried back up the ramp, around the corner and out of sight.

'Come on,' Anna said to Patti and the two women ran after them. 'Eva! Wait!' Anna shouted.

People coming down the ramp jumped aside to let them through. Anna, ahead of Patti, shouted Eva's name. It echoed through the tunnel.

Suddenly someone took Anna firmly by the arm, spun her around and she was face to face with a tall policeman. Callahan, his name tag said. 'What do you think you're doing?' he demanded.

'Let go of me,' she said, twisting free, and as Patti watched from the side Anna started after Eva, Yuri and Grigori. She had taken only a few steps when Callahan grabbed her again, this time with a firmer grip. 'Lady, what is your problem?'

'Let me go,' she repeated. 'You have no idea what's going on here.'

'Why don't you tell me?'

Anna looked up the ramp. Eva and the two men were long gone. 'Never mind,' she said dejectedly.

'Never mind!' Callahan said with a cynical

laugh. 'I don't think so. You can't harass people like that.'

She worked to compose herself. 'You're right. I'm sorry. I saw someone I know. I thought she was having trouble with two men who were following her. I apologize.'

He considered her thoughtfully, clearly trying to decide whether to release her.

'I assure you I am not a crazy person,' Anna said and added irrelevantly, 'My boyfriend is a police officer.'

'Who is that?'

'Santos Reyes.'

He smiled broadly. 'Reyes is your boyfriend? Great guy.'

'Yes, he is.'

'All right,' Callahan said, still reluctant, 'you can go. But watch yourself.'

Back in her office, Anna called Santos while Patti lay on the love seat reading a cover story in the *Star* about celebrities without makeup. Anna told Santos what had happened.

'She was escaping,' Anna told Santos. 'Then Yuri and Grigori came after her and dragged her back.'

'Did you see where they took her?'

'How could I with your friend Officer Callahan holding on to me?' In her agitation Anna tapped a pen repeatedly on her desk.

'Don't sound so bitter,' Santos said. 'Think how it must have looked.'

'Don't be such a cop. We have to do something.'

'I'll go see Grigori again.'

Anna tapped the pen especially hard and it flew out of her hand, landing between her desk and the wall. She leaned over to retrieve it and came face to face with another dead mouse.

'Ew!'

'What is it?' Santos said.

Patti sat up. 'What's wrong?'

'Another one,' Anna told Patti, who came over and looked.

'Another what?' Santos asked.

'I'll call you back,' Anna said and put down the phone.

'At least this one isn't bloody,' Patti said. 'What are you going to do?'

'I'm going to have a chat with Mr Fox.'

'Would you mind if I left now?'

'To go where?'

'Explore, like I was saying.'

Anna hesitated. 'All right,' she said at last, 'but let's agree you'll be home by six for dinner. Deal?'

'Deal.'

Anna found Fred coming out of the men's locker room, his hair still wet from the shower. 'My office,' she said and he followed her downstairs.

'What is it?' he asked when they reached her office.

'I want to show you something.'

She pointed to the mouse. He looked. 'It's a mouse.'

'I know it's a mouse.'

Fred frowned. 'What's it got to do with me?'

'A lot, since you put it there.'

He looked at her as if she were insane. 'Why would I put it there?'

'You're mad at me for reprimanding you about the ice.'

'I'm not mad at you.'

'I understand you told Bill Hogan you were tired of taking orders from a broad.'

His eyes bulged in surprise. 'Who told you that? Bill?'

'No, it wasn't Bill.' Apparently he'd forgotten Patti was there, or he hadn't noticed her in the first place. 'It doesn't matter who told me. What matters is that this is how you express your resentment of me. Your communication skills need a lot of work.'

'You gotta believe me,' he pleaded. 'I did not put that there. I admit I was ticked off when you talked to me like that about the ice. You embarrassed me in front of everybody. But I wouldn't do something like this, you should know that about me. I been working with you for a long time.'

Anna decided to believe him. 'I apologize for blaming you. Do you have any idea who might have done this? It's not the first time.'

'You mean somebody keeps leaving you dead mice?'

She nodded.

'I'm sorry, I got no idea.'

Thoughtfully she watched him go.

What happened to Irena after the doctor's thorough examination of every inch of her body bordered on the surreal. When she had dressed, Dr Renser took her down the corridor to a suite and ordered her to sit in a chair in the center of the living room. After a few moments the door opened and a gray-haired man with a mustache entered. He was in his shirtsleeves, a tape measure dangling from his neck. He nodded to Dr Renser who left the room.

'I am Mr Martin,' he said, eyeing Irena appraisingly. 'Stand up,' he said in a businesslike tone, 'and strip to your underwear.'

He proceeded to take her measurements, marking them down on a pad.

'Why are you doing this?' she asked but he shook his head.

'Sorry, only English. Turn, please.'

Finally he was finished and motioned for her to get dressed. Then he left the room and two women entered, one tall and skinny, the other dumpy and short.

'Hello,' they said in unison, smiling warmly. The tall one pointed to the chair in the center of the room and indicated that Irena should sit.

Suddenly they were all over her, the tall woman unpinning her hair, moving it around her face, backward and forward, up and down.

132

At the same time the short woman stood back as if to study a work of art, tilting her head from side to side. 'Minimal,' she finally pronounced. 'A natural look. What do you think?'

'Absolutely,' the other woman said. Then without another word they left the room, leaving her alone.

A few minutes later Dr Renser returned and took her to a room down the corridor, locking her in. There was a clean, neatly made twin bed. A dresser and a chair. No phone, no TV. A window near the bed looked out on an air shaft. There was a closet near the door and next to it a tiny bathroom stocked with towels. Irena took a shower. She hated putting her dirty clothes back on but they were all she had.

She sat down on the bed and tried to figure out what to do.

The following morning Yuri came to Irena's room and took her back to the suite. Dr Renser and Mr Martin were there and also the hair and makeup women. To one side stood a rack of gowns in various colors.

Irena was ordered to sit in the chair, whereupon the tall woman draped a towel over her and began to cut and style her hair. It took a long time but when it was finished Irena was allowed to look in a mirror and had to admit it was the most beautiful style she had ever had, still long but gracefully shaped over her shoulders, and with bangs, which she had never had before. She turned to Dr Renser and, pointing to her hair, her body, said, 'Why?'

'Why? To make you even more beautiful, my dear.' He stood back so that the short makeup woman could start her work. When she was finished Mr Martin helped Irena put on one of the gowns from the rack, a diaphanous white creation. When she turned around everyone gasped.

'A goddess,' the hair woman said.

'A movie star,' the makeup woman said.

'So graceful,' Mr Martin said.

Dr Renser studied her for a long time, then broke into a slow smile. 'Perfect.'

Tears ran down Irena's cheeks, making little tracks in her makeup.

During the afternoon Allen Schiff called Anna to his office. 'I want to discuss our holiday duties,' he said. Looking at Anna he wrinkled his brows. 'Are you all right?'

She'd been thinking about Eva, then about the dead mice. 'I'm fine,' she said, forcing a little smile.

He nodded. 'Let's start with Times Square.' He meant the cleanup after the New Year's celebration. Times Square was in Anna's section. Allen always liked to discuss the cleanup ahead of time, even though every year the drill was pretty much the same.

At eleven o'clock, even before the ball dropped for the countdown, approximately ninety sanitation workers under the command of the Sanitation Department's deputy chief assembled at the edge of Times Square's tightly controlled security area known as the 'frozen zone.' The previous year these workers had been armed with thirteen mechanical brooms, nine collection trucks and seventy-five hand brooms and blowers.

Until the ball dropped the cleanup crew kept out of sight. When the new year had arrived and revelers began to either head home or escape the cold in neighborhood bars, the workers moved into action, beginning to clean even as the grips and roadies broke down the stage used by the performers.

Anna recalled that the previous year an especially bitter wind had hindered the crew's efforts by whipping up confetti, plastic souvenir bags and other refuse and swirling it into the sky in small tornadoes. But the workers had persevered, deployed by the deputy chief to sectors marked on a map. The cleanup yielded forty-two tons of garbage, which was pretty much typical.

'I want you to make sure every member of your crew is proficient in operating the mechanical broom,' Allen said. She knew why. The previous year Bill Hogan had accidentally knocked over one of the metal barricades the police used to partition and control the crowd. A grip had had to jump out of the way.

'Absolutely,' she said.

'Let's move on to Christmas tree recycling. January third through fourteenth. We're taking a tougher stance this year. If residents don't follow the rules we don't take the tree. They've got to remove stands, tinsel, lights and ornaments. They can't put the tree in a plastic bag. This is a good program when it runs smoothly.' Collected trees were chipped and turned into compost that was processed and ultimately spread on parks, ball fields and community parks throughout the city.

'I want you to make sure everyone on your crew knows about Mulchfest. Technically it's not part of Sanitation, it's Parks and Recreation, but we've got to be able to give residents information if they ask. It'll be held on Saturday, January eighth, and Sunday, January ninth, at more than eighty sites around the city. They can find locations on the P and R Web site. People can drop off their tree and pick up free mulch.'

Anna's cell phone rang.

'Sorry,' she said, about to turn it off.

'That's OK, we're done here.'

She gave him a nod and went out to the corridor to take the call. It was Mary Jean.

'I'm sorry I haven't called sooner,' she said. 'How's the visit going?'

'It's going well. We've already ruled out Sanitation as a career path. I was going to call you. Patti wants to be free to explore New York on her own. Are you OK with that?'

'I suppose so. She's fine on her own. It's just

136

that I don't know how much good that's going to do her.'

'Maybe it's exactly what she needs. Who knows what ideas she'll get?'

'Good point. I can't thank you enough for having her.'

'No thanks needed. I'm glad to have this chance to get to know her better.'

This conversation was still on Anna's mind as she walked home later that afternoon. It was as she approached her building that she had an idea. In her apartment she called Beth.

'How are you fixed for staff?' Anna asked.

Beth laughed. 'I have a staff of one – me. This is a Cheap Shop, remember. I'm keeping overhead as low as possible.'

'Then you'll probably like my idea. Patti won't be coming to the garage anymore. How about letting her help you in the shop?'

'That's an excellent idea,' Beth said. 'Make sure she comes to my grand opening party tonight. I'll speak to her then.'

Back in her room Irena took a shower. She carried the chair to the window and as she gazed into the air shaft she began to cry, thinking about her parents, how afraid they must be for both their daughters. In Irena's case they weren't even able to tell themselves she was all right because she hadn't furnished them with a story; she had simply disappeared.

In the late afternoon there was a soft knock on

her door. As if she could let someone in if she wanted to. Puzzled, she went to the door and said, 'Yes?'

'Housekeeping. May I come in?'

'Yes, yes,' Irena said and watched as the bolt turned and the door opened. It was a middle-aged woman in a maid's uniform with an armful of fresh towels and bed linens. She had tightly curled gray hair and a kindly face.

'I'm supposed to come right in and lock it again,' she said, doing so and then pocketing her key.

For the briefest moment Irena considered attacking her and taking the key. But even if she escaped from this room she doubted she would make it to the street.

'What's your name, honey?' the woman asked.

'Irena.'

'Russian, are you?'

'I am from Ukraine.'

'That's interesting,' the woman said, barely listening as she replaced the towels in the bathroom. 'Another maid here, girl name of Marfa, she's Russian too.'

'Your name?' Irena asked.

'Me? I'm Roberta, nice to meet you.' She used one of the dirty towels to wipe down the bathroom. Then Irena watched her strip and remake the bed.

'I almost forgot,' Roberta said. 'I'm to take your clothes to the laundry. There should be a robe in the closet you can wear.'

There was. Irena changed into it in the bath-room.

'This girl Marfa...' Irena said as she handed her clothes to Roberta.

'Yes?'

Irena spoke several sentences very fast in Ukrainian. When Roberta stared at her help-lessly Irena repeated them. Then she screwed up her face as if she were going to cry.

'Now, now.' Roberta put a comforting arm around her. 'I've got just the thing. Next time I see Marfa I'll send her up. She'll know what you're trying to say. How's that?'

Irena thought she understood and nodded enthusiastically.

She tried one more thing before Roberta departed.

'Why I am here?' she said, pointing to herself and then indicating the room.

'Why are you here?' Roberta shook her head regretfully, but Irena knew it wasn't because she didn't know, but rather because she was afraid to say. Carrying the dirty towels Roberta let herself out and quickly relocked the door.

Nettie peered out from behind the window blind, waiting for nightfall. Eddie hadn't return-ed since she'd spotted him, but she knew that was because he knew she'd seen him and was waiting elsewhere. He was down there, she had no doubt of that, so even when she went out under cover of dark she must be careful.

And go out she must. She had never been so hungry. She had long ago run out of Charleston Chews and Suzy Q's. She had then drunk the peach Snapple and squirted the remainder of the whipped cream into her mouth.

She still had no coat. It was especially cold tonight, twenty-three degrees according to the TV, so she piled on the layers, finishing with an oversize sweatshirt and a black watch cap. She was reaching for the doorknob to leave when her phone rang.

Her phone almost never rang. She had no family except Uncle Allen, her parents having died years ago. No siblings, either, and no close friends. No caller ID. She supposed this could be one of the people she blogged for, nagging about some overdue piece, though they rarely called this late. It had occurred to her that Eddie, being a cop, might have succeeded in obtaining her unlisted number, so now whenever she lifted the receiver she simply listened, waiting for the other person to speak. She picked up the phone, said nothing.

'Hello? Nettie?'

She recognized the strong voice of Jane Stuart.

'How are you?' Nettie asked. 'Are you calling with good news?'

'Good news?' Jane sounded puzzled. 'You mean an offer? No, sorry. I'll be in the city tomorrow and wondered if I could take you to brunch. I realize it's short notice but I figured I'd take a chance and see if you were available. I thought we could talk about future projects.'

Nettie frowned into the phone. 'Future projects? But we haven't sold *New York Super-Women* yet.'

'And in this market, who knows if I will?'

Nettie didn't like this kind of talk. Perhaps it was time to hire a new agent. For now she'd play along, not wanting to alienate Jane while she still needed her. 'Of course, I'd love to see you,' she said, dreading the thought of going out in daylight. 'Where and when?'

'How about The Palm on West Fiftieth Street between Eighth and Broadway? Eleven.'

'Perfect. Can't wait. See you then.'

Nettie hung up, returned to the door and with a deep breath slipped out to the landing.

When Irena awoke from her nap her laundered clothes were in a neat pile by the door. As she finished putting them on Grigori came and took her back to the suite. This time a photographer was there, all set up with a white-draped stool for her to sit on and a white backdrop. A good-looking dark-haired man in his late twenties, he reminded Irena of Alex.

'You look as if you've seen a ghost. I'm Ian,' he said, pointing to himself. He handed her a plain white robe and indicated that she should go into the bedroom and put it on instead of her clothes. When she came out the hair and makeup ladies were there. Irena sat on the stool and the tall lady made sure her hair was perfect while the short one applied makeup. Grigori had stepped out to the hall and now reappeared pulling the rack of gowns. Irena was instructed to put on the white goddess one and then sit again on the stool. With hand movements Ian instructed Irena to take different poses as he flashed away. 'How 'bout a smile?' he said and she managed one. He flashed some more.

'Very, very beautiful.' Ian set down his camera and walked over to Irena. 'You're going to make some lucky man very happy,' he said, holding her chin gently between his thumb and forefinger.

Suddenly Grigori stormed over and threw down Ian's hand. 'What do you think you are doing?'

'Nothing,' Ian said, hands palms-out at his sides.

'Never touch!' Grigori said.

Not another word was said as Irena returned to the bedroom to put her clothes back on.

That evening there was a soft knock on Irena's door. 'Housekeeping.'

Irena expected Roberta but it was a different woman, around Irena's age, with dark hair and wary eyes. She entered with an armload of towels and relocked the door. Then she turned to Irena and said in Ukrainian, 'My name is Marfa.'

Irena ran to her. 'You are from Ukraine?'

Marfa nodded. 'Odessa. You?'

'Kiev. Please, you must help me. They are holding me prisoner. Call the police.'

'I can't do that.' Looking sorry, Marfa set the towels on the dresser. 'If I do they'll kill me.'

'What is this place?'

'It's a hotel. The Taylor Hotel.'

'Why am I here?' Irena asked desperately. 'What are they going to do with me?'

'I don't know, honestly. I'm only a maid.'

'Only a maid,' Irena said disgustedly. 'You are a criminal, as bad as they are. You could let me out but you do not. There are other maids from Ukraine?'

'No ... but the *girls* have all been from there.'

Irena's breath caught in her throat. 'Who?'

Marfa searched her memory. 'Six including you.'

'Was one named Dasha?' Irena asked.

'Yes, she was the latest one. She looked like you.'

'She is my sister. Please, do you know what they have done with her?'

'Same as the other girls. Taken her to the Kirkmore.'

Irena frowned. 'What is the Kirkmore?'

'A sort of hotel near Times Square. Very fancy.'

'What happens to these girls in the Kirkmore?'

'I don't know,' Marfa said apologetically. 'I

143

guess you'll find out. I'd better go.' As if in fast motion she grabbed the towels from the dresser, hurried into the bathroom and reappeared with the dirty ones. 'Good night,' she said and let herself out.

Irena stared at the door as Marfa relocked it from the outside. Dasha had been there. Then they had taken her to this place the Kirkmore. Marfa had implied Irena would be going there, too.

Hope filled her.

TEN

Beth's Cheap Shop was located on Third Avenue between 61st and 62nd streets, between a bookstore and a pet boutique. As Anna and Patti's taxi pulled to the curb, Anna peered out at the sign Beth had had made, designed to look as if someone had scrawled out the shop's name with a paintbrush. Through the window a good-size crowd had already gathered.

Beth greeted Anna and Patti warmly, then put her arm around Patti's shoulder and led her off to the rear of the shop to chat.

Santos appeared and greeted Anna with a kiss. He surveyed the crowd. 'I see everyone who came to Libby's reception.'

'Plus Beth's friends from work.'

His face grew serious. 'Can I talk to you a second?' They moved to one side. 'I went to see Grigori again.'

'And?'

'He wasn't home but I spoke to his wife Vicky. I told her about how you spotted Eva escaping under Grand Central yesterday, how Grigori and Yuri caught up with her and dragged her back.'

'What did she say?'

'This time she was happy to tell me anything she could about Grigori, because she's thrown him out. Seems he was gone for a week, and during that time Vicky found some emails between Grigori and his mistress. Turns out the desk he bought from you was a present for her.'

'Where had he gone?'

'She doesn't know. She said he's been disappearing like this periodically for the past year or so, but he would never tell her where he was going. He got back from this latest trip late yesterday. Before she told him he was no longer welcome she heard him talking on his cell phone. He was speaking Ukrainian, she doesn't know to whom. Having been married to him for five years she understands some Ukrainian, and she thinks he said, "She won't be able to tell anyone anything."'

'What do you think that means?' Anna asked. 'Do you think he was referring to Eva?'

'No idea,' Santos said with a shrug. 'From Brighton Beach I went up to West 113th Street to talk to Yuri. He wasn't home but I spoke to a woman in the next apartment. She said Yuri had been gone for a week and she heard him get back late last night.'

'Same as Grigori.'

Santos nodded, then shrugged again to indicate he didn't know what it all meant. 'How about some wine?' he said with forced cheerfulness.

'I'd love some,' she said and watched him head for the refreshments table. While he was gone, Patti returned from her chat with Beth.

'That was a surprise,' Patti said.

'A good one, I hope.'

'I'll give it a shot, see how it goes. I'm starting tomorrow.'

Santos returned with two glasses of wine. 'Sorry, Patti, would you like some wine?'

'I'll get it.' She smiled politely. 'I'm heading in that direction anyway.'

As Patti walked away Anna had the distinct feeling Patti didn't want wine so much as she wanted to get away from Anna.

Grigori and Yuri came to Irena's room and took her down to the service area behind the hotel. An olive-green pickup truck was parked there. They marched her toward it.

'I am freezing,' she said, 'I have no coat.'

They ignored her. Grigori pushed her to the middle of the front seat and they got in on either side of her, Grigori driving.

'Don't try anything,' Yuri said as Grigori put the truck in gear.

The streets teemed with people but Irena didn't dare try to get anyone's attention. They passed through Times Square – Irena recognized it from TV and movies – and Grigori found a parking spot in front of an ice cream shop. As they crossed the sidewalk Irena realized they were going to an unmarked glass door beside the shop. A uniformed doorman saw them and hurried out. He nodded curtly at the two men, who called him Michael as they greeted him. Then Michael tipped his cap at Irena, at the same time looking her up and down appreciatively.

'What is this place?' Irena asked the two men as they crossed a small lobby.

'The Kirkmore,' Yuri replied.

Excitement filled Irena as they took the elevator to the nineteenth floor and went down the corridor to a door marked 1910. Grigori unlocked it and they entered a beautiful marble foyer with a garden in the center. Off this foyer were many rooms, all of them lavishly appointed.

'Who lives here?' Irena asked.

'Dr Renser,' Yuri replied.

At that moment Dr Renser himself appeared in the archway leading to the living room. He wore a dark suit. He came forward and held Irena's chin in his hand as Ian the photographer had done. 'Welcome, my dear.' He turned to Grigori and Yuri. 'How is the one with the flu?'

'The same,' Grigori replied.

'You can go,' he told them. They left and he used a key to lock the door behind them.

'I'm afraid I must go out,' he said to Irena. 'Make yourself at home. I think you'll find everything you need.'

With a smile he let himself out, relocking the door.

The suite was very quiet. Irena began to explore, first entering what must be the master bedroom. It was the most beautiful bedroom she had ever seen, a vast room in shades of cream and gray, like something out of the decorating magazines her mother loved to read. Off this room was a dressing area, a room in itself. Shelves, drawers, closets and cupboards held what must be Dr Renser's clothes, an endless wardrobe. Then she noticed, on the other side of this room, a woman's wardrobe – pants, shirts, dresses, shoes, coats. She wondered who it all belonged to.

She wandered into the bathroom. It was unlike any bathroom she had ever seen, a huge room done in cream-colored marble with a rough, natural surface. In the center was a flower garden with a silent fountain in it. There was a large shower in a sort of grotto and a tub with an odd channel around it that Irena couldn't figure out.

She moved through the suite's many rooms, awestruck. A gleaming ultramodern kitchen looked as if it had never been used. A service door at the back was locked. The kitchen drawers were empty, as was the refrigerator.

A library filled with books and overstuffed leather furniture had windows that extended from the floor to the ceiling. She looked down at the street nineteen stories below and felt a wave of dizziness. None of the surrounding buildings were close enough that she might attract someone's attention. There were no terraces from which she might have screamed for help and it wouldn't have mattered if there had been because none of the windows opened.

Back in the foyer she noticed a TV monitor built into the wall. On the screen was the lobby she had passed through. She could see Michael the doorman standing just outside and cars passing in the street. There were buttons underneath the monitor that must be for the intercom but they appeared to have been turned off. Anyway, who would she call through the intercom?

In a den there was a large flat-screen TV. She found the remote and switched it on. A movie called *The Stepford Wives* was on and she sat down to watch it but her mind was elsewhere.

Was Dasha still here at the Kirkmore?

Anna placed the antique angel at the top of the Christmas tree, then stepped back to survey her and Santos's creation.

'Wait,' Santos said and switched off the light.

Anna let out a little gasp. On the tree jewel-tone lights glowed. Gold-colored ornaments and silver tinsel sparkled. 'It's the most beautiful tree ever.'

'You say that every year.'

'Because it's true. I'll be right back.' She went into the bedroom and returned with an armful of presents which she arranged artfully under the tree.

'Good idea.' Santos retrieved a shopping bag

150

he had left behind the sofa and brought out more brightly wrapped boxes. He mixed these in with the ones Anna had just put down. Anna knelt to look at Santos's gifts. Several had her name on them. She picked one up and shook it.

'No fair,' he said, and with a laugh she put it back. Then she put her arms around Santos and hugged him tight. When she finally drew back, her face was troubled.

'I know what you're thinking,' he said. 'Eva.'

'Of course. Here we are, getting ready for Christmas, while she's being held prisoner, afraid for her life.'

The phone rang. 'I hope it's not Patti saying she doesn't want to work at Beth's shop,' Anna said.

It was Gloria.

'I spoke with my friend Toby at NewYork-Presbyterian,' she said. 'She'll be happy to talk to you but she can't leave work. Can you be there at noon?'

'She's working on Sunday?'

'People are always being admitted to the hospital. Go to Admitting and ask for Toby Eisenberg.'

The check room attendant at The Palm smiled at Nettie. 'May I take your coat?'

'I'm not wearing one,' Nettie replied. The woman's smile turned to a look of puzzlement.

Nettie gave Jane's name to the maître d'.

'She's already arrived. This way, please.'

Jane was at a table in the corner. When she saw Nettie she waved and stood to greet her. Nettie had met Jane only once before and had forgotten what a striking woman she was, with her strong features, shoulder-length auburn hair and tall, shapely figure. They exchanged kisses, then Jane drew back and studied Nettie.

'That's an odd outfit, if you don't mind my saying so,' Jane said.

Nettie did mind her saying so but didn't tell Jane that. Jane was known for her bluntness and Nettie would have to keep reminding herself of that. She looked down at her outfit – an over-size black Mickey Mouse sweatshirt over a pink mock turtleneck sweater over black leggings. 'It is Sunday,' she said lightly.

Jane gave a little frown of bewilderment. 'I get cold just looking at those leggings. But of course your coat would keep you warm.'

Nettie smiled. She wasn't about to tell Jane she didn't have a coat because she'd left it in the Kirkmore when she was snooping around. 'What brings you to New York?' she asked Jane, changing the subject.

'I came in with my son, Nicholas, and his girlfriend. They're ice skating at Rockefeller Center. I'm meeting them later. We've got tickets to the Radio City Christmas Spectacular. Corny, I know, but Caitlyn – that's Nick's girl-friend – she's had her heart set on it.'

'Are they very serious, your son and his girl-friend?'

152

'As serious as two high school juniors can be. But tell me about you. How is the writing coming along?'

'Really well,' Nettie lied, for in truth she was still in the research phase and had written nothing beyond the two chapters she had produced for the book proposal. She knew, however, that this was not what Jane wanted to hear. 'As you know, I managed to snag an apartment right above Anna Winthrop. I'm getting some really good stuff.'

'Like what?'

Nettie reminded her about the two Ukrainian men and the beautiful young woman, then told her about infiltrating the Kirkmore and her close call with Mr Eckart. (She left out the part about blackmailing him.)

As Jane listened her face grew alarmed. 'This sounds dangerous. I think you should stay out of it.'

'But I told you, these two men came out of Anna Winthrop's apartment. Somehow they're linked to her.'

'You said they were carrying a desk out of her apartment. Maybe that's all it was – they were buying her desk.'

'Maybe, but we don't know, do we? Maybe that was a cover. If they *are* linked to Anna this could be terrific material for the book.'

'Just be careful.' Jane took up her menu. 'Salad for me,' she said, quickly putting it down again. 'I'm getting as big as a house.' She glanced at Nettie.

Nettie knew what Jane was no doubt thinking – that Nettie could stand to put on a few pounds.

Jane went on, 'My husband Stanley says I'm perfect, but he loves me so it doesn't count.'

'I think you look fabulous,' Nettie said as the waiter appeared to take their order. She ordered an omelette. Not that she had any intention of eating it. But she could cut it up, move it around, and no one would be the wiser.

'What have you written so far?' Jane asked when the waiter had gone. 'I mean in addition to what you wrote for the proposal.'

Inwardly Nettie groaned. This subject again. She would simply have to lie some more. 'I've been working on the Anna Winthrop chapter.' She figured that made the most sense. 'Since I'm living right over her.'

Jane nodded. 'She certainly belongs in the book. Her father a Greenwich billionaire, brother an investment banker, sister a doctor, another sister a lawyer, and she goes into ... garbage!'

'And her boyfriend is a cop. How's that for a culture clash?'

'What do you mean?'

'White collar versus blue collar. It rarely works.'

'My husband is a police officer,' Jane said, 'and we're quite happily married.'

Nettie felt herself flush. 'I mean in general. Of course there are exceptions. Anyway,' she

154

rushed on, 'it's going very well.'

'May I read it?'

'Read what?'

'What you've written so far.'

'Not quite yet. It's still a bit rough, needs editing.'

'I understand. What about your other Super-Women? When will you get started on them?'

'When I'm finished with Anna. There's no rush, right, because when you sell the project I'll still have some time to complete it. I'm thinking I'll need six months.'

'If you can deliver that fast, terrific. But what if we can't sell the book? In this crazy market you never know what will and won't sell. I think we need a contingency plan.'

There was that talk again. Nettie worked to control herself. 'Shouldn't we be optimistic, tell ourselves the book *will* sell?'

'You can tell yourself anything you like, but the reality is that it may not, and if you want a career as a book writer you'll have a project waiting in the wings. So what else've you got?'

'I'm developing some other things,' Nettie said, her mind working a mile a minute as she tried to come up with something. Not that she would necessarily stay with Jane – her negative attitude was unacceptable – but Nettie would play along for the time being. 'How about a book on the Ukrainian mob?' she said off the top of her head.

'Been done.'

'Not the way I'm going to do it.'

'And how is that?'

'Um ... from the women's point of view.'

Jane drew down the corners of her mouth, weighing this idea. 'Interesting. Tell me more.'

More? 'What is life like for the wives, the mothers, the daughters of these ruthless men? And what about the women who are themselves involved?'

'Are women involved?' Jane's eyes were wide.

'Most certainly,' said Nettie, who had no idea.

'Love it. My partner, Daniel, handled a book in a similar vein, a study of children soldiers. It's selling quite well.'

'Very promising,' said Nettie, who didn't see how the two books were related.

Their meals arrived and Nettie was glad to get off this topic.

Jane wasn't. 'What other book ideas are you developing?' she asked.

'Um...' said Nettie, who wished she'd never agreed to brunch.

Around noon Irena was in the den watching a movie called *The Shape of Things* when she heard the door being unlocked. She went out to the foyer. It was Michael, the doorman, with a cart bearing a tray of food.

'There you are,' he said, his eyes raking her body. 'They're short-handed today so I offered to bring up your lunch.'

She said nothing, looked at him blankly. It was as his eyes devoured her again that she had an idea.

She gave him her most beguiling smile.

'That's better,' he said. 'You are so beautiful...'

'A waste,' she said with a sad expression, then looked at him from under her lashes. 'Dr Renser...' She held out her hands to indicate his great bulk, blew out her cheeks. 'You ... nice.'

'I am nice,' he said, encouraged. He was breathing hard. 'Maybe we could ... get together.'

'I would like.'

His eyes widened in shocked delight. 'We'd have to be careful. But I know when Renser, Grigori and Yuri go out – I'm a doorman, right? That's when we could do it, but we'd have to be fast.'

'Better than nothing,' she said, and walked up to him and placed a light kiss on his lips. Then she plucked a grape from the cart and sauntered back to the den, knowing his eyes were on her.

She heard him let himself out and smiled.

Anna was about to leave for her appointment with Toby Eisenberg when Beth called.

'It's not going to work out with Patti,' Beth said.

'Why? What happened?'

'She seemed preoccupied from the minute she got here.'

'Like she wasn't interested?'

'More like she has something troubling on her mind. Around noon she said she had a stomach ache and left early. What did she say to you when she got home?'

'Nothing, because she still hasn't come home.'

'So much for the stomach ache.'

'I'm sorry,' Anna said.

'You have nothing to be sorry about. I'm worried about her. Something is definitely wrong.'

ELEVEN

Toby Eisenberg, an attractive woman in her early sixties, had silver neck-length hair and an intelligent face. She and Anna sat at a small café table in the lobby outside the hospital's gift and snack shop.

'I appreciate your seeing me,' Anna said.

'Don't be silly.' Toby unwrapped her egg salad sandwich. 'Gloria's a great gal. I'm happy to help in any way I can.'

'What can you tell me about Dr Jeremiah Renser?'

Toby took a bite of her sandwich. 'It's been so long since I've thought about him. He retired ten years ago. I would say the best word to describe him was *arrogant*.'

Anna waited for Toby to explain.

'Huge ego,' Toby said. 'I guess if you're a brain surgeon you're allowed to have an ego, right? But this man, he acted like he was a god or something.'

'How so?'

'For instance, when he did his surgeries here. I was friends with several of the O.R. nurses and they said he was like a drill sergeant. If he

159

gave an order you'd better follow it fast or you were out.'

'Out?'

'If someone displeased him he would demand that they leave, right then and there.'

'Was that allowed?'

Toby laughed. 'Allowed? In this world I've learned you're "allowed" to do whatever you can get away with. No one ever challenged him, I guess because he was really needed. He was after all a brilliant surgeon.'

'According to whom?'

'Everybody. The toughest cases always went to Dr Renser. He was considered the finest neurosurgeon in the city.'

'Then suddenly he retired,' Anna said.

Toby nodded. 'Right after a patient died, so I think people connected the two events.'

'What was the patient's name, do you remember?'

Toby knit her brows, thinking.

'Was it Heather Montgomery?'

'Yes! She had a brain tumor. Dr Renser couldn't operate so he treated her with drugs, but they did no good. Toward the end, when she was much worse, he moved her to a rehab facility he owned in New Jersey. My friend Dottie worked there as the receptionist. She was the one who told me Heather had died.'

'What can you tell me about this rehab facility?'

'Only that it was "state-of-the-art." That's

what Dottie called it. Dr Renser closed it when he retired.

'I understand Heather's father Cyrus had also been a patient of Dr Renser's.'

'Yes, for his Parkinson's. Dottie told me Dr Renser tried some experimental procedure on him but it didn't do any good. But Cyrus must still have believed in Dr Renser, because he and his wife brought Heather to him later.'

'I would like to talk to Dottie if possible. Do you have her number?'

'It's in my office. She lives here in New York now.'

Patti finally came home – seven hours after leaving Beth's shop. Anna decided to play it cool. She'd had another idea. 'I understand you didn't like working at the shop,' she said, looking up from her book.

'No.' Patti hung up her coat and hat in the hall closet. 'It's just not me.'

'Beth said you had a stomach ache.'

'I did, but it went away.'

'So what have you been doing all this time?'

'Just exploring.' Patti came in and sat down.

'I've been thinking...' Anna said. 'You've mentioned that you're interested in art. How would you like to take a class?'

'What kind of class?'

'Drawing. Painting. Whatever you like.'

'Where?'

'I understand the Metropolitan Museum has

161

excellent classes. Students work from models and also from the pieces in the museum.'

Patti hesitated, looking thoughtful. 'Would it be every day?'

'I don't know. I can certainly find out.'

'All right. But don't sign me up for anything before checking with me.'

'Of course not. Let me make a phone call.'

Anna called Henry Burton, an old friend of her father's who was an Egyptologist at the Metropolitan Museum of Art.

'Lovely to hear from you,' Henry said. 'Merry Christmas.'

'Thank you, Henry, the same to you.'

'How are your parents?'

'Doing wonderfully, thanks.'

'Please give them my best wishes. Now, what can I do for you?'

'I understand the museum offers art classes.'

'Absolutely. Are you interested?'

'No, it's my cousin Patti. She's visiting from out of town. She might like to take a class and I thought of your program first.'

'Lecture classes, or studio?'

'Studio.'

'Those are very much in demand, always full, but here's what we'll do. You have Patti go to the museum's website and pick the class or classes she's interested in, then let me know and I'll get her in.'

'That's wonderful. When could she start?'

'Officially the classes follow the academic calendar, so the next classes begin in January. But if you call me within, say, an hour, I can make a phone call and reserve her a spot. She could start tomorrow.'

'I can't thank you enough.'

'Don't be silly. What good are connections if you don't use them?'

Patti selected a still-life class that met Monday through Friday, from nine in the morning until four in the afternoon. The instructor would have Patti's name when she appeared for class the following morning.

'I'm excited,' Patti said, watching Anna remove a roast chicken from the oven. Anna had decided to make Sunday dinner. 'I don't know why I didn't think of it.'

Working at the counter, Anna smiled. She was pleased Patti had agreed to take a class. Mary Jean had been pleased, too, when Anna called and told her.

Santos arrived with eggnog and a fruitcake. They ate at the dining-room table with the lights turned low and the Christmas tree sparkling in the corner.

'By the way,' Patti said to Anna, 'did you ever speak to Fred about the dead mice?'

Santos frowned. 'What dead mice?'

Anna told him.

'How do you know someone's putting them there?' he said. 'Maybe they died there.'

Anna nodded. 'That's what I said.'

'It's too much of a coincidence,' Patti said, taking more cranberry sauce. 'Besides, one of them had a crushed head.'

'Thanks,' Santos said, 'but I don't need the details while I'm eating.'

'Sorry.'

'What does Fred have to do with it?' Santos asked.

'He's mad at Anna,' Patti said. 'He doesn't like takin' orders from a broad. I heard him say that in the break room.'

Santos looked at Anna in puzzlement.

'He forgot to put sand on some ice outside the garage and an elderly woman slipped and fell.'

'So Anna reamed him,' Patti said.

'I didn't "ream" him, I reprimanded him. That's my job.'

Santos turned to Patti. 'So you think he did this to get back at Anna?'

'Wait a minute.' Anna put up her hands. 'Fred did not do it. I spoke to him. He admitted he was angry with me, but he swears he didn't do it and I believe him.'

'Then who did?' Patti said. 'You'd better get to the bottom of it. I have experience with this kind of thing.'

They both turned to her. 'What do you mean?' Anna asked.

Patti set down her fork. 'When I was a freshman in high school, someone started leaving Chucky dolls for this teacher named Mrs

Archer.'

'Who's Chucky?' Santos asked.

'You don't know who Chucky is?' Patti looked amazed. *'Child's Play, Bride of Chucky, Seed of Chucky...'*

Still Santos shook his head, looking even more bewildered.

'I know who Chucky is,' Anna said. 'He's this creepy little doll in some horror movies.'

'I see,' Santos said.

'Anyway,' Patti went on, 'this kept happening. Chucky in her desk drawer, Chucky in her car. Chucky at her back door. No one could figure out who was doing it. Then one day she was found dead in her house. Murdered. Her throat cut ear to ear.' She drew her finger dramatically across her neck.

'Patti!' Anna said.

Patti laughed.

'You sure you don't want to pursue a career in acting?' Santos said.

'It's true,' Patti said, taking up her knife and fork again and cutting off a piece of chicken.

'So who did it?' Anna asked.

Patti gazed at them, eyes immense. 'They never found out...'

'Oh, brother,' Anna said and shook her head.

Who *was* doing this?

A maid brought dinner and Irena carried the tray to the den. As she unrolled her white linen napkin she had to laugh. The eating utensils

165

they brought her were always plastic, incongruously inelegant but necessary.

About an hour later there came the sound of the foyer door being unlocked. Irena went out to see who it was. It was Michael. 'They'll be gone for a while,' he said and slipped in, relocking the door. As soon as he was finished he spun around, whipped off his cap and took Irena in his arms, kissing her deeply.

It occurred briefly to Irena that under other circumstances she would have enjoyed this. Michael was handsome and kissed quite well. But she wasn't looking for enjoyment.

When he released her she smiled, made her eyes bright. 'I am glad you come.'

'Will I ever,' he said and led her to a room she hadn't noticed behind the kitchen, a small bedroom she realized must be for a maid. He closed the door and immediately began removing his clothes. She removed hers at the same time. When they were both naked he pushed her back on the bed and began making love to her.

Anna leaned over the railing and waved goodbye to Santos before he went out the front door. She heard him greet someone and then Nettie came up the stairs.

'Hi,' Anna said. 'No coat?'

'Nah, just ran out for a minute.'

'We didn't have a chance to talk on Thursday morning.'

Nettie looked puzzled. 'About what?'

'About Eddie coming here looking for you.'

Nettie reached the landing. 'What is there to talk about? Now that he knows where I live I avoid going out because he's always out there, watching, waiting for me. If I have to go out – like just now, for instance – I'm especially careful and avoid the shadows.'

Anna nodded, her face troubled. 'Would you like some tea?'

'Sure,' Nettie said, and followed Anna into her apartment.

Nettie sat on a stool at the breakfast counter while Anna put out a plate of cookies and made the tea.

'I know it's none of my business,' Anna said, 'but doesn't it alarm you that Eddie is stalking you? Stalking is a crime because these cases so often end violently. It's not enough to avoid going out. What if he gets into your apartment? You said he wants to kill you.'

Nettie nodded solemnly, her hair plume bobbing. 'You raise some excellent points. Let me give this some serious thought.'

'I hope you will. If you ask me, what you need is a restraining order. And though I'm delighted to have you for a neighbor, I think you should consider moving again.' Anna added the cookies to the tea tray she had assembled. 'And now I'll mind my own business. Come, let's go in the living room.'

Sitting down on the sofa, Nettie took in the sparkling Christmas tree surrounded by presents and for a moment looked a little sad. 'Beautiful tree.'

'Thank you. Santos and I had fun decorating it.'

'Love the angel.'

'It's an antique, belonged to my great-grandmother.'

'Blog idea!' Nettie said with a smile, raising an index finger. *'Heirloom Christmas Ornaments.'*

'Ooh, you're good.'

'Yeah, well, it's what I do,' Nettie said modestly. 'I had another idea the other day for a piece called *The Vintage Office.'*

'That sounds interesting. What would that be about?'

'Going back to the old way of doing business. Typewriters instead of computers. Fountain pens. Antique office furniture. Which reminds me ... that was a lovely old roll-top desk those two men were carrying out of here Monday afternoon.'

'That's right, you went out while they were here.'

'I came out when I heard the men speaking Ukrainian. Eddie's Ukrainian and we were together a couple of years, so I'm pretty fluent.'

'How interesting. Did you make out anything they said?'

'As a matter of fact, I did. It was the tall one. He called the other one stupid – *"Durnyj!"* – and he also said, "Hurry up! If she gets away

I'll kill you.'"

'You're sure he said that?'

'Absolutely. Who *are* those men?'

'Grigori, the tall one, came to buy the desk...'
Anna trailed off, studying Nettie, trying to
decide how much to tell her. She was odd, no
doubt about it, but who in New York wasn't?
Clearly she was intelligent ... a successful
writer. Her perspective might prove helpful.
Yes, she would confide in her. 'Something
troubling happened when they were here...'

Nettie leaned toward Anna intently. 'Yes?'

Anna told her everything, right up to talking
to Toby Eisenberg about Dr Renser earlier in
the day. 'I'm convinced they're holding Eva
prisoner. I want to help her.'

Nettie looked thoughtful. She seemed to make
a decision. 'Can I level with you?'

'Of course.'

'I don't only write blogs. I'm also an investi-
gative journalist. When I heard that man
Grigori say those things to Yuri on the stairs, I
figured something must be up, sensed a story ...
so I followed them.'

'You what?'

'Followed them. Jumped in a cab and went
after them.'

'So that's where you were going.'

Nettie nodded. 'Now let me tell you what I
know.' And she told Anna about her stint as a
maid at the Kirkmore, about her encounter with
Mr Eckart and leaving her coat and bag behind.

169

(She left out her blackmail scheme.)

'We can work together on this,' Nettie said. 'We'll help Eva and I'll get a great story.'

Anna thought this over. 'It makes sense. And I know exactly how we can begin.'

Nettie waited.

'I want to meet this Lucy. It's my turn to clean at the Kirkmore.'

As Michael had warned Irena, he couldn't stay long. He had to get back to work. 'Are you sure you're OK?' he asked her as he finished dressing.

'I am fine. You will come again?'

'You better believe it.' He examined the sheets. There was a spot of blood in the center. 'I'll take care of this,' he said and pulled the sheets off the bed. 'We're in luck, it didn't go through. He balled up the sheets under his arm. 'To the incinerator we go. The maid will think another maid forgot to finish changing the bed.'

He kissed her at the door. 'I guess I don't need to tell you, if anyone finds out about this we're both dead.'

She understood, nodded. 'Return when he is gone.'

With a quick nod he slipped out and locked the door. She hurried to the shower to wash him from her. As the hot water coursed down over her, her gaze wandered and she smiled, thinking of Dasha.

TWELVE

Later, Anna and Nettie walked to Crazy Ice Cream. Arnold remembered Nettie – how could he not? – and immediately ushered the two women into his office.

'You want to go in again?' he asked Nettie. 'It's going to cost you even more.'

'Not me, my friend here,' Nettie said, 'but she's not paying any more than I did.'

'Three hundred,' Arnold said.

'Come on, Anna, let's go,' Nettie said and they started out.

'Wait. I'll call Lucy. She's at home. When do you want to go in?' he asked Anna.

'Tonight?'

'Sure, they've got maids on all kinds of shifts.' He called Lucy, mumbled something into the phone. 'She'll be here in ten minutes.'

'Let me give you a tip,' Nettie said to Anna while they waited. 'Leave your coat and hand-bag at home.'

An hour later, in the uniform that had been too big on Nettie but fit Anna perfectly, she entered the Kirkmore by the rear service entrance. She made her way down the corridor, passing other maids beginning their shift, and found Carmela in her supply closet. Lucy had told Anna that if Carmela questioned her, she was to say the Kemp Agency had sent her. But Carmela could barely keep up with the maids approaching her for instructions, so when Anna stepped up to the half-door Carmela gave her an indifferent look and said, 'Suite twelve sixteen.'

Anna nodded curtly but had no intention of cleaning suite 1216. Nettie hadn't known what she was looking for beyond two Ukrainian men with a beautiful young woman – was 'cleaning blind,' so to speak. Anna knew exactly what she was looking for.

Still on the first floor but at the front of the building, she came to a suite whose door was propped open with a supply cart. The maid it belonged to was just inside, cleaning the floor.

'Excuse me,' Anna said. The woman turned. 'I'm looking for Dr Renser's suite. I'm new.'

'Who?'

'Dr Renser. Carmela told me to clean his suite.'

The woman put her hands on her hips. 'If she told you to clean his suite, why don't you know the number?'

Anna feigned embarrassment. 'Actually, I think she did say the suite number but I was so nervous I don't remember what she said.'

The woman gave a nod. 'One sec.'

She grabbed a walkie-talkie from her cart and

172

was about to press a button when Anna said, 'Wait! Who are you calling? Not Carmela?'

'I wouldn't do that to you. Hold on.' She pressed the button and this time a voice squawked out. 'I need a suite number. Renser.' She waited.

'Right now he's in nineteen ten,' the voice said.

The maid switched off the radio, put it back in the cart. 'Nineteen ten.'

'Not the penthouse?' Anna asked facetiously.

'No, we can't get up there anyway.'

'Why not?'

'Because it's locked, that's why not,' the woman said impatiently. 'Special staff only. There are no suites up there anyway.'

'What *is* up there?'

The woman shrugged indifferently. 'No idea. Listen, I got work to do.'

Anna hurried off. *The twentieth floor is locked. Interesting ...* But she couldn't pursue that now. She pushed her cart to the elevator and took it to the nineteenth floor. There she followed the suite numbers in search of 1910. Suite 1906 ... 1908 ... The corridor turned to the left. Rounding the corner, Anna found herself face to face with Dr Renser. He wore a tuxedo. Behind him stood Eva in a flowing gold strapless gown. Over it she wore a sumptuous sable stole. She took no notice of Anna.

Dr Renser looked right at Anna. Her heart began to pound. But, miraculously, he looked away. He hadn't recognized her. Maids were invisible. He had produced a key and was unlocking the door to the suite. Anna had turned away but his deep voice came from behind her: 'It's all right if you want to clean in here, we're leaving in a few minutes. I just came back for my wallet.'

'All right, thank you, sir,' Anna said in a soft voice. When she was sure he and Eva were inside she turned around. He'd left the door ajar. *Here goes*, she thought, and went in, pushing her cart in front of her.

She was in a large, beautiful marble foyer with a garden in the center. A number of rooms branched off this foyer and from one of them, the master bedroom, she heard Dr Renser's voice.

'I'm half tempted not to go out after all. Come here.'

Anna grabbed a feather duster from the cart and got busy on the low wall around the garden while keeping her eye on the bedroom. Suddenly Renser came into view. He opened his arms and Eva walked into them.

'I want you to kiss me,' he said. Smiling, Eva leaned her head back on her beautiful long neck and their lips came together in a long kiss. When it ended, Eva's smile was gone, replaced by an expression completely devoid of affect, her eyes glassy. She turned and walked away.

He was drugging her.

'Let's go, I'm hungry,' he said. He emerged

174

from the bedroom and walked past Anna, whose back was to him as she continued dusting. A moment later Eva walked past, her movements fluid and serene.

Once they had left the suite Anna waited no more than thirty seconds before hurrying out without her cart. Eva and Dr Renser had turned the corner of the corridor and were heading for the elevator. Anna followed silently. When she reached the door to the service elevator she summoned it and took it down to the first floor. There she hurried down the corridor to the lobby at the front of the building in time to see Dr Renser and Eva approaching the entrance.

'Find your wallet OK, Dr Renser?' asked the doorman, an older man with white hair.

'Yes, thank you, Archie.'

A black limousine waited at the curb, the driver standing by the open door.

It was a risk but Anna had to know. She ran across the lobby, past the doorman and stopped six feet behind Eva. 'Miss!' she said. Eva stopped. Dr Renser turned and looked at Anna, still not recognizing her from Victoire.

'What is it?' he said irritably.

Anna had pulled off one of her earrings. She held it up. 'I found this earring, sir, and thought the lady might have dropped it.'

Renser looked from Anna's hand to Eva's ears, where two huge diamonds sparkled. 'It's not hers.'

'Are you sure you didn't drop this, miss?'

175

Anna said, knowing she sounded like an idiot, willing Eva to turn around.

At last she did, slowly, smoothly, with a peaceful expression, and her gaze rested on Anna's face.

She registered no recognition whatsoever.

Dr Renser had seen Anna only once, at Victoire. Eva on the other hand had seen Anna three times, had stared at her ... yet it was clear from the blank look in her eyes that she had no memory of it, that she did not recognize Anna.

'Sorry, my mistake,' Anna said quickly and turned and went back inside.

She left the building by the rear service entrance and hurried home.

Patti was still asleep when Anna left for work the following morning. The still-life class didn't start until nine, which meant Patti could sleep until seven thirty, shower, eat breakfast and taxi up to the Met in plenty of time.

It had been after eleven when Anna got home from the Kirkmore the previous night, too late to tell Nettie how her turn as a maid had gone. She called her as soon as she got to her office, thinking only after she had dialed that Nettie might still be asleep. The phone rang several times and Anna was about to hang up when it was answered but no one spoke.

'Hello? Nettie?'

'Anna?'

'Why didn't you say anything?'

'I did. Must be something wrong with the line. How was it?'

'Extremely interesting.'

'Did you find Eva and Renser?'

'Sure did, got into his suite.'

'Wow. What happened?'

'They were all dressed up. He was in a tuxedo and she was in a gown. They were going out. She looked more beautiful than ever, but...'

'But what?'

'There was something wrong.'

'What do you mean?'

'She was completely calm, I'd even say happy. He told her to kiss him and she kissed him – willingly. She was like an automaton, blank face and all. He's drugging her. She didn't recognize me. She's seen me three times but this time she had no idea who I was.'

'What are you going to do now?'

'I'm not sure. I've got to think.'

She decided to do her thinking at lunchtime. She walked over to her and Santos's favorite coffee shop, Sammy's Coffee Corner at Tenth and 45th.

'How's my girl?' Sammy shouted to her from behind the counter.

'Good, you?'

'Eh.'

She took a small booth and ordered coffee and a chicken salad sandwich. She wished she could tell Santos what had happened at the Kirkmore the previous night but she hadn't told

177

him she was going there in the first place and that would have to come first. As if reading her thoughts, he called.

'Where are you?' he asked.

'Sammy's.'

'Mind if I drop in for a few minutes? I can't stay long but I've got something to talk to you about.'

'Sure. See you in a few.'

Did he somehow already know? No, how could he? She waited for him to arrive, had a coffee waiting for him.

'Everything all right?' she asked as he sat down.

He looked uncomfortable. 'Yeah, sure.'

She laughed. 'I'm supposed to believe that? What's going on?'

He wrinkled his brow and stared at the Formica table as if unsure how to begin. 'I probably shouldn't even be telling you this...'

'What is it?' She smiled, put her hand on his.

'There's this place on Ninth Avenue in the forties called Kitty Kat Palace...'

Where on earth was he going with this? 'Yes?'

'It's one of those peep show strip club places. You know.'

'I gathered that from the name.'

'Anyway, I was about a block up from it, walking toward it and...'

'And?'

'And Patti came out.'

She stared. 'Patti?'

He nodded. 'She didn't see me.'

'When was this?'

'About an hour ago.'

'An hour ago? But she's supposed to be at her art class. What was she doing there?'

He gave a helpless shrug, looking more uncomfortable than ever.

'Let's be logical about this,' Anna said. 'There are actually two issues here. First, why didn't she go to her class? Second, what was she doing at the Kit Kat Palace?'

'Maybe she did go to her class but she was on her lunch break,' he said.

'Maybe.'

'As for the Kit Kat Palace, maybe she...'

'Was curious?'

Santos shrugged and shook his head.

'Where did she go from there?' Anna asked.

'She headed south.'

'South? The Met is *north*.'

'I don't know what to tell you. I just thought you should know.'

'I appreciate it.'

'Are you going to say anything to her?' he asked.

She considered this for a moment. 'I don't think so. I'm going to give her the benefit of the doubt. I'm going to figure she went to her art class, was on her lunch break and popped in their simply to satisfy some healthy curiosity, which is none of my business.'

Santos gulped down the remainder of his coffee. 'I think that's the way to go. By the way, delicious dinner last night. Thank you again.'

She smiled. 'My pleasure.'

'Wish I could have stayed later.' He gave his dark brows a wiggle.

'I know, me too. But Patti will only be visiting for a month.'

'Only!'

She laughed. 'I'm glad you're missing me.'

'You better believe I am. Had a terrible night. What about you?'

'Same,' she said, taking his hands in hers, but in her head was a picture of Eva's blank stare outside the Kirkmore.

On the way back to the garage she found herself passing the Kit Kat Palace. A young man in a knitted cap stood near the door holding some leaflets. Whenever a male passed he slapped the leaflets on his hand, held one out and cried, 'Girls, girls, girls! Come on, check 'em out. Girls, girls, girls!'

Anna hurried past, forcing herself not to look in the window. At the corner she crossed to the other side of the street and continued south. She paused for a moment to look in the window of a job lot store at a display of colorful, whimsically painted ceramic flower pots. She considered buying them, then decided she had no room for them and continued on her way.

'Ms. Winthrop?'

The voice was so low she wasn't sure she had heard it. She thought it had come from behind her but when she looked there was no one there.

'Ms. Winthrop?' This time it came from the left and she turned to find a woman walking along beside her. She was of medium height, neither thin nor fat, with an intelligent face and piercing blue eyes. Her dark hair was cut in a short no-nonsense style.

Anna stopped.

'Please keep walking,' the woman said softly. 'I need to speak with you but not here. There's a McDonald's on the next block. Can you meet me there?'

'Who are you?'

'I'll explain everything,' the woman said and fell back so that she was a few steps behind Anna.

Anna's first instinct was to walk right past the McDonald's, get away from this woman who somehow knew her name. But there was something about her that signaled OK to Anna and she found herself entering the McDonald's and taking a seat near the window. After a few moments the woman entered, went to the counter and bought two cups of coffee which she carried back to Anna's table.

'I'm sorry if I frightened you,' she said, sitting down and sliding a coffee to Anna.

'Who are you?'

'My name is Margo Rayburn.' She brought out a badge and opened it for Anna. 'US Immi-

181

gration and Customs Enforcement.'

'What do you want?'

'I want to talk to you. About Grigori Sidorov.'

THIRTEEN

'What about Grigori Sidorov?' Anna asked Margo.

'We've had him under surveillance for some time now. I've been watching him, following him. I saw you and a police officer go to his house in Brighton Beach, saw you enter the Kirkmore impersonating a maid.'

'Then you're not just watching Grigori, you're also watching me.'

'You're with the Sanitation Department. Why are you interested in him? What's going on?'

'Why don't you finish telling me what's going on with you first.'

'Fair enough.' Margo took a sip of coffee, put down the cup. 'You probably won't be surprised to hear Grigori's running a sex trafficking ring out of Ukraine. He lures girls with promises of jobs in New York – modeling, that sort of thing. Once they get here they're his prisoners.'

Margo took a breath, let it out. 'What we know so far is that he's bringing the girls in by way of Mexico, crossing the border in Tijuana because that's the easiest place to get through.

He sends some of them straight to strip clubs and brothels in Tijuana where he's made deals or has a financial interest. The rest of the girls are flown from San Diego to New York, where they're taken to a hotel on the East Side where Grigori's also made a deal.'

'The Taylor Hotel?' Anna ventured.

'That's right. You know more than I thought. The Taylor Hotel is basically Grigori's brothel. But it's not as simple as that. We've had the hotel under surveillance for some time, building our case. During this time we've seen Grigori and an associate, Yuri Morozov, transport six girls from the Taylor to the Kirkmore. But once these girls go in we have no idea what's happening to them. That's what we're trying to find out.'

'You need my help...?'

Margo nodded. 'You've succeeded in infiltrating the Kirkmore. From what I could tell, you left without having aroused any suspicion. That's valuable to us.'

'It wasn't difficult to do. Can't one of your agents do it?'

'Two of our agents have tried. We never saw them again.'

Anna's eyes grew wide.

'We want to know everything before we bust Grigori's operation,' Margo said. 'That's where you would come in. If you agree to work with us we would ask you to enter the Kirkmore as a maid on a regular basis. You would be provided with detailed instructions on what to do, what to look for, once you're in there. Any interest?'

'Maybe.'

'Of course, before going forward with this plan we need to know what your interest is in this case.'

Anna told her about Eva, beginning with the note dropped from the pickup truck and ending with Eva's blank look before she got into the limousine. 'So I've been trying to help her, get her out of there. What is Dr Renser's role in all of this?'

'We don't know. He's a doctor so it's likely he's in charge of drugging the girls. He may also have a financial interest.' Margo leaned forward. 'Will you help us?'

'Of course. We want the same thing – to help Eva, to help these girls.'

'Excellent. Needless to say, you can't tell anyone you're working with us.'

'Of course not.'

'How can I reach you?'

Anna jotted her cell phone number on a napkin and slid it to Margo, who pocketed it and rose. 'Thank you. And welcome to ICE. I'll be in touch.'

At three o'clock that afternoon Anna headed out in her department car to follow up on a complaint filed by a resident that morning. According to the complaint, sanitation workers collecting garbage had torn a plastic bag and its contents had spilled out all over a snow bank. The mess wasn't hard to find. A mound of plowed snow on West 56th Street was dotted with aluminum cans, apple cores, banana peels and who knew what else. It looked like a giant scoop of ice cream with sprinkles. As Anna switched off the ignition a young man ran out of a nearby apartment building.

'I've been waiting for you,' he said in a belligerent tone as Anna got out of the car.

'I can see that.'

'You think this is funny?'

She came around the car, gave him a mild smile. 'Not at all, sir. I'm sorry about this. We'll clean it up right away.'

He looked surprised and a little resentful that she had taken the wind out of his sails.

'However,' she added, 'I would suggest you switch to stronger bags.'

'So you're saying this is my fault.' He looked pleased to be arguing again.

'Not at all. It's simply a suggestion.' She wished him a good day and went back around the car.

'Make sure they come soon,' he hollered as she closed the door and took out a pad to make some notes.

Suddenly the passenger door was yanked open.

Shocked, Anna said, 'Sir, I've told you the mess would be cleaned up right—'

Her words froze on her lips. Grigori Sidorov

jumped into the car, slammed the door shut and spun around to glare at her with his ugly face.

'What do you think you're doing?' she demanded and started to get out.

'Don't,' he said. 'I want to talk to you.'

'About what?'

'About your new career.'

She frowned, not understanding, as he drew a folded sheet of paper from his coat pocket. Wordlessly he unfolded it and held it in front of her.

Her eyes bulged at what she saw: herself, in her maid's uniform, crossing the lobby of the Kirkmore. The printout was grainy but there was no question that it was her. Her eyes shifted to him and she said nothing.

'What kind of game are you playing?' he asked. 'I buy a desk from you and now I cannot get you out of my life.'

'And you won't, not while you're holding Eva and all those other girls prisoner.'

He let out a mirthless laugh. 'There is no one named Eva. You have a vivid imagination. Very James Bond. Maybe this is what rich girls who pretend to be blue-collar do, play a game of making things up.'

He had checked up on her. 'This is no game,' she said, hatred in her voice.

'Whatever you call it, do it somewhere else, do you understand? If I see you in the Kirkmore again – and believe me, I will be watching for you – I will kill you.' He flung the security

187

printout at her. 'A souvenir,' he said and before she could respond he threw open the door and was gone.

She reached over and pulled the door shut, her heart hammering. Her mind raced as she drove back to the garage. Returning to the Kirkmore as a maid was of course out of the question now. She would explain this to Margo immediately, she decided – only to realize a moment later that she had no idea how to reach her.

Anna couldn't believe her eyes. She stared down at the floor in front of her office door. This time it was a rat, very large and very dead. It lay on its side, a little pool of blood running from its mouth.

Big blond-haired, blue-eyed Hal Redmond, supervisor of section two, was just entering his office one door down. He gave her a grin, noticed the distressed look on her face and followed her gaze downward. 'What is that?'

'It's a rat.'

'Why?'

'Your guess is as good as mine.'

He shook his head. 'I'll help you get rid of it,' he said gallantly and hurried off.

She entered her office, stepping over the rat. Who was doing this? Would the animals keep getting bigger? Hal returned and she gave him a grateful smile as he bent over to clean up the mess.

*   *   *

Patti arrived home at six o'clock, two hours after her art class ended. Anna was on the sofa with her mystery and a cup of coffee. 'How was it?'

'Great,' Patti replied distractedly and headed for the guest room. She looked tired, drained.

'Wait a minute,' Anna said with a laugh. 'Tell me about it.'

Forcing a little smile, Patti came in and sat down. 'We did a still life today. Some fruit.'

'Do you like the teacher?'

'Yeah, she's great.'

'So the class is all-around great.'

'Mm-hm.' Patti nodded simply.

'I assume they gave you a lunch break,' Anna said, remembering what Santos had said about seeing Patti exiting the Kit Kat Palace.

'Sure. Why?'

'Did you grab lunch at the museum? I think their food is terribly overpriced.'

'I ... grabbed a sandwich at some deli. I'm beat. Mind if I take a shower and lie down?'

'Of course not.'

Eyes narrowed pensively, Anna watched her go.

Anna dreamed she was in Dr Renser's bedroom in the Kirkmore.

'I want you to kiss me, Eva,' Dr Renser commanded.

Eva, seated at a vanity applying her makeup, rose in one fluid motion and turned to him. On her lips was a loving smile but her eye sockets were dark empty holes. 'Of course, Jeremiah,' she said. 'I love you...'

At the moment their lips met a shrill alarm went off. Anna started and opened her eyes.

It was the telephone beside her bed. The clock beside it said TUES 5:16 a.m. She grabbed the phone.

'Anna.' It was Santos.

'What's wrong?'

'I need to see you.'

'What is it? Are you all right?'

'I'm fine. Can you meet me somewhere?'

She shook her head, combed her hand back through her hair. 'Where?'

'Sammy's. Come as soon as you can.'

She found him in a booth at the back, in uniform. He looked up from his coffee, expression grim, and waved. She hurried over.

'What is it?' she asked, sliding into the booth.

He put his hand over hers. 'There's no easy way to tell you this. Early this morning a woman's body was fished out of the Hudson by Pier Forty off Houston Street. There's a daisy tattoo on the left ankle. It's Eva.'

FOURTEEN

Anna stared at Santos, fury rising in her. 'Grigori did this.' She began to cry. 'Eva needed our help and we let her down.' She remembered what Margo Rayburn had told her: *But once these girls go in we have no idea what's happening to them.*

There could be no more secrets.

'I have some things to tell you,' Anna said.

Santos looked surprised, waited.

She told him how she and Nettie had gotten into the Kirkmore posing as maids ... about her encounter with Margo Rayburn ... about Grigori dropping into her car and threatening her.

He shook his head as if dazed. 'I don't know where to start. I guess you see now what a risk you and Nettie took sneaking into the Kirkmore like that.'

'Yes. Those other women ... maybe they're dead, too.'

He gave a little nod to say it was possible.

'But why?' she said.

He thought for a moment, shrugged. 'Some kind of snuff thing?' He looked her in the eye. 'If Grigori threatens you again I want you to tell me immediately. Tell this ICE agent you've changed your mind and won't help her.'

'I would if I knew how to reach her,' she said dryly.

'She said she'd be in touch with you.'

'But maybe if I help her we'll find out who killed Eva ... find out what's happened to those other girls. Are we sure I should tell her that?'

'Yes, because helping her would involve going back into the Kirkmore and you're not going to do that, remember?'

Reluctantly she nodded.

'There's something you do need to do,' he said. When she looked up he said, 'You need to speak to the homicide detective assigned to Eva's case.'

Sharply she met his gaze. 'It's not—'

'I'm afraid it is.' He grimaced. 'Rinaldi.'

At the NYPD's Midtown North station house on West 54th Street, Anna and Santos sat facing Detective Elena Rinaldi across her gray steel desk. She was a petite woman in her mid-thirties with an olive complexion, catlike almond-shaped eyes and lots of glossy black hair that she kept pinned to her head. She was beautiful but appeared to do everything in her power to conceal it, perhaps in an effort to be taken more seriously by her male colleagues.

Anna and Santos had just finished telling her everything they knew, everything they had done, pertaining to the case.

'Unbelievable,' Rinaldi muttered, gazing down at her notes.

'Horrible,' Anna agreed.

Rinaldi looked up at her. 'No, I mean it's unbelievable that I'm sitting here talking to you.'

Anna made no reply. It was true – she and Rinaldi had had their share of run-ins over the past few years. There had been the murder of a homeless man behind Anna's brownstone ... the murder of one of Anna's crew members right in the garage ... and a string of murders in mews and courtyards around the city. All cases Anna had been instrumental in solving. But she made no attempt to point this out to Rinaldi. It would have done no good.

For a long moment Rinaldi glowered at Anna across the desk. Behind Rinaldi, her partner – tall, lanky, red-haired Detective Sean Roche – glowered along with her.

'OK,' Rinaldi said suddenly, as if she'd pulled her thoughts together. 'First, you will tell this ICE agent you won't be assisting her, won't be playing spy anymore at the Kirkmore. It's bad enough you keep interfering in police business. I won't have you sticking your nose in the business of Homeland Security.'

'I just finished telling you I'd decided not to help her.'

Rinaldi ignored this. 'Tell her I want to talk to her.' She gave Anna one of her cards. 'I also want to talk to Nettie Clouchet.'

Anna wrote down Nettie's number and gave it to Rinaldi.

'Second,' Rinaldi went on, 'if Grigori Sidorov threatens you again you are to tell us immediately.'

'Just told you that, too.'

'Third, you are to say nothing about any aspect of this case to anyone, do you understand?'

'Yes.'

'Officer Roche is going to sit down with you now and get every detail you can give him – names, descriptions, events.' Rinaldi gave Anna a sneer, eyelids lowered sardonically. 'You got time for that, or you got some important garbage to collect?'

Anna began to seethe.

'Easy,' Santos whispered beside her.

Anna took a deep breath. 'I'm at his disposal,' she said and immediately realized her unfortunate play on words.

Fortunately Rinaldi didn't catch it. She got up and walked out, Detective Roche taking her place.

On her way back to the garage Anna called Nettie. Once again the call was answered but there was silence.

'Nettie?'

'Sorry, Anna. Still having trouble on this line.'

'I'm calling to give you a heads-up.'

Anna brought Nettie up to date, ending with Eva's murder and her and Santos's meeting with Rinaldi and Roche. 'Rinaldi wants to talk to you. She'll be in touch.'

There was dead silence on the line.

'Are you there?' Anna said.

'Yes, I'm here,' came Nettie's voice, very faint. 'I can't believe you've done this.'

'Done what?'

'Told the police about me.'

'Of course I told them about you, you're involved.'

'You don't get it, do you?'

'Get what?'

'Why do I not speak when I answer the phone?' Nettie's voice began to rise. 'Why do I rarely go out? Why, Anna?' Now she sounded nearly hysterical.

'Because of Eddie?'

'Yes, because of Eddie. Who is *a cop*! And now you've pulled me into this mess with *the cops*. That's it. I'm dead.'

'Don't be so melodramatic. One thing has nothing to do with the other. An innocent woman has been murdered. You should be thinking only about how to get justice for her. Isn't that why you snuck into the Kirkmore in the first place?'

'No, it isn't why!' Nettie screamed. 'I couldn't give a rat's ass about some Ukrainian girl dumb enough to get lured into slavery. I snuck into the Kirkmore because I thought Grigori and Yuri and Eva were somehow connected to you!'

Anna frowned into the phone. *'Me?* I don't understand.'

'I'll spell it out. I'm writing a book called *New York SuperWomen.* As you might imagine, it's about extraordinary women from all walks of life in New York City. You are one of them. No, scratch that. You *were* one of them. You've betrayed me. You will not be in my book.' Nettie let out panicky giggle. 'But there won't be a book, will there? How can I write a book *when I'm dead*?' And she hung up.

Dumbfounded, Anna put away her phone.

Nettie ran from room to room making little squeaking noises. What should she do? She threw herself into a chair at the dining table, gazed absently at a piece she'd been writing on garden pests.

Think, Nettie, think.

Anna had said this Detective Rinaldi would be in touch. If she were to call, Nettie would as always answer but not speak. Then she realized that would do her no good because Rinaldi would know she was home and come over. If only Nettie could afford caller ID. But she couldn't. The only thing to do was simply not answer the phone. If Rinaldi came to see her she wouldn't answer the door.

But she knew she was postponing the inevitable. Cops didn't simply give up. Rinaldi would do what she had to do to speak to Nettie. Would that include breaking down her door? Nettie had seen lots of TV shows where cops had done that, often with little provocation.

Now she had not only Eddie to worry about but also this Rinaldi.

She nibbled a fingernail, began to cry, pressed her knuckles hard against her forehead.

With a sudden thought she ran to the window and peeked out. There he was! Dressed as an old woman this time, in a long coat and a scarf on his head, stooped over, but it was Eddie, of course it was. Watching. Waiting.

She had no choice. She had to get out of there.

'Got a minute?' Anna asked Allen, standing in his doorway.

He looked up, his expression distracted.

'It's about Nettie,' Anna said.

Allen looked up warily. 'What's she done?'

'Nothing. I'm worried about her.'

He focused sharply on her. 'In what way?'

'She's very ... excitable. This business with Eddie...'

'She told you about that?' Allen looked surprised. 'It was a very bad situation.'

Anna nodded in agreement. 'She's trying very hard to put it behind her.'

'And when she does, she should calm down ... somewhat.' Allen gave Anna a sudden smile. 'What's on tap for you this afternoon?'

'I'm starting the mechanical-broom practice.'

'Good. Make sure Bill Hogan gets lots of time behind the wheel.'

Bill was the first to speak up when Anna announced the exercise. 'We've never had to do this before,' he whined, gazing up at the boxy white vehicle equipped with rotating brushes sitting in the middle of the garage floor.

Fred Fox threw back his head and laughed. 'She's hoping you won't kill anybody this year.'

Bill flushed and turned to Anna. 'Is that why we're doing this? I told you, that was an accident.'

'An accident we can't let happen again,' Anna said. 'I'm not singling anyone out. Everyone is expected to practice.'

With a groan Bill hopped aboard and shut the door. 'What do you want me to do?'

'Drive to the end and clean up,' Anna instructed him.

She had created a mess for the crew to practice on – a thin layer of debris contained on three sides by the same metal barricades the police used in Times Square on New Year's Eve.

Bill nodded and Anna and Fred watched as he advanced on the rectangular setup. All went well ... until he knocked over one of the barricades and began dragging it along with him.

'Stop! Stop!' Anna cried. Behind her she heard Fred convulsing with laughter.

Bill stopped the machine and opened the door.

'The space was too small.'

'It's exactly the size of the spaces in Times Square. Come on,' she said to Fred, 'help me get this into place,' and they put the barricade back in position. 'OK, try it again,' she told Bill, who shut the door, leaned forward with grim determination and started up again.

Anna sighed. It was going to be a long afternoon.

At a quarter past four, as Fred started practicing, Anna remembered she'd told Patti she would be home when Patti returned from her class and that they would go Christmas shopping and have dinner out. Patti would be home around four thirty. Anna called Patti's cell but the call went straight to voice mail. Anna considered phoning the apartment periodically until Patti picked up, then decided she would set a better example by leaving a message for Patti at the museum's school office.

'I'm calling to leave a message for my cousin,' Anna told the young man who answered. 'She's in your still-life class. I hate to trouble you but I can't reach her on her cell.'

'No problem,' the young man said. 'Her name?'

'Patti Fairchild.'

'One moment.'

Anna heard the clicking of keys. There was a brief pause, then he came back on the line. 'Sorry, not here.'

'Excuse me?'

'She's enrolled, but she hasn't come to class yesterday or today. Never showed up at all.'

Anna thanked him and hung up. She told Bill and Fred practice was finished for today. Then she headed home, trying Patti's cell several times along the way and each time going directly to voice mail.

'Hey,' Patti greeted Anna when she walked into the apartment a little after six o'clock.

'Hey,' Anna called from the kitchen where she was washing dishes.

Patti appeared in the doorway.

'Stop for a bite on the way home?' Anna asked.

Patti nodded.

'I thought we were going Christmas shopping,' Anna said pleasantly.

'Sorry, I completely forgot.'

'That's OK.' Anna indicated a counter stool. 'Have a seat, talk to me a minute.'

Warily Patti came over and sat down.

'How was class today?' Anna asked.

'Fine.'

'What did you do today?'

'Uh ... we worked some more on the same project.'

'What project is that?'

'The still life.' Patti met Anna's gaze. 'You know, don't you?'

Anna gave a sad nod.

'I'm so sorry, Anna, I—'

Anna put up her hand. 'While you're staying with me it's my responsibility to ensure your safety, but you're making it impossible for me to do that. What the blazes is going on?'

Patti lowered her gaze to her lap. 'I hated lying to you, but I knew you and Mom wanted me to take those classes.'

'Only if you wanted to. You said you did.'

'I know, but yesterday I got to the entrance of the museum and couldn't go in.'

'Why not?'

'I guess I'm not as interested in art as I thought I was. The thought of sitting there all day, four days a week ... I couldn't do it.'

'Why didn't you tell me?'

'I knew you and Mom would be disappointed.'

'You thought we wouldn't find out?'

'I'm sorry.'

'What were you doing instead?' Anna asked, a picture of the Kit Kat Palace flashing in her mind.

'Exploring. I told you, that's what I really want to do. Please don't tell Mom about this.'

'I won't ... because you're going to. She only wanted you to take art lessons because she thought you would enjoy them. Tell her you changed your mind.'

'OK. Thanks.' Patti rose and walked out of the room.

Anna went to the living room but it was a long time before she picked up her book. As she did the buzzer sounded. She went to the intercom. 'Who is it?'

'Rinaldi.'

Anna's heart sank. 'Just a minute.' She buzzed her in and opened the door to wait for her.

'This certainly isn't what I expected,' Rinaldi said as she came up the stairs.

'What do you mean?'

'You don't even have an elevator. Rich girl like you, I thought you'd be in a doorman building, luxury all the way. Place is a dump, you don't mind my saying so.'

'Actually, I do mind your saying so. Where I live is none of your business. What can I do for you?'

'Don't be so touchy. I'm looking for your upstairs neighbor, actually. Miss Clouchet. She's never home. Just buzzed her apartment again. No answer. I've tried calling but it just rings and rings. No answering machine, I guess. Who doesn't have an answering machine?'

'Nettie, obviously.'

'Next time you see her I want you to tell her to call me. Here's another card. Tell her I'm trying to reach her.'

Anna nodded. 'Have you made any progress?'

Rinaldi snorted out a laugh. 'You don't listen so good, do you? I told you, this is police business and doesn't involve you. Then again, I've told you that a lot of times and you've never

202

paid any attention. Guess I can't expect different this time.'

'Expect what you like,' Anna said and closed the door in Rinaldi's face. When she turned around, Patti was standing in the doorway.

'Was she a cop?' Patti asked.

'Yes.'

'What did she want?'

'It's about Eva. I haven't had a chance to tell you. She's been murdered.'

Patti put her hand to her mouth. Then she burst into tears and ran out of the room.

At that moment there was a thumping in the hall, followed by a knock on the door. *Oh, no*, Anna thought. She looked out and saw Mrs Dovner's glowering face.

Anna opened the door. 'Good evening, Mrs Dovner. Would you like to come in?'

'You know I wouldn't. You always ask me that.'

'I guess I don't want to give up hope.'

'Don't be smart. What's going on around here?'

'What do you mean?'

'That woman cop who was just here, for one thing. That was the fourth time she's been here. What does she want?'

'She's looking for Nettie.'

'Why?'

Anna shrugged.

'What's the story with that Nettie?'

'How do you mean?'

'I saw her creeping down the stairs this morning, peeking out the front door like she's afraid of somebody. Who's she afraid of? That Eddie who was here?'

'You'll have to ask her that yourself.'

'I've tried. She's never home.' Mrs Dovner turned and started down the stairs, thumping her cane. 'Big help you are.'

FIFTEEN

By morning, Anna realized leaving it to Patti to tell Mary Jean she wasn't taking the art class after all had been a mistake. Anna would call Mary Jean and tell her, but first she would let Patti know she was doing it.

It was five thirty, at least two hours before Patti's normal rising time, when Anna finished dressing and passed the guest room on the way to the kitchen. Patti's door was ajar and Anna happened to glance in. Frowning, she opened the door. Patti's bed was empty.

From the living room came the sound of the apartment door softly closing.

'Patti?'

Anna hurried across the living room, opened the door and heard Patti clattering down the stairs. 'Patti,' she called again but if Patti heard her she didn't respond. Anna heard the sound of the front door opening and closing. What was going on?

Anna hurried back into the apartment, grabbed her coat and purse and ran out, pulling the door shut. She flew down the stairs and out the front door into the early-morning darkness, looking quickly in both directions. She spotted Patti halfway up the block, walking fast, heading toward Ninth Avenue. Anna opened her mouth to call out to her, then abruptly closed it and quickened her pace.

She followed Patti up Ninth Avenue. As they approached 45th Street Anna wondered if Patti was heading for the Kit Kat Palace. But she went right past it, continuing north.

Then, suddenly, she was gone.

Anna hurried to the spot where Patti had vanished. It was another peep show. Over the entrance was a sign that said XXX DVD XXX. She peered in. In front of the doorway was a partition to shield the shop from passersby, but by moving a little to one side Anna could see inside. She caught a glimpse of Patti walking toward the back.

What to do now?

She decided to wait. She crossed to the opposite side of the street and stood in the shadow of a narrow storefront restaurant. The sign above the roll-down metal security gate said Hell's Chicken. Cute.

It was getting lighter, Ninth Avenue becoming busier. Anna was considering moving somewhere less conspicuous when Patti emerged from the peep show. As she turned to head up the street a dark-skinned young man in a beret suddenly stepped into her path. He said something to Patti and she responded, then tried to get by but again he blocked her. Now the man's back was to Anna so that Patti was mostly obscured. He put his hands on Patti's upper arms, then jumped back, hands fully raised. A second later Patti was on the move, the man watching her go.

Now Anna stayed on the opposite side of the street and a little behind as she followed Patti. At 49th Street Patti disappeared into a building marked Hotel Shropshire. It was a run-down six-floor pre-war dump, the kind of place hookers took their johns. Anna crossed the street and walked nearer to the hotel, looking for a place to watch and wait. As she settled on the recessed doorway of a psychic reader two doors down from the hotel, Patti suddenly re-emerged. She was walking fast, away from Anna. A moment later a middle-aged man ran out of the hotel after her, catching up with her and tapping her hard on the shoulder. Patti spun around and they began to argue. Anna leaned out of the doorway, straining to hear.

'I told you before, she's not here,' Anna heard the man say. 'Why you goin' to the cops?' Patti said something back but Anna couldn't make it out. The man stormed back into the hotel, Patti spun around – and her gaze landed on Anna.

Patti froze. Anna walked up to her. For a moment they simply looked at each other.

'Now,' Anna said quietly, 'would you like to tell me what's going on?'

Patti gave one small nod. Anna looked around and realized Sammy's was only a few blocks away. They walked there without speaking, took a booth at the back.

'Coffee?' Anna asked Patti, who was staring down at the table. She nodded. The waitress brought two mugs and filled them.

Finally Patti looked up. She looked miserable. 'I don't know where to start.'

'Anywhere you like,' Anna said pleasantly, adding Splenda and milk to her coffee, and waited.

Patti took a deep breath. 'Back home there's a girl named Sarah. Sarah Williamson. She's my best friend; I've known her since kindergarten. Sarah ... has problems.'

'What kind of problems?'

'She makes bad choices. Gets mixed up with the wrong people. The wrong guys. The latest one was her boyfriend Roy. A real scuzzbucket. He drank, did all kinds of drugs, never had a job. He treated Sarah like dirt. When they'd been going together for a month he beat her up. Split her lip, gave her a black eye. I asked her why she stayed with him, but I knew why. It was because Sarah's never thought she was worth anything and Roy treated her the way she thought she deserved to be treated.' Patti met Anna's gaze. 'Do you know what I mean?'

'I know exactly what you mean. I couldn't have put it better.'

'That's not what Sarah said, of course. She said she loved him, which was pretty much what I expected her to say, but I begged her to drop him. She wouldn't listen.'

Patti sipped her black coffee, set down the mug. 'About a month ago Sarah announced she and Roy were going to New York. But I knew it was more like Sarah was going to New York with Roy.'

'Why was he coming here?'

'Who knows? To buy drugs, fence something ... you can be sure it was something bad. When I asked Sarah how long they would be gone she said she didn't know but probably a couple of weeks.'

'Where were her parents all this time?'

Patti let out a disgusted laugh. 'Nowhere. Not literally. But they might as well have been nowhere for all they cared about Sarah. See, they're kind of like Roy. They drink too much, do drugs, get into horrible fights the cops have to break up. Years ago Sarah had a little brother named Dennis who wandered out of the house while their mother was passed out drunk on the sofa. He fell into a well and died. He was four. Get the picture?'

Anna nodded sadly.

'Anyway, Sarah and Roy went to New York. During the first week she called me once on her cell and said everything was fine, they were having a good time. She told me they were stay-ing at that hotel I was just in, the Shropshire. A week passed and I didn't hear from Sarah so I called her. The first few times I called she didn't answer. Then I got a recording that her number had been disconnected. I started to worry. But then, out of the blue, Sarah called me. She sounded weird. She said everything was fine, that she and Roy were having a "nice time" and had decided to stay longer. I told her she sounded funny, not fine. She gave me this strange phony laugh and said she'd see me soon. Then she hung up. I tried calling her again and got the disconnected message. I know Sarah better than I know anybody. Roy forced her to make that call. A week later he came back to Cincinnati ... alone.'

'Alone?'

'When I asked him where she was he said they'd broken up and Sarah had decided to stay longer. I asked him if she was still staying at the Shropshire. He said, "How would I know? I told you, we broke up."'

'I went to see Sarah's parents and told them everything. They listened to me but they were so stoned they nearly passed out while I was talking. I told them they should file a missing-persons report. They said they would but I knew they wouldn't. Roy had told them what he'd told me – that he and Sarah broke up and Sarah decided to stay in New York – and that was good enough for them. Later I found out Sarah had a huge fight with them before she left. She'd asked them for money for her trip and of course they'd turned her down. Bottom line, they weren't much interested in what had happened to her. In fact, I think they were relieved to be rid of her.'

'Why didn't you tell your mother all of this?'

'For the same reason I didn't file a missing-persons report myself in Cincinnati. Sarah was always ... well, the town bad girl. Like I told you. Ran with a bad crowd, got into trouble. To the cops she was trash and they wouldn't have cared what happened to her any more than her parents did.'

'You said she "was" trash.'

Patti's mouth twisted and she began to cry. 'Because I think Sarah is dead. I don't want to believe it, I want to find her, that's why I'm really here, but something inside me says she's dead and I'll never find her.' She met Anna's gaze. 'But I have to try, right?' Her tone was pleading.

'I admire your loyalty to your friend. I only wish you'd been honest with your mother and me about why you were coming here.'

Patti shook her head quickly. 'If I'd told Mom the real reason I wanted to come here she would have killed the trip in a second. And no offense, but if I'd told you why I was really here you'd have sent me home.'

'That's not fair.'

'I'm sorry.' Patti took a sip of coffee. 'I was the one who put the idea of this trip into my mother's head. I said I admired you – which I do, that's not a lie – and that maybe I could get some ideas about what to do with my life if I spent some time with you. But I'm really

211

here to find Sarah. That's what I've been doing – going to hooker hotels, peep shows, strip clubs...'

'Why? What do you think has happened to her?'

'*If* she's even alive, I think she's working for someone who won't let her go. Hooking, stripping, something like that. I think that was why Roy came to New York, to sell Sarah to somebody. Because that happens, you know it does. These girls are kept so scared or so drugged-up or both that they can't escape. It's what must have happened to that poor girl Eva before she was murdered.'

Anna only nodded.

Patti's eyes still brimmed with tears. 'I suppose you're going to put me on the next plane back to Cincinnati.'

Anna's smile was kind. 'Of course not. You're here to help your friend. It's the right thing to do. I only take issue with how you've gone about it. I'll do anything I can. But I think we need some professional help.'

'What do you mean?'

'We need to go to the police.'

Patti smiled sardonically. 'I forgot to mention – that was the first thing I did when I got here. I went to a police station near Times Square and told them I was looking for my friend, that I thought something bad had happened to her.'

'What did they say?'

'They laughed at me. I think they thought I

212

was a hooker.'

Anna had to smile. 'You do have a distinctive way of dressing.'

Patti let her jaw drop. 'You think I look like a hooker too?'

'I'm taking the Fifth on that one. Patti ... who was that man in the beret?'

'Some pimp, kept trying to recruit me.'

'You scared him off pretty good outside the peep show.'

Patti looked sharply at Anna, whose gaze was on Patti's purse. 'May I have it, please?' Anna said.

Wordlessly Patti opened the purse and brought out a small pistol. Anna put out her hand and Patti placed the hand gun in it.

'Where did you get this?' Anna asked.

'Some guy I know in Cincinnati. They're easy to get.'

'You could have killed someone with this.'

'If necessary,' Patti said easily.

Anna placed the gun in her purse. 'Come on,' she said, dropping a few bills on the table. 'Let's go talk to Santos.'

'That's a sad story,' Santos said to Patti and Anna across a desk at the police station. 'I'm sorry you weren't taken seriously the first time you came to us. I assure you I am taking you very seriously.'

He took a pad from his desk and began to jot notes. 'First, we need to get out that missing-persons report. I don't suppose you have a picture of Sarah?'

'I do!' Patti said, remembering, and began pressing buttons on her cell phone. Then she held it up for Anna and Santos to see, a photo of two girls with their arms tight around each other. Sarah was a plain girl with straight dark hair and a serious face.

'You can e-mail that to me,' Santos said and passed her his card. 'Now I need to find out more about what happened.' He looked at Anna. 'If you need to go, we'll be fine.'

Anna rose. 'Thanks, I should get to work. One thing, though.' She looked at Patti. 'I have to tell your mother everything.' Patti opened her mouth to protest but Anna put up her hand. 'That's not negotiable.' She smiled. 'I'll see you both later.'

Mary Jean was crying. 'I'm so sorry.'

'For what?' Anna asked.

'For putting you in the middle of all of this. Patti should have told us about Sarah. If she had we could have started looking sooner. I hope it's not too late.'

Mary Jean had given voice to something that had also occurred to Anna. 'Now that we know,' Anna said, 'we'll do everything we can to find her.'

'Of course. In the meantime, Patti must come home.'

'I had a feeling you would say that,' Anna

214

said sadly.

'You don't agree?'

'I didn't say that. It's probably the best thing. But I can imagine how she'll feel. Like she's leaving her friend behind, abandoning her.'

'There's nothing Patti can do to help her. This should be left in the hands of professionals. You've been a saint. I can't thank you enough. Please, when she gets home, have her call me so we can arrange her flight.'

'I won't go!' Patti said and stormed out of the living room. Anna heard the guest room door slam.

Anna felt very tired. Was this what having children would be like?

She went down the hall and knocked on Patti's door.

'Forget it,' Patti said. 'I'm not leaving New York. If you don't want me here, fine, I'll find someplace else to stay.'

Anna opened the door a little. 'Of course I want you here. But it's not up to me. Your mother wants you home. There's not much you can do here anyway. The police are on the case now. Let them do their work.'

'I can't leave Sarah,' Patti said, crying into her pillow. 'I can't!'

Anna decided there wasn't much more to be said. Gently she closed the door and returned to the living room. Later, when she looked in, Patti was sound asleep.

215

Twenty minutes later Anna was chatting with her brother Will, just back from Aruba, when her cell phone rang. 'Can you hold a second?' she asked him.

'I'll let you go. I have to help with Nina's bath.'

She said good-bye and took the other call. It was Margo Rayburn.

'Can you meet me now?' she asked. 'I have some things to tell you.'

'Where and when?' Anna heard herself saying.

'There's a coffee shop on Forty-Fourth between Tenth and Eleventh called Cynthia's. South side of the street.'

Anna left a note for Patti saying she'd had to run out. The temperature had dropped considerably and Anna huddled into her coat as she made her way along the quiet streets.

Cynthia's was long and narrow, a counter on the left and booths on the right. Margo sat at the rearmost booth sipping a coffee. She waved to Anna.

'Thanks for coming,' Margo said. 'I think you'll find what I have to tell you quite interesting.' The waitress brought Anna a coffee. When she'd gone, Margo put her hands on the table and leaned forward slightly. 'I've been watching the Kirkmore. Yesterday one of the doormen, a man whose name we've ascertained is Archie, came out with a young woman – the third of the six women brought over from the

Taylor Hotel. They got into a limo. I followed them to LaGuardia where they checked in for a flight to Las Vegas. I called one of our agents in Vegas and he picked up the trail. He followed them to the Bellagio Hotel. There they were greeted by a man we've identified as Jean-Pierre Roussard, a French billionaire.'

Anna's eyes widened.

Margo went on, 'Roussard took charge of her, and Archie returned to the airport for a flight back to New York.'

'Did the young woman appear drugged?'

'Yes, our agent said she seemed oddly passive. I think what we saw is a clue to what's happening to these girls they're taking to the Kirkmore.'

'I've got another clue for you. Two days ago Eva's body was fished out of the Hudson.'

Margo's gaze drifted as she took this in. She looked back at Anna. 'How do you know this?'

'From my boyfriend. He's a cop.'

'Do you have the M.E.'s report yet?'

Anna shook her head.

'It doesn't make sense,' Margo said. 'These girls are the product. Why would they kill one? I'm going to keep watching the Kirkmore, see if they ship out any more.' She slapped down a few bills and rose. 'I want to know what the M.E. says about Eva's cause of death. I'll be in touch.' With a curt nod she walked out into the night.

* * *

Nettie scurried along the sixteenth-floor corridor of the DeLuxe Hotel. As she searched for room 1678 it occurred to her there was probably no hotel in New York City that deserved the name DeLuxe less. Once one of the wonders of the Times Square area, the massive 24-story building extending from 40th Street to 41st Street between Seventh and Eighth avenues was now a haven for pimps, whores and transients. Horrible things happened here all the time – suicides, murders, beatings. Nettie knew from a blog piece she'd written entitled *Hygienic New York* that the DeLuxe had also been named the city's filthiest hotel six years in a row. In her piece she'd advised against staying here, yet here she was. But she had no choice. The cash she had withdrawn from the ATM with the new card the bank had sent her was nearly gone and she didn't dare take out more for fear the transaction would get back to Eddie. The DeLuxe was all she could afford.

From behind a door on the left came the sounds of a man hollering in Spanish and a woman wailing. In a room on the right a baby was crying hysterically. Farther up on the right a door opened and a young woman who couldn't have been more than sixteen emerged in bra and panties. Ignoring Nettie she leaned against the door frame, lit a cigarette and looked up the hall expectantly.

Finally Nettie found room 1678 and let herself in. The room was oppressively hot and smelled of onions but the door had a bolt and a chain and she was safe here, at least for the time being.

The space certainly lived up to the hotel's reputation. Grit in the matted tan shag carpet crunched under her feet. Dust coated the top of the dresser. The bedspread, though tucked neatly around the mattress, looked as if a Luminol test would light it up like the Christmas tree. Nettie would have to remove that. On second thought, she would not sleep in the bed at all. But where *would* she sleep? She started to cry.

She wrapped her hand in toilet paper from the small moldy bathroom and removed the bedspread from the bed, throwing it in a heap in the corner. Then she turned on the TV and perched on the edge of the bed with the remote. She found *My Fair Lady* starring Audrey Hepburn and Rex Harrison, one of her favorites, and found herself drawn in, momentarily forgetting where she was.

From the corridor came a woman's shout followed by the slamming of a door. Jarred back into grim reality, Nettie looked through the peephole but saw nothing. Another door slammed. Cautiously, silently, leaving the chain on, she turned the bolt and opened the door just enough to peer down the hall. Immediately she closed it again, eyes huge.

It was Eddie. Down the hall on the other side. Dressed as a vagrant this time, he was going door to door asking for handouts. But he didn't fool Nettie. Eddie had done plain-clothes work, knew how to become someone else. She had to give him credit – checking rooms under the guise of panhandling was a stroke of genius. He was dangerously close but he wouldn't find her. Fortunately he was moving in the opposite direction. She peeped out again. Eddie was out of sight, having turned a corner in the corridor. Heart racing, she slipped out and scurried down the corridor away from Eddie. It turned a corner and ended. Terror filled her. She was trapped. Then she realized one of the doors here led to the service stairs.

The stairwell was poorly lit and she had to be careful because there were people here – a man shooting up, a woman smoking a joint, two young men doing who knew what. But they paid her no attention and she squeezed past, excusing herself. Sixteen flights was a long way but she reminded herself of the brave people who had descended dark stairs in the besieged World Trade Center, some over a hundred flights, and besides, what was running down some stairs compared to her life?

Eventually, breathless, she burst into the DeLuxe's dim lobby and scampered out to the dark safety of 40th Street.

The apartment was silent as Anna let herself in at ten thirty. Patti's door was closed. Carefully Anna turned the knob and opened it a crack.

Not again.

Patti was gone. Really gone this time – her clothes, her suitcase, everything. The dresser was bare, the linens tangled on the bed.

Anna hurried out to the kitchen, switched on the light and scanned the counters for a note. She found only the one she had left for Patti. She checked the living room. Nothing.

She hurried to the apartment door, opened it and looked out. The landing, the stairs, all quiet.

She considered calling Santos, then decided that could wait. Pulling her coat back on she locked the apartment and returned to the cold darkness of the street. She headed east, then turned up Ninth Avenue. Outside the Hotel Shropshire a young Asian woman in boots, miniskirt, tank top and goose bumps gave Anna the once-over and looked away. Anna went inside.

The once grand low-ceilinged lobby was a study in umber – empty oversize sofas and chairs, a couple of dying ficus trees. A disturbing odor pervaded the place, a blend of must and sweat and fried food. To the left stood the reception desk. As Anna had expected, a heavy Plexiglas barrier reached to the ceiling. Behind the desk an elderly man sat with his chin propped up on his hand, apparently asleep. 'Excuse me,' Anna said through a small window in the barrier.

The man lazily opened his eyes. 'Sixty dollars

for two hours, twenty-five dollars each addi-
tional hour,' he recited.

'I don't want a room,' Anna said.

Finally his eyes focused on her. 'Then what
do you want?'

'I'm looking for someone.'

He scowled, puzzled. 'Yeah?'

'I saw her come in here once. Her name is
Patti Fairchild.'

'Let me check the register, maybe she reserv-
ed the Presidential Suite. You for real?'

'All right, I'll describe her.'

'Won't do no good. They all look alike to me.'
He rolled his eyes, then closed them and placed
his chin back in his hand.

Anna wandered back outside. The Asian
woman was gone and in her place was the dark-
skinned man with the beret who had accosted
Patti outside the peep show. Leaning against the
building, hands in the pockets of his hoodie, he
gave her a self-satisfied smile. 'Not much luck
in there, huh?'

She made no reply, watched him.

'I might be able to help.'

'How?'

'You lookin' for the that girl who came out of
the DVD store?'

'How do you know?'

He smiled. 'Saw you watchin' from across the
street.'

'Do you know her?'

He shrugged. 'Don't know her name, if that's

222

what you mean. But I seen her again, know where she is.'

'Where?'

Out came his hand, palm up.

She gave him a ten.

'You gotta be kiddin'.'

'How much do you want?'

'Lot more than that.'

She gave him two more tens. 'That's it.'

He peeled himself off the wall, passed in front of her. She followed. He led her to Tenth Avenue and north to a hotel at the corner of West 52nd Street that could have been the sister to the Shropshire. This one was called the Barrington. 'She just went in 'bout twenty minutes ago,' the young man told Anna over his shoulder, cocking a thumb in the direction of the entrance, and kept walking.

'Wait, aren't you—?' But he had turned on 52nd. She hurried after him but when she looked around the corner he was gone.

She returned to the Barrington and went inside. Another study in umber except that there were people in this lobby, a homeless man sleeping on a sofa and three young women in miniskirts and tank tops sitting in chairs, eating Chinese food out of Styrofoam containers.

'I'm looking for a girl who just came in here,' Anna told a middle-aged woman behind the Plexiglas.

'Lot o' girls just came in here.'

'This one *just* came in. She's tall, very thin,

223

dark hair, Cleopatra haircut.'

The woman stared at her.

'Maybe I need the police,' Anna said. 'She's underage.'

'Hold it.' The woman spun her chair around and gazed up at an old-fashioned board with keys on hooks. She pointed to a hook without a key. 'Three twenty-two. Elevator at the back.'

The elevator operated so slowly that Anna wasn't sure it was moving. Finally the doors opened on the third floor and she followed the dimly lit corridor to room 322.

She stopped short, listened.

From behind the door came the sound of a woman moaning.

SIXTEEN

Anna banged on the door. No response. She banged harder. After a few moments the doorknob turned, even as the moaning continued. The door opened a crack and Patti peered out and let out a gasp. Anna forced the door open and stepped into the room. A young woman with straight dark hair had just gotten off the bed and was rushing into the bathroom. From inside came the sounds of her retching violently.

'I'm sorry,' Patti said. 'I hated running out on you like that but you were going to make me go home and Sarah needs me.'

'How did you find her?'

'She found me. She got free from where they were keeping her. Someone let her use a phone and she called me. It was while you were out. She hid in an alley until I could come for her. I checked us in here.'

Anna went into the bathroom. Sarah was kneeling at the toilet bowl waiting for another round of retching. She glanced up miserably at Anna, was overtaken by another urge and returned to the bowl.

'She's so sick,' Patti said, standing beside Anna. 'Vomiting, seizures, acting crazy, she can't sleep...'

'What's wrong with her?' Anna returned to Patti.

'She's trying to get off crack. Roy got her hooked before he sold her to a pimp.'

'She should be in a hospital.'

'No hospitals!' Sarah stood in the bathroom doorway, shaking. She walked to the bed, grabbed the blanket and wrapped it around her shoulders. Then she sat down on the end of the mattress.

'Why not?' Anna asked.

'Because I'm a minor and they'll call my parents and I'm not going back there. I'd rather die.'

'You see what I mean about her parents?' Patti said.

'You don't know the whole story,' Sarah said to Patti. 'They're drunks and drugheads but there's something else.' Her face convulsed and she bent her head and cried.

Anna went over and sat close beside her. 'What else?' she said softly.

'My father...'

'Did he abuse you?' Anna asked.

Sarah silently nodded. 'And there's more.'

Anna met Patti's gaze. Patti shrugged and shook her head. They waited.

'I heard Roy talking to Jimmy – he's the guy Roy sold me to. My father ... sold me to Roy.'

'I don't understand,' Anna said. 'Why would your father have had to sell you? Couldn't Roy have simply taken you?'

'My father said if Roy paid him he wouldn't go to the police when I went missing.' Sarah gave a bitter laugh. 'Roy didn't know my father wouldn't have done that anyway. But if some hospital social worker calls my parents, they'll have to take me back ... and then I would have to run away ... and I'm tired of running.'

Sarah pulled the blanket tighter around her and shivered. Then she jumped from the bed and ran back into the bathroom. Anna and Patti stood in the bathroom doorway, watching helplessly.

When Sarah finally returned to the bedroom and lay down, Anna said, 'Being underage doesn't mean you have to go back to your parents. No social worker will send you home if you tell them what you've told us.'

Sarah looked up, listening.

'Your father will be arrested and your mother too if she was complicit in the deal with Roy. You're safe. Please ... you need medical attention.'

For the longest time Sarah stared into nothingness, weighing what Anna had said. Then, almost imperceptibly, she nodded.

Anna got out her phone.

Nine blocks away, on West 41st Street between Eighth and Ninth avenues, Nettie walked slowly along the shadowy sidewalk, casting her gaze wildly about for any sign of Eddie.

Across the street lay the dark bulk of the Port Authority Bus Terminal. To the right stood large industrial buildings with the occasional brownstone and shop between them.

Just ahead of her and to the left, something rustled behind a pile of garbage bags left out for pickup. Nettie stopped, stood absolutely still. Suddenly a dog appeared. It was on a leash whose other end was held by a man who now also appeared. The dog pulled on the leash. 'Sheba,' the man reprimanded the dog.

Nettie moved silently to the left, taking shelter in a brownstone's dark stairwell. As she watched, the man and the dog passed close in front of her. The man – he wasn't Eddie, she could see that. But the dog ... Wouldn't that be just like cunning Eddie to disguise himself as a dog, recruit a man to walk him, as he searched for her? She studied the animal carefully as it crossed her view. Yes, that was definitely Eddie. Sheba! She laughed to herself. She wasn't fooled. She waited several moments after they were gone, then left the darkness of the stairwell and continued down the street toward her home. Only two blocks to go. Get in, shower, get out.

When she had nearly reached Eighth Avenue she stopped, an odd feeling coming over her. Déjà vu, that's what it was. She'd been here before. Up ahead, the bar with the triple red awning: Pool Tables, Free Hot Dog, Marty's, it said. She walked a little farther. The doorway beyond the bar, a glass door in the gray-brick face of the narrow building. She stared, began breathing harder.

This was where she had lived with Eddie.

She approached the doorway, peered in. There was that long flight of stairs. Their apartment had been at the top, on the right. It had always smelled of cat urine up there because Carolyn, who rented the other apartment, boarded cats and didn't change the litter boxes often enough.

Her gaze drifted and she remembered, like it was happening at this moment...

It was late, dark, like this. She trudged up the stairs, making as little noise as possible so as not to wake Eddie. But he was awake. He opened the door as she stepped on to the landing.

'Why are you looking at me that way?' she asked.

'What way? I'm just wondering where you've been.'

She laughed scornfully. 'No, you've decided where I've been, what I've been doing. You think I'm having an affair with David.'

'Who's David?'

'Go ahead, play stupid. You know exactly who David is. He's the guy I've just started blogging for, owns EthnicFairsNY.com. We're doing a special project and he needed me to stay late.'

Eddie shrugged. 'It's your story.'

'How dare you accuse me?' she said, her voice rising.

'I'm not accusing you of anything. Come inside.'

She rushed at him, hands like claws to his eyes.

He jumped back into the open doorway. 'Stop it! Get a hold of yourself! Stop! Don't make me...'

She and Eddie struggling ... moving back out to the landing...

Abruptly the memory shattered, replaced by a high-pitched sound like a siren inside her, so loud she thought her head would burst. She shut her eyes tight against the pain, pressed her hands to each side of her forehead.

More flashes of memory ... voices...

'It was an accident.'

'I heard them arguing ... it woke me up.'

'No one saw what happened...'

'It would be better for you if you moved away...'

And she had. Hidden from Eddie. But now he had found her, which was why she was out here in the middle of the night, scrambling to keep a step ahead of him. Why she would stay in her new apartment only long enough to shower, then hit the streets again.

A car turned on to the block and came toward her. She squinted to make out the driver's face. Eddie!

She ran into Marty's and slammed the door.

The crowded bar grew silent, all eyes on her. The bartender approached from behind the counter, blinked in surprise. 'That you, Nettie?'

'No!' she cried and scrambled back outside. Ran toward Ninth Avenue.

Kept to the shadows.

When Anna and Mary Jean entered Sarah's room at St Luke's Roosevelt hospital the following day, Sarah and Patti were chatting quietly. Sarah looked better. There was color in her cheeks and she appeared rested.

'I can see the patient is improving,' Anna said.

Patti looked up, saw her mother and ran to her. Mary Jean hugged her tight. 'I'm so sorry.'

'*You're* sorry?' Patti said through her tears.

Mary Jean nodded. 'For trying to push you into doing things you're not interested in.'

'You didn't push me. I was the one who put the idea of coming here into your head, so I could look for Sarah. I'm sorry I lied to you.'

'Now that we've established that you're both sorry,' Sarah said with a smile from the bed, 'what do we do now?'

Mary Jean, a tall, attractive woman with black hair cut close to her head, went over to Sarah and gave her a gentle hug. 'You look better than I expected.'

'Thanks ... I think.' Sarah laughed.

'What we do now,' Anna said, addressing Sarah's question, 'is find you a place to live. The social worker has been told everything and agrees that's the right move.'

'Live with us,' Mary Jean said. 'We'd love to have you, wouldn't we?' This with a look at Patti.

Patti nodded emphatically. 'We've suggested it in the past but she was never interested,' she told Anna.

'It's true,' Sarah said. 'I was interested in a whole bunch of other stuff, all of it bad. I'd love to live with you. Thank you.'

'Speaking of bad,' Anna said to Sarah, 'the police are going to want to ask you some questions about your father, Roy, Jimmy and anyone else you need to tell them about.'

'No problem. Soon as they let me out of here.'

As Sarah spoke a young doctor entered the room. 'I don't think we'll need to keep you much longer,' he said to Sarah. 'But from here you need to go to a rehab center. We can make some recommendations.'

They all looked at Sarah for her reaction. She smiled. 'Great.'

The doctor examined Sarah briefly, nodded approvingly and left.

'A new beginning,' Mary Jean said, looking from Sarah to Patti.

'No more lies,' Anna said.

Patti bit her lower lip and nodded. 'No more lies.'

Sitting at her desk the following day, Anna sensed movement and looked up to find Allen

Schiff in her doorway. 'See you a sec?' he said, beckoning, and she followed him to his office. There he pointed. In the middle of his desk lay a dead pigeon. Anna looked at Allen.

'I understand you've been getting gifts like this,' he said. When she nodded he said, 'Why didn't you tell me?'

'What's to tell? It's someone's idea of a sick joke. Whoever is doing it will get tired of it.'

'What's been left for you so far?'

'Two mice and a rat.'

'Who's angry at both of us?' he wondered aloud.

Anna shrugged. 'I'm not going to put any energy into trying to figure that out. In the grand scheme of things, it's not important.'

Allen didn't look so sure.

A short time later Anna was working on her computer when she heard something scrape the outside of her closed door. She jumped up and whipped it open. There was no one in the corridor. She looked down. At the threshold lay a half-eaten pastrami sandwich on a wrinkled sheet of waxed paper.

From across the garage came the clang of metal hitting the floor. Anna looked up sharply. The sound seemed to have come from the vicinity of a stack of discarded tires in the corner. Crossing the garage she saw something move behind the pile. At last she would learn the identity of the mysterious gift-giver.

Silently she crept forward. Then with sudden

speed she ran behind the tires.

At first she saw nothing. Then her eyes adjusted to the shadows and she saw, sitting in front of the tires, a cat.

It was entirely black. It had big green eyes with which it stared at Anna. It let out a plaintive meow.

She took a tiny step closer. 'Hey, boy,' she said in a gentle voice. 'Or are you a girl?' Now she could see that its fur was matted and dirty. 'Looks like you've had a rough time. Thanks for the presents.' Another step.

The cat darted away, scurrying out from behind the tires and making for a row of parked collection vehicles. It ran under one of them.

Anna bent down, looking for it, moving from truck to truck.

'What are you doing?'

Anna stood up.

Brianna was watching her. 'Lose something?'

'Yes, a cat.'

'A *cat*?'

Anna nodded. 'That's who's been leaving the dead animals.'

Now they both peered under the trucks.

'I see it. Come on,' Brianna coaxed the cat, 'don't be afraid. We're your friends.'

It flew out from under the truck and out to a courtyard adjacent to the garage. The two women followed. The courtyard was surrounded by a twelve-foot-high cinder-block wall. The cat sauntered along the top, watching them.

Then it stopped and, its eyes still on Anna and Brianna, let out another mournful wail.

'We've got to help it.' Anna turned to Brianna. 'Or do you think it's feral? They can be dangerous, I think.'

Brianna laughed. 'No way is this cat feral. It's a stray. Someone discarded it. It needs love, wants to be friends. That's why it's been leaving food.'

'If it wants to be friends, why doesn't it come down?'

'Because it's afraid. You would be, too, if you'd gone through what that cat has probably gone through. Who knows how long it's been fending for itself?'

'What's going on?' came Allen's voice from behind them. He stood in the courtyard doorway.

'We've found the culprit,' Anna said and pointed to the cat, who mewed a greeting to Allen.

'Well I'll be ... Hey,' he said to the cat, 'next time you want to bring me something, could you make it a liverwurst on rye?'

As if responding to Allen's request the cat jumped off the wall into the alley on the other side.

'We've lost him,' Anna said.

Brianna gave her head a confident shake. 'He'll be back.'

Leaving the garage that afternoon Anna heard

someone call her name. She turned. It was Detective Rinaldi, crossing the street toward her.

'Don't look so pleased to see me,' Rinaldi said.

Anna forced a polite smile. 'What can I do for you?'

'What you can do for me is put me in touch with that ICE agent you told me about.'

'Why?'

Rinaldi gave her a withering look. 'I don't have to answer that question but I will. Because I realized she probably has information that will help us solve Eva's murder. We're all on the same side, right? So how can I reach her?'

'Uh ... you can't.'

'What do you mean, I can't?'

'I don't have her number. She gets in touch with me.'

'Gets?'

'Got.'

Rinaldi's exotic eyes narrowed suspiciously. 'No problem. She's gotta work out of the New York office on Twenty-Sixth. I'll look for her there. Why are you staring at me?'

Anna shook herself. 'I don't know. I mean, I'm not. Sorry.'

'I think those garbage fumes are getting to you,' Rinaldi muttered as she walked away.

Anna hurried back into the garage, switched on her computer and looked up the address of the Immigration and Customs Enforcement

New York office: 601 West 26th Street, between Eleventh Avenue and the West Side Highway. She ran back outside and grabbed the first cab she saw. She was there in less than ten minutes. She passed through security, then found the office and spoke to the receptionist.

'I'm here to see one of your agents,' Anna said, a little breathless.

'Do you have an appointment?'

'No, but she'll want to see me. If she's here, of course.'

'The name, please?'

'Margo Rayburn.'

The receptionist gave a mild frown. 'Just a minute.' Her fingers flew over her keyboard, she gave her mouse a few clicks, then she gave one decisive nod and turned back to Anna. 'It's as I thought. We have no agent by that name.'

SEVENTEEN

Anna wandered out in a daze. *We have no agent by that name.* How was that possible? Who was Margo? Suddenly Anna remembered Rinaldi was going to try to find Margo – which was the reason Anna had hurried down, hoping to alert her – and as Anna had this thought her cell phone rang. It was Rinaldi.

'I don't know what kind of game you're playing, garbage girl, but there is no agent at ICE by the name of Margo Rayburn.'

'I just found that out.'

'How?'

'I went to the office looking for her.'

'Why?'

'To give her a heads-up that you would be in touch with her.'

'Why?'

'Because I had told her I wouldn't tell the police I was working with her.'

'This is a royal mess,' Rinaldi muttered. 'Now listen to me. You said she gets in touch with you. The next time she does, tell her you want to meet. Then I want you to call or text me where that meeting's going to take place, you got that?'

'Yes.'

'If she finds you somewhere I want you to secretly text me your location.'

'All right.'

'You see now why we don't want you meddling in police business? Stick to your trash and we'll all be better off!'

Word of the cat had spread through the garage. Everyone was on the lookout. On Saturday morning it was spotted twice, once streaking out from under a mechanical broom and once on top of the courtyard wall again. Benny Klurman, a sanitation worker in section three whose father had been a veterinarian, tried coaxing it down with a dish of cat food but the cat only mewed and ran away.

Around noon Anna got a call from Rinaldi. 'Hear from Margo yet?' Rinaldi asked.

Anna said she hadn't.

'Don't forget what I told you,' Rinaldi said and hung up.

Anna sat with her chin in her hand, wondering again about Margo Rayburn, when something brushed her shoulder. She started, spun around. The black cat stood on her desk, inches away, staring at her with those enormous beautiful green eyes.

'Hey,' Anna said, 'you wanna be friends now?'

She sat very still. The cat came closer and

rubbed the top of its head against her upper arm. Then it let out a tiny mew, gave her another long look ... and collapsed on to the desk.

Pierre Bontecou, who had two cats, went home to get his carrier. In the meantime, Anna placed the unconscious cat in a cardboard box with a screen on top. Pierre returned with the carrier, helped Anna get the cat into it and gave her the number of his veterinarian, whose secretary agreed to squeeze Anna in. She placed the carrier on the back seat of her Department car and drove uptown.

Dr Rekani was a trim man around fifty with heavy black-framed glasses. Carefully he removed the cat, conscious now but weak, from the carrier. 'You have been through the ringer, haven't you?' he said to the cat, then turned to Anna. 'We will need at least a few days for this fellow.'

'It's a boy?'

'Yes. He is severely dehydrated and near starving. He will need vaccinations and we will also test for leukemia and FIV – feline immunodeficiency virus. We will check for parasites – very common in strays – and this poor gentleman also has fleas and ear mites that we will get rid of. And last but not least, we will give him lots of lovely food and water and a good bath. In the meantime, you can be preparing for his return.'

She frowned, not understanding.

'You are keeping him, are you not?'

She gazed down at the cat lying sluggishly on the examination table. One green eye gazed up at her.

'I suppose I am,' she replied in a marveling tone. 'After all, I was the one who found him.'

'No,' Dr Rekani said with a knowing smile. 'He found you.'

Santos, beside Anna in bed, propped himself up on his elbow. 'Good morning.'

Anna yawned. 'A very good morning. No work today.'

'Just think,' he said. 'In a few days we'll be waking up to a cat sitting on our heads.'

She laughed. 'After what he's been through, he can sit anywhere he likes.'

She made coffee while he showered. Often she liked to pick up something special for breakfast on Sunday. She poked her head into the bathroom. 'I'm going out for bagels. Would you like anything else?'

'Crumb cake. And a *Times*, please. I want to do the crossword.'

'You got it.'

Heading out she reflected that she was relieved Patti was no longer staying with her. Mary Jean had taken a hotel room for them near the hospital.

Anna went around the corner to a place she liked called Bagels & Such. The line was out the door, nothing new on Sundays, but it always moved quickly. She took her place like a good New Yorker. It was warmer today, in the forties, the sun bright, so standing outside like this was actually pleasant. She took a deep breath, got a nose full of diesel fumes and laughed to herself.

The line moved forward a little. Someone in line behind her jostled her. 'Excuse me,' the person said.

'No problem,' Anna said, turning, and stared. It was Margo.

'Can we talk?' Margo said in a low voice.

'Where?'

'Starbucks a block up. Meet you there.'

On the way Anna called the apartment but Santos didn't answer. He must still be in the shower. She left a message on his cell that she would be out a little longer than usual. As she entered the coffee shop she had to work to behave normally – or at least she hoped she was behaving normally. She remembered Rinaldi's instructions but wouldn't follow them quite yet. First she wanted to hear what Margo had to say.

'Did you get the M.E. report on Eva from your boyfriend yet?' was the first thing Margo said. Two coffees sat on the small round table.

'Not yet,' Anna replied, sitting down. 'How are things going on your end?'

'Nothing new to report.'

'That's not surprising, since you're not really an ICE agent.'

Margo glared at her. Anna could practically

see the wheels of her mind turning.

'Who are you really?' Anna asked.

'My real name isn't important. I used to work with Grigori.'

Anna blinked in surprise. 'In what capacity?'

'In the capacity of helping him bring girls over from Ukraine. That's right,' the woman Anna knew as Margo said sardonically, 'I'm a very bad person. Now that we've gotten that out of the way...' She leaned back in her chair. 'We had a simple operation. We procured the girls in Ukraine, brought them over, used them in several brothels in Brooklyn, Queens and Man-hattan, including the Taylor Hotel. It was quite lucrative. Things were going well and I had no intention of stopping.'

'Then why did you?'

'Because Grigori pushed me out. He wouldn't say why, but I know it was because his opera-tion was changing – changing in a big way – and he didn't want to share the money anymore. He recruited Yuri Morozov, a less successful trafficker, to work for him. He also hooked up with Dr Renser.'

'Why? What does Renser do?'

'I was telling you the truth when I said I didn't know.'

'What is it you want?' Anna asked.

'I want back into Grigori's operation. The only way that's going to happen is if I black-mail him. I could use what I know about the brothels but I need more and I know there is more, much more. You can help me there because you can get into the Kirkmore.'

Anna flashed on Grigori jumping into her car and showing her the security printout, threatening her.

'Why would I help you?' Anna asked.

'We could be a great team. You can't be happy with what you're making in the Department of Sanitation. This is your chance to make some real money.'

Obviously Margo didn't know Anna's background.

'So what do you say?' Margo asked.

Anna made a point of looking at Margo for some time. Finally she said, 'What you say is extremely interesting. You've given me a lot to think about.' She rose. 'Excuse me, I'll be right back.' She looked around for the rest rooms.

'That way,' Margo said, pointing to the back.

In the women's room, Anna called Rinaldi and got her voice mail. 'I've got Margo Rayburn at the Starbucks at Forty-Third and Ninth,' she said in a low voice. Then she texted Rinaldi the same message.

When Anna returned to the table, Margo was gone, a man with an iPod in her place.

It wasn't until Anna had returned to her apartment and hung up her coat that she realized she'd bought neither bagels, crumb cake nor a *New York Times*. Santos gave her a wondering look.

'Let's go out for breakfast,' she said, 'and I'll tell you what's going on.'

They went to Sammy's. Over pancakes Anna told him about Margo.

'She's dangerous,' Santos said when she had finished. 'And she's on to you.'

'That's OK, because I'm on to her, too.'

He didn't look convinced that this was enough. As he signaled the waitress for more coffee, Anna's cell phone rang. The caller ID said NewYork-Presbyterian.

'It's Toby Eisenberg. Can you come see me again? I need to talk to you. Same place.'

They quickly finished breakfast and took a cab to the hospital.

At the table outside the gift and snack shop Toby looked troubled. Anna introduced Santos.

'You said you wanted to talk to my friend Dottie – you remember she worked at Dr Renser's rehab center, told me Heather had died. She's eager to talk to you, too.'

'Why?'

'She wouldn't say.'

'Where does she live?'

Toby handed Anna a slip of paper. 'I'll tell her you're coming. Now I'd better get back.'

Dottie Lange lived in a luxury high-rise not far from an apartment Anna's parents owned in Sutton Place. Dottie's building was called The Larimore. The doorman already had Anna and

Santos's names and directed them to the elevator.

Dottie was a woman in her sixties with white cotton-candy hair, vivid blue eyes and very red lips. Red, white and blue. She wore a beige pant suit and lots of gold jewelry. She led Anna and Santos through an all-white living room adorned with colorful paintings of birds. On a glassed-in terrace with a million-dollar view of the East River a wrought-iron table had been set with coffee, tea and cookies.

'I couldn't believe it when Toby called me,' she said. 'As she told you, I was the receptionist at Dr Renser's rehab center.'

'What was it called?' Anna asked, taking notes.

'The Renser Rehabilitation Institute. It was in Alpine, New Jersey.'

Alpine, Anna knew from her father who paid attention to such things, had been the most expensive zip code in the United States for 2009, according to *Forbes* magazine.

'Being the receptionist,' Dottie said, 'I knew only so much. For instance, I knew Heather Montgomery was a patient, but I never knew what was wrong with her and I never actually saw her.'

Santos frowned. 'You never saw her?'

Dottie shook her head. 'She was put in a special private wing to which only certain staff had access – Dr Renser, of course, and the nurses who worked only in that wing.'

'Are you in touch with any of these nurses?' Anna asked.

'No ... though I don't know whether they would tell us anything even if I were. You see, Dr Renser paid us all well for our loyalty, our discretion. He paid me extremely well and helped me invest my money so that I was later able to finance a business for my late husband that did quite well.' She looked around appreciatively.

'I did meet Heather's parents,' she went on. 'A nice couple, Edwina and Cyrus. Cyrus had very bad Parkinson's and was a patient of Dr Renser's. The doctor did some kind of procedure on him and Cyrus spent time at the rehab center, in the regular wing. I liked him very much and we had some nice chats about birding.'

Dottie sipped her tea. 'One day about a year later, Cyrus and Edwina walked in. I asked what they were doing there and they told me their daughter Heather was a patient at the Institute. I had no idea because, as I told you, she was in the private wing and we never knew the names of patients there. While I was chatting with Cyrus and Edwina, Dr Renser came in. He was very upset. He interrupted us and asked to speak to Cyrus and Edwina privately. The three of them left the room and I never saw the Montgomerys again.'

Her face grew troubled. 'The next day I asked Dr Renser why Heather was there. He told me

247

never to speak of Heather again to anyone. Then a strange thing happened. Two weeks later he came to me and told me Heather had died.'

'Why is that strange?' Anna asked.

'No one in the private wing ever talked about the patients there. Dr Renser himself had told me never to speak of her again. Yet here he was making a point of telling me she had died. But that wasn't the most troubling thing.'

They waited.

'We were a rehab center, not a hospital, so patients didn't die very often. But once in a while someone did and it was my job to make arrangements. So I told Dr Renser I would call the funeral home. But he said no, I shouldn't do that, because the family had already made arrangements.'

Anna and Santos waited for Dottie to continue.

She leaned toward them, blue eyes wide. 'But no funeral home ever came for her.'

Santos asked, 'Would you necessarily have known if one did?'

'Oh yes. If a patient died, whether from the regular wing or the private wing, it was my job to liaise with the funeral home. There was a strict policy about that.'

'So what are you saying?' Anna asked.

'That I don't believe Heather Montgomery really died.'

'What *do* you think happened?' Santos asked.

Dottie shrugged. 'Her parents took her home? Why, I wondered, would Dr Renser lie like that, say Heather was dead when she wasn't? It bothered me and finally I had to ask him – not why he had lied, of course. I told him that no one had ever come for Heather's body.'

'What did he say?' Anna asked.

'He gave me the oddest look and said, "That's not for you to worry about. It's part of the discretion I pay you for. In fact, I think it's time you received a bonus."'

'And did you?'

'Did I ever! Twenty thousand dollars.'

'Had he ever done that before?'

'Given me a bonus? Never. But he was to give me an even larger one, and that was when he closed the center about six months later. He said, "You've been a loyal employee. I know you will continue to be loyal and discreet, and never talk about anything that happened at the Institute." He gave me one hundred thousand dollars.'

Dottie looked ashamed. 'I'm not stupid. I knew I was being bought off. But I needed the money and I didn't think any harm was being done. But it's troubled me ever since.'

'Can you think of anyone else who was there at this time who might be able to give us more information?' Anna asked.

Dottie thought for a moment. 'I haven't kept up with anyone I worked with there. There is someone who might know something, but I don't know if he's still there or even if he's still alive.' When Anna nodded encouragingly Dottie said, 'The Institute was in a big old mansion Dr Renser had renovated. There were acres of grounds and on them was a cottage the caretaker and his wife lived in. His name was Perry Stanton.'

'What became of the mansion after Dr Renser closed the Institute?'

'I have no idea.'

'If someone else moved into the house, would Perry still be the caretaker?'

'He might. He had been the caretaker for the people Dr Renser bought the house from.'

'Do you remember the address of the Institute?'

'Of course. Sixty-three Warren Lane, Alpine, New Jersey.'

Nettie drew her knees closer to her chest and adjusted the blanket around her. She had positioned herself in the underground passageway that connected Times Square to the Port Authority Bus Terminal. Subway riders hurried past, most of them ignoring her, a few tossing coins and the occasional bill into the empty aluminum can she'd set out figuring she might as well make some money.

After fleeing the DeLuxe she'd thought she'd outsmarted Eddie. But she'd stopped at a Quik-Mart for Suzy Q's and Charleston Chews and there he was at the milk case, pretending to look

250

at the fat-free. This time he'd been disguised as a little girl but he hadn't fooled her. She dropped the cakes and candy bars on the counter and ran out, not stopping until she had lost herself in the tangle of subway tunnels beneath the streets.

She had once written a blog about the mosaics that decorated the walls of this tunnel, brightly colored depictions of people blowing party horns and donning party hats. The artist, Jane Dickson, had been selected by the Metropolitan Transportation Authority from among about thirty artists. While viewing and photographing the mosaics Nettie had seen the homeless people who leaned against the walls for hours on end, sleeping or panhandling, seemingly immune to police harassment.

Earlier with money from her aluminum can she had purchased a few Charleston Chews – the newsstand at the Port Authority end of the passageway didn't carry Suzy Q's. The Port Authority rest rooms were safe and relatively clean and she had gone there twice now to wash with the aid of a microfiber dishcloth she'd bought at an odds-and-ends shop not far from the newsstand. There she had also found a toothbrush, toothpaste and a small can of deodorant.

But despite the washing and the deodorant she was beginning to smell and her hair, which she couldn't very well shampoo in the Port Authority women's room, felt greasy and lank.

She'd considered buying a small can of dry shampoo, favored among many homeless people, but she knew from a traveler-tips blog piece she'd written entitled *Personal Care While You're in the Air* that the job it did was less than satisfactory.

To remain here for any length of time she would have to be truly clean and that meant a real shower. Homeless shelters were out – they asked for your name and ID which would go straight to Eddie. No, eventually she would have to slip back into her apartment, quickly shower and get out. Perhaps tonight. She would of course first watch the building from across the street to make sure Eddie was nowhere in sight.

She was shaken from her thoughts by the clink of coins tossed into her can by a slim dark-skinned woman who gave her a loving smile and said, 'Bless you.'

Anna turned off the Palisades Parkway on to Closter Dock Road, then took a right on to Warren Lane. To each side, private driveways led through masses of trees to homes hidden from view. Alpine was all about privacy and discretion for the very wealthy. Word was Stevie Wonder had lived in Alpine for years. Other celebrity residents included the comedian Chris Rock and the hip-hop mogul Sean Combs.

Anna had had a roommate at U. Penn named

Eloise who had grown up in Alpine, and once during Christmas break Anna had gone home with her. The daughter of a media tycoon, Eloise had proudly told Anna the town had only one school and no commercial area but that nearly all of the houses were mansions.

A few of the houses on Warren Drive had signs at the road displaying their street numbers, but most of them did not. By extrapolation, however, Anna was able to locate the drive for number 63.

The trees lining the drive, mostly evergreens, were so overgrown that branches scraped the car and little sunlight shone through from above. For nearly half a mile the potholed road twisted through the woods. A faded wooden sign came up on the right: Renser Rehabilitation Institute.

Finally the trees ended and the house stood before her. It was clear no one inhabited it now and probably hadn't in the ten years since Renser had closed the Institute. It was an imposing two-story structure of stucco with two gables protruding from the front of the roof and a semicircular pillared portico in front. The small windows in the gables were black gaping eyes, the glass gone. The dozen or so tall windows at the front of the house had all been boarded over with plywood. The shingles covering the upper right portion of the front roof were covered with a greenish-black substance, probably mold.

Anna parked in a small lot to the right of the drive and walked up to the house. Except for the soft whistle of the wind it was quiet here, so quiet that Anna could imagine she was the first person to visit this place since it was closed down. Walking under the high portico she climbed the wide steps to the front door and tried it. It was locked. She came back down the steps and walked around to the side of the house.

Now she could see an addition jutting from the back of the house – one story, long and low, with a flat roof and large windows that had also been covered over. Walking around to the back of this addition she came to an unmarked door. She tried the knob. It was locked but loose. She cast a furtive look around, then rattled the knob hard. The four screws securing the escutcheon plate to the door popped up slightly. She rattled some more and they protruded farther. With her fingers she was able to slowly remove them. As she pulled out the fourth one the plate fell to the top step with a dull clink. She looked around once more, then pushed the door open.

She was in a small waiting room with chairs against the walls and a glassed-in reception desk. Thick dust covered everything. Anna sneezed. In the center of the waiting room was a low table piled with magazines. She picked one up, blew off the dust, sneezed again. *Ladies' Home Journal*, February 2000. *Good Housekeeping*, January 2000. All the magazines were dated either January or February 2000.

She went through a door to the receptionist's desk behind the glass. An old CRT computer monitor sat on the Formica desk but there was no actual computer she could see. The desk itself was bare except for a large Rolodex with no address cards in it, and a four-button phone whose cord had been ripped from the wall. There was no chair at the desk. She tried the drawers and found them empty except for a few pencils and pens, rubber bands, bottles of Liquid Paper, little paper packets of salt and pepper.

A door at the back of the reception area led to a corridor with a number of doors. The nearest of these doors revealed what appeared to have been a small break room. A microwave oven with its door hanging open sat on a counter alongside a coffee maker with no carafe. In the center of the room was a bare table surrounded by vinyl chairs.

The next room contained an examining table, a counter and cupboards containing only a few boxes of gauze and a bottle of alcohol. There were two more rooms like this. The next room was large and clearly the physical-therapy room, its variety of machines layered in dust. Moving on, Anna came to a room with a bed. Opposite the bed was a TV shelf without a TV. On a side wall were doors to a closet and a tiny bathroom.

The next door led to an identical room except

that there was also a doctor's scale. Turning to leave the room, Anna froze. Listened.

She thought she had heard a sound ... a footstep. She waited, barely breathing, and it came again, a slow, deliberate footfall, as if whoever it was did not want to be heard.

Anna's heart began to pound.

Another footstep, closer this time.

Silently she slipped into the closet and pulled the door shut. She held her breath. Another footstep came, this one in the room. Another, closer...

The closet door was thrown open and Anna jumped. Standing in front of her was an elderly man, very thin, with a white crew cut. He wore baggy jeans and a heavy flannel shirt over his spare frame. In his hand was a gun pointed at Anna's middle.

EIGHTEEN

'Who are you?' the man demanded.

'Are you Perry Stanton?'

'I asked who you were.'

'My name is Anna Winthrop.'

'Why are you here?'

'If you'll lower that gun I'll be happy to explain it to you.'

'Explain it to me and I'll decide if I want to lower the gun.'

She gave a quick nod. 'It's complicated, but basically I'm here about Heather Montgomery.'

His white brows lifted. 'What about her?'

'Please...' she said, eyeing the gun. Slowly he lowered it. 'I'm looking for information on Dr Jeremiah Renser, the man who used to own this clinic.'

'I know who he is.'

'Then you are Mr Stanton?'

'That's right. How did you know that?'

'From Dottie Lange.'

'She still alive?' he asked with a wondering smile. When Anna nodded he said, 'She was a cute little thing.'

'She still is, actually. After all, she was here

only ten years ago.'

'A lot can happen in ten years.'

'True. Dottie said you might be able to give me some information.'

'About Heather?'

Anna nodded.

'Come out of there,' he said.

Sticking the gun into the waistband of his jeans, he led the way outside. 'I live over there,' he said, pointing, and through the woods Anna made out a small patch of white. She followed him to the edge of the lawn and on to a dirt path that snaked through the trees and finally came out at a small cottage. She followed him inside. The front door opened on to a living room cluttered with books, magazines, files and assorted dirty plates and silverware. It was stiflingly warm, the air pervaded by the smell of decay.

Her revulsion must have been clear from her expression because he said, 'Wife passed away five years ago. Doin' the best I can without her but it's not easy. You want a glass of water or something?'

'No, thank you.'

He shrugged and vaguely indicated she should sit. She chose an armchair that had somehow evaded the clutter and he sat opposite her on a sofa whose cushions were covered with newspapers. They crinkled under him. 'I wondered if anybody would ever ask me about Heather,' he said.

'Why? What can you tell me about her?'

Perry wrinkled his white brows, remembering. 'I was the caretaker – but I guess you know that from Dottie. It was my job to keep the lawns mowed, shrubs trimmed, flowers planted, repairs made, anything that needed doing.'

His gaze drifted as if he were trying to see back through the years. 'The way the clinic worked, there were two kinds of patients. At the front, as we used to call it, was the regular wing. That was for the less serious cases. In the private wing, where I found you snoopin', they had the "difficult" cases, as the doctor and the staff used to say.'

'What did they mean by *difficult*?'

'More serious medically, people in terrible accidents, that kind of thing. But it was more than that. It was very private, a place where famous people could come and not have reporters all over them. Heather was in the private wing. No one at the front knew what was wrong with her and normally I wouldn't have wondered...'

'Why did you wonder in her case?'

'I was friendly with a man who cleaned in the regular wing, man name of Wesley. One day I was working on a flower bed when Wes came up to me and said, "Bad news from the private wing." I asked him what and he said, "Girl name of Heather Montgomery died." You see, that was odd in itself, that Wes knew. That anyone would know. Because no one ever told us anything about what happened in the private wing. I asked him how he knew and he said a nurse at the front named June told him.'

'Why do you think people up front knew this?'

'It was almost like ... somebody wanted the story to get out that she was dead.' He gave his head a little shake. 'But I don't think she was.'

He shifted on the sofa, the newspapers crinkling. 'It was because of something that happened about a week later. One night around midnight Agnes, that was my wife, she woke me up and said, "Something's going on over at the clinic." I went outside and looked through the trees and sure enough she was right. There were lights on at the back of the private wing. I followed that path you and I were just on and watched from the edge of the woods. There was an ambulance parked at the door. Two EMTs came out with someone on a stretcher. Then I noticed there was a car parked behind the ambulance. The doors of the car opened and a man and a woman got out. They walked beside the stretcher. The woman said, "Heather, we're going to take a nice plane trip now. Everything will be all right." The woman was crying.'

'Did Heather answer?'

'No, not even a grunt or a moan. Then I heard one of the EMTs speak to the woman. He said, "All right, Mrs Montgomery, we're going to put her in the ambulance now."'

'The next day I asked June if she knew about

any ambulance during the night and she looked at me like I was crazy. She knew nothing about it. I asked someone else up front and got the same response. I never heard another thing about it. Never really thought about it much until you just brought it up.'

'Who owns the house and this land now?' Anna asked.

'Renser still owns it.'

'And he's letting you live here?'

'Letting me?' Perry snorted. 'I pay rent every month, high rent, takes up most of my Social Security. I've lived here since 1971, worked as caretaker for the couple who owned the house before they sold it to Renser. I'll have to leave soon, though.'

'Why?'

'Renser's just sold the place. Some rich executive and his wife are going to "restore" the place.'

'And you can't go on living here?'

He shook his head. 'Right where we're sitting is going to be the tennis court. I asked the Realtor to ask Renser to make it a condition of the sale that I can go on living here. She came back to me and said Renser laughed and said I should be in a nursing home anyway. You wouldn't be asking me about him unless you thought he'd done some bad things. I hope what I've just told you helps you nail the SOB.'

Anna sat at her kitchen counter, before her an

apple from which she had taken one bite.

She thought about what Dottie Lange had told her and Santos, what Perry Stanton had told her. Heather Montgomery was alive, no doubt about it. Why had Dr Renser wanted the world to think she was dead? Why had Edwina Montgomery come running after Anna expressly to talk about how Heather died?

If Heather was still alive, wouldn't her parents be in contact with her? Maybe. If so, they might sometimes call her, maybe also visit, depending on where she lived.

Anna knit her brows, concentrating. It was time for a few leaps in logic.

The Montgomerys were for whatever reason hiding Heather's existence. Edwina had told Heather they were going on a 'nice plane trip.' Both of these things suggested Heather was not close by. In which case, if Cyrus and Edwina did visit her, they would most likely fly. And they would most likely do so from nearby Newark Liberty International Airport, from which it was possible to travel virtually anywhere.

Cyrus Montgomery was disabled. To get to the airport he would most likely use a handicap accessible van service.

Anna went to her laptop in the bedroom and googled 'handicap accessible van service Montclair, NJ.' A short list of companies came up, in various locations around New Jersey: Pompton Plains, Ledgewood, Bogota, Jersey

City, Teaneck, Dumont ... Clifton. Clifton was close to Montclair. Garden State Invalid Coach Service, the company was called. Anna grabbed the phone from her nightstand, dialed 67 to block her caller ID and dialed.

The phone was answered by a bored-sounding woman with a low voice. 'Invalid.'

'Good evening,' Anna said pleasantly. 'This is Mr and Mrs Montgomery's assistant, Carol.'

'Yeah?'

'I wonder if you could help us with something. It's the end of the year and I'm gathering tax information for our accountant. I'm going over the Montgomerys' records and I seem to be missing the amounts for their most recent trips to and from the airport.'

'Hold,' the woman said. A few moments later she came back on the line. 'November twenty-second.'

The week of Thanksgiving.

'Found the itemized list,' the woman went on, and read: 'Coach service from Upper Montclair to Newark Liberty Airport. Assistance to gate, Terminal C, for Continental flight to Sarasota-Bradenton Airport. As a courtesy we arranged for coach service from Sarasota-Bradenton to Ocean Springs. That company would have billed you directly.'

'Yes, I have their bill,' Anna said.

The woman went on, 'Return November twenty-eighth. Assistance from gate at Newark Liberty. Coach service to Upper Montclair.

263

Pretty much the usual. Total fee seven hundred fifty-eight dollars, not including tolls.'

'Perfect. Thank you so much, you've been enormously helpful.'

'Welcome,' the woman said and hung up.

Anna googled 'Ocean Springs, FL' and perused several informational sites. Located on Florida's gulf coast, Ocean Springs was barely a town. Its only entity of any importance, it seemed, was a place called Harbor Memorial Hospital.

Anna picked up the phone again.

'Ladies and gentlemen, we have started our descent in preparation for landing. Please make sure your seat backs and tray tables are in their full upright position...'

Anna gazed out the window and saw vivid green grass, graceful palm trees waving in a gentle breeze, here and there the sparkling blue water of a swimming pool. Within twenty minutes she was walking across Sarasota-Bradenton Airport toward the exit.

Passing through the sliding doors she breathed deeply of warm, jasmine-scented air. Seventy-eight degrees, the flight attendant had said. She closed her eyes and let the sun warm her through.

As she joined the taxi line her cell phone rang. It was Santos. Though she had left a message on his voice mail that she had called in sick today, she hadn't told him where she was going, hadn't been sure she was going to. It was one thing to talk to Dottie Lange and learn Heather Montgomery was almost definitely alive, quite another to go in search of her.

'I've seen the M.E.'s report on Eva's body,' he said. 'She was suffocated.'

'Suffocated...' Anna repeated thoughtfully.

'Why'd you call in sick? Did you catch the cold that's going around?'

'No, I'm fine. I'm also in Florida.'

'You're *what*?'

'I've just landed. It's a long story. I'll be home tonight. I'll call you when I get in.'

'Anna,' he said, his voice stern, 'what is going on?'

'Santos, we're breaking up. Can you hear me? Hello? Hello?' With a little sigh of regret she closed her phone. She'd listen to Santos's lecture that night. Right now she had no time to spare.

'Morning, ma'am,' the taxi dispatcher said. 'Where to?'

'Harbor Memorial Hospital.'

The driver of the cab that had just pulled up heard her and nodded. She hopped in. 'How far is it?' she asked him.

'About half an hour.'

Gazing out at the sunny landscape rolling by, Anna felt a building sense of dread. She was taking a risk, a big risk, but it was the only way.

In her mind she rehearsed what she intended to say, at the same time checking her outfit. She had worn a businesslike tan pant suit, a conservative cream-colored blouse and low cocoa heels. The leather briefcase on the seat beside her was full and well worn.

They had left the city, passed through suburbs and were now on a highway with nothing but trees and wild grasses on either side.

'Here we are,' the driver said as a magnificent white building came into view at the top of a low hill. It was ten floors high, with a central tower and wings curved forward and slightly inward like welcoming arms. A wide circular drive planted with high banks of pink and white flowers carried them to the entrance under a low portico. Nurses in white uniforms walked in and out of the front door. A white-coated doctor wheeled an elderly man in a wheelchair toward a waiting car.

Anna paid the driver and strolled confidently into the large, bustling lobby. A tall, burly security guard appeared as if from nowhere, blocking her way. 'Good morning, ma'am. May I ask what your business with us is today?'

'Of course,' she said with an easy smile. 'I'm an attorney representing the parents of one of your residents.'

'And who is that?'

Here goes. 'Heather Montgomery.'

He gave a small nod and indicated, in the center of the lobby, a circular information desk staffed by four people. 'Please register.'

A wave of trepidation overtook her as she

approached the desk. A woman with glasses perched on the end of her nose gave her a tiny, mechanical smile. 'Good morning. Your name, please?'

'Anna Winthrop.'

'May I please see some ID, Ms. Winthrop?'

She handed the woman her driver's license. The woman glanced at it, then at her and passed it back. 'Thank you. And who are you here to see today?'

'Heather Montgomery.'

'In what capacity?'

'I'm an attorney representing her parents.'

'And the name of your company?'

'Schutz Fine Kovner,' Anna said, again using the name of Beth's old firm.

'One moment, please.' The woman's fingers flew over her keyboard. She gave a tiny frown and typed some more. She glanced up. 'I don't have you in our system.'

Anna feigned surprise. 'This is my first visit, but our office manager told me she had made this appointment for me.' Surprise turned to businesslike distress. As if to herself she said, 'Don't tell me I've come all the way from New York for nothing.'

'You say someone at your firm made the appointment?' When Anna nodded the woman said, 'I'll need to give your office a call, just to confirm.'

'Of course.' Anna gave her the number.

'Good morning,' the woman said into the telephone. 'I'm calling from Harbor Memorial Hospital in Ocean Springs, Florida. I need to confirm that someone from your firm is scheduled to visit us today. Yes, her name is Anna Winthrop ... That's right, representing the Montgomerys.' The woman smiled. 'Very good. I appreciate your help ... Yes, I'm sorry to tell you it's a beautiful sunny day here today. You make it a great day now. Good-bye.'

The woman smiled up at Anna. 'That's all right, then. We always check. You never know, especially these days.' She rose slightly, pointed with her pen. 'You're going to go to the end of that corridor, turn left and you'll see the elevator. Ninth floor.'

Anna thanked her, wished her a wonderful day and walked briskly away, making a mental note to tell Patti what a good job she'd done impersonating Anna's office manager.

A male nurse at the ninth-floor reception desk who said his name was Rudy asked Anna all the questions the woman downstairs had asked, except that this time Anna was in the system. He smiled. 'Come with me, please.'

She followed him down a corridor with rooms on each side, all the doors closed. A female nurse wheeling a cart came in their direction and wished them a good morning. Rudy stopped at a door on the left and spoke to Anna in a low voice. 'This is your first time here, right?' When Anna replied that it was he said, 'Don't be deceived by what you see. Inside that shell she's as sharp as you and me, she just can't break through, can't see, can't move. She can hear perfectly, though. Don't talk down to her or treat her like a child. She's a twenty-nine-year-old woman.'

Anna nodded that she understood. Rudy rapped softly on the door and opened it. 'Somebody here to see you,' he said cheerfully.

The room was bright and airy, not like a hospital room, more like a bedroom, with pale blue walls, framed prints of Central Park on the walls and a picture window with the curtains drawn back to let in the sunlight. From a CD player on the windowsill came Dionne Warwick singing 'Don't Make Me Over.' In a corner sat a miniature Christmas tree with twinkling lights.

Heather sat strapped into a wheelchair, her head lolling, a thin line of drool hanging from the lower corner of her mouth, her arms and legs twisted and stiff. In a grotesquely distorted face beautiful long-lashed blue eyes stared vacantly at the floor. Her naturally blonde hair was cut short and shaggy. A long blue breathing tube snaked from a hole in her throat to a ventilator standing a few feet away that emitted a steady, rhythmic whoosh. From a gap in her loose pink blouse came a feeding tube plugged into her stomach, its outer end stoppered.

Anna noticed a large brown teddy bear on the nightstand. Attached to the bear's hand with a ribbon was a Mylar helium balloon with *Happy*

269

Birthday! on it. Rudy followed her gaze. 'It was Heather's birthday last month, few days before Thanksgiving. Her parents brought her that.' Silently he shook his head, disapproving of the childish gift. He gently wiped Heather's mouth and expertly checked the machinery. Then he stood back and crossed his arms, waiting for Anna to do whatever she had come to do.

What *had* she come to do? To see Heather, to find out what Renser had done to her. But she was expected to say something...

'Hello,' she said warmly to Heather. 'My name is Anna Winthrop. I'm an attorney with the law firm representing your parents. I've come to check on you, make sure you're all right.'

Heather, of course, made no response, no movement, only gazed unseeingly. Suddenly Anna felt ashamed for lying to her. Then she reminded herself that information about Heather could lead to information about Dr Renser, which could in turn lead to solving Eva's murder. With a smile she turned to Rudy and nodded that she was done. He led the way out of the room and gently closed the door.

'I hope you'll encourage her parents to come more than once every couple of months,' he said. 'I realize it's hard for them as they get older, and him with his Parkinson's. But they are her parents, the only family she's got. Their visits have got to mean a lot to her.'

'Have you spoken to them about visiting

more frequently?'

'Yes, and it's always the same reply. It's expensive for them to travel because of his disease. I gently pointed out that Mrs Montgomery could come on her own, but they would have none of it. They come together or not at all.' Rudy nibbled his lower lip as he framed his next words. 'It's like this is some kind of endurance test they have to take together, that they need each other for. And I guess I can understand that. It must be incredibly difficult for them to see her like this. There must be tremendous guilt there.'

Anna nodded in understanding, at the same time mentally recording every word he said. He started to turn in order to lead her back to the elevator. She couldn't let him go, not without learning what she had come to learn.

'As I said, I'm new to Heather's case.'

He nodded, watching her, waiting for what she would say next.

'I'm new to Heather's case and not yet familiar with all the details. I'll be reading through the entire file carefully, of course, but in the meantime ... can you tell me what it was Heather was given?'

His eyes narrowed and he tilted his head ever so slightly. 'Given? I don't understand.'

'Yes, what drug or drugs did this to her?'

For a moment he just looked at her. Then he nodded. 'I have some literature on it I can give you. Come with me and I'll get it for you.'

She followed him back to the reception area where he went behind the desk, sat down and began rummaging in a low file. As he continued to search, it occurred to Anna that he was taking an inordinately long time.

The realization of what he was doing hit her just as the elevator door opened behind her. She turned. The big security guard who had spoken to her in the lobby stepped out, his gaze fixed on her. 'Ma'am,' he said in a low voice, 'I need to ask you to come with me, please.'

She glanced back at Rudy, who now stood behind the desk and was watching her and the guard, his expression impassive.

Her heart pounding, she followed the guard into the elevator. He pressed L and they silently descended, both facing forward. 'This way, please,' he said as the doors opened on to the lobby. To her surprise he didn't take her arm but walked just ahead of her. She followed him along the corridor to the central lobby area. As they neared the circular desk the woman with her glasses at the end of her nose scowled hatefully at her. *You tricked me,* her look said.

The guard led Anna down another corridor that ended in a T intersection and they went to the left. He stopped at a door marked Security, fished for his key and in that instant she bolted.

At the end of this small corridor was a door marked EXIT with a window showing trees and flowers. She ran as fast as she could on her low heels, bursting out into bright sunshine. A brick path led around to the circular drive in front of the hospital. A taxi that had just discharged its fare was nearly out of the otherwise empty drive, about to turn on to the road. She scrambled after it.

'Stop!' came the voice of the guard behind her but she didn't look back.

'Taxi!' she called. The driver didn't hear her. *'Taxi!'* she screamed. This time he heard and stopped short. She sprinted to the door, flung it open and jumped in. 'Keep driving!'

Wordlessly he obeyed, leaving the drive and pulling on to the road.

'Faster,' she said. 'A car may come after us. I'll give you a hundred dollars if you can lose it.'

'Whatdja do, rob the hospital?' the driver said with a laugh.

Making no response she watched out the rear window but no one seemed to be coming after her. Suddenly a police siren pierced the air.

'Sounds like they're playing your song,' the driver said.

She couldn't tell which direction the siren was coming from. It grew louder and in the next instant a police car appeared on the road ahead, coming toward them, lights flashing. It was going very fast. She expected it to stop short, spin around to stop them, but it kept on going, racing toward the hospital.

'Idiots,' the driver said with a chuckle.

'Go faster,' she told him. 'They'll figure it out.'

'OK, but I don't know where I'm goin'.'

'Airport.'

He gave a single nod, gave the car more gas and they sped toward Sarasota-Bradenton.

A couple of minutes later they heard the police siren again. 'Better duck down,' the driver said and she hit the floor. The whooping sound grew louder ... and then receded. 'Went right past us!' the driver said, shaking his head, clearly enjoying this. 'Keystone Cops.'

At the airport she hurriedly purchased a ticket for a flight to LaGuardia leaving in forty-five minutes. She half expected her name to be on some no-fly list, but she sailed through security and sat down at the crowded gate, gaze fixed on the corridor.

Twenty minutes later she boarded, and twenty minutes after that she was in the air.

Nettie stepped out of her shower, dried herself and quickly dressed. Normally she would blow-dry her hair, fashion the fountain-like spray on top of her head that men found so attractive, but there was no time for that now. She'd been in her apartment more than an hour, far too long, and needed to get out as quickly as possible. She brushed her teeth, applied deodorant. When she had first fled the apartment she had been so distraught that she hadn't thought to take a bag of essentials with her. This time she took a reusable shopping bag and quickly filled it. She added all the Charleston Chews and Suzy Q's in the cupboard. Then she put her various layers back on – she still hadn't bought a coat – and headed for the door.

There was a knock. She froze. Barely dared breathe. The knock came again. She stared at the door, eyes immense.

'Nettie, I know you're in there.'

She stood motionless, gaze still fixed on the door.

'Please open up. I just want to talk to you.'

'Eddie, go away! I won't let you hurt me.'

Silence. Then, 'Come on, Nettie,' in a pleading tone. 'I'm not going to hurt you. Please, all I want to do is talk to you. I love you.'

'Do you, Eddie?' she asked, mouth twisting as she began to cry. 'Do you really?'

Slowly she moved toward the door. Undid the chain, threw the dead bolts. Opened the door.

Stared as he advanced on her, his expression cold as stone.

NINETEEN

On Tuesday afternoon Anna drove Mary Jean, Patti and Sarah to LaGuardia and saw them off. When she arrived home Mrs Dovner was at her door speaking to the landlord, Mr Vickery. He was carrying a tool box. 'Here she is,' Mrs Dovner said.

Mr Vickery turned around. In his late sixties, he was painfully thin with sharp, craggy features. He stood with his hand on his completely bald head, a gesture that indicated he was angry or upset.

'Have you seen Nettie?' he asked Anna without preamble.

'How could I have seen Nettie,' she replied pleasantly, 'if I'm just now arriving home?'

He rolled his eyes in exasperation. Behind him, Mrs Dovner did the same.

'I mean since yesterday,' he said. 'I've been calling and knocking on her door. She wanted me to fix her leaky faucet.'

'You've got a key,' Anna said. 'Why don't you let yourself in?'

Mr Vickery looked reluctant. 'All right,' he said at last and turned to Mrs Dovner. 'Do me a favor and come up with me, will you? I need a witness. I let myself into her apartment once before and she accused me of reading what's on her laptop. I don't even know how to turn on a laptop. Woman's a kook.'

'I can't go up two flights.' Mrs Dovner indicated Anna with a fling of her hand. 'Take her.'

Mr Vickery turned to Anna with a questioning look.

'All right,' Anna said on a sigh. 'Will it take long? If so I want to grab my book.'

'Five minutes.'

Together they climbed the stairs to the third floor.

'She had the lock changed not long ago,' Mr Vickery told Anna as they approached Nettie's door.

'Why? Had she had a break-in?'

'I asked her the same thing. She said no but wouldn't explain.'

Anna shrugged. Mr Vickery unlocked the door and pushed it open. They both gasped.

The apartment was in a shambles, as if a terrible struggle had taken place. Chairs knocked over, the coffee table on its side with its glass top smashed. Nettie's laptop lay open face-up on the floor, its screen fractured.

Mr Vickery let out a low whistle. He stepped back to let Anna enter first.

'Nettie!' she called. She crossed the living room, glanced into the kitchen and made her way down the hall, Mr Vickery not far behind. The apartment was the same as Anna's. The room Anna had turned into a guest room was Nettie's storage room, cardboard boxes stacked against the walls, in front of them an exercise bike with a blanket draped over it.

Nettie's bedroom door was closed. Slowly Anna pushed it open, drew in her breath. More signs of a struggle. A plant lay on the floor, dirt everywhere. Decorative pillows from the bed were strewn about.

'Nettie?' Anna called again.

Silence.

From behind her came the sound of Mr Vickery gasping. She spun around. He had opened the closet door. She followed his gaze. Nettie hung from a hook like a coat, her head on its broken neck twisted unnaturally, her face calm as Anna had never seen it.

'Police,' Mr Vickery croaked.

'Why is it every time I see you it's about a murder?' Detective Rinaldi asked when Anna opened her apartment door to her. Behind Rinaldi, Roche nodded to second the question.

'Have you heard from Margo?' Rinaldi asked, strolling in.

'I told you I would contact you if I did.'

'Like you contacted me when you met her for coffee at Starbucks?'

'I *did* contact you.'

'Yeah, after your third venti.'

It was true Anna hadn't contacted Rinaldi immediately. She made no response.

'So where's the victim?' Rinaldi asked.

'Third floor,' Mr Vickery said.

Anna led the way upstairs. On the third floor landing Mr Vickery unlocked the door to Nettie's apartment.

'You can both wait out here,' Rinaldi said to him and Anna before entering the apartment with Roche.

Anna and Mr Vickery waited, not speaking, until the two detectives re-emerged a few minutes later.

'I want to talk to you both. Can we use your apartment?' Rinaldi asked Anna.

'Of course.'

They went down one flight and Anna let them in. Rinaldi and Roche sat on the sofa, Anna and Mr Vickery in chairs facing them.

'Would you like some coffee?' Anna asked them all.

'No, thanks,' Rinaldi answered. 'I'll stop at Starbucks on the way back to the station.' She gave Anna a meaningful lift of her eyebrows.

Anna ignored the remark.

The phone began to ring.

'I'll let the machine get it,' Anna said.

The machine clicked on, played her outgoing message and beeped. From the speaker came, 'It's Beth. Call me.'

'Who's that?' Rinaldi asked Anna.

'None of your business.'

'Sounds pissed.'

It was true, Beth had sounded angry. Anna would call her as soon as everyone left.

With an uncaring shrug Rinaldi brought out a pad and pen. 'So how did this go down? Who found her?'

'We both did,' Anna said.

'Nettie had asked me to fix her leaky faucet,' Mr Vickery said.

'When did she ask you?' Rinaldi asked.

Mr Vickery thought a moment. 'Maybe a month ago, when she first got here.'

'Real speedy service. Go on.'

'I've been calling her and knocking on her door but she hasn't been home. So today I let myself in. I asked her –' he tilted his head in Anna's direction – 'to come in with me.'

'Why?' Roche asked, proving he had a voice.

'Because another time I let myself in to fix something for Nettie she accused me of snooping in her laptop.'

'Did you?'

'Of course not.'

'OK, so Ms. Winthrop entered the apartment with you,' Rinaldi said. 'Then what happened?'

'It was a mess,' Anna said. 'We checked the rooms and found her in the closet.'

Rinaldi nodded. 'Ms. Clouchet have any family, do you know?'

Suddenly Anna thought of Allen. 'Her uncle works with me at the garage. Allen Schiff, our district chief. Nettie's late mother was his

280

sister.'

Rinaldi frowned. 'A strange coincidence, wouldn't you say? That you work with her uncle.'

'Actually it wasn't. Allen had heard the apartment above me was vacant and told Nettie.'

'Any other family that you know of?'

Anna shook her head.

Rinaldi said, 'No other family, or no other family that you know of? Which is it?'

'None that I know of. Listen, do you mind if I tell Allen about Nettie? I think it would be better coming from me.'

'Sure, knock yourself out. Tell him we'll want to talk to him.' Rinaldi tapped her pen on her pad, thinking. 'OK. We've asked Mrs Dovner downstairs if she's seen any strangers, anyone suspicious, in the building, and she said no. Ditto for the other tenants. What about you two? You see anybody who shouldn't have been here?'

Anna shook her head. 'I wasn't here.'

'Where were you?'

'Driving some people to LaGuardia.'

Rinaldi looked at Mr Vickery. 'What about you?'

'I don't live in this building. My apartment is on West Forty-Sixth Street.'

Rinaldi turned back to Anna. 'Mrs Dovner said Ms. Clouchet had an ex-boyfriend she was trying to avoid. You know anything about that?'

Anna nodded. 'Yes, I was going to tell you.

Nettie said he'd been abusive. She was hiding from him.'

'She tell you anything about him?'

'His name is Eddie and he's a cop.'

'That's a big help, since there are nearly forty thousand cops in New York City and Edward is a pretty common name,' Rinaldi said tiredly.

'He's Ukrainian,' Anna said.

'Now that narrows it down.' Rinaldi made another note. 'You ever see Eddie the Ukrainian? Probably not, if she was hiding from him.'

'Actually, I did see him,' Anna said. 'He was here looking for Nettie.'

Rinaldi blinked. 'I thought you said she was hiding from him.'

'It's complicated. She knew he'd found out where she lived but she was careful to watch for him when she went out.'

'When did he come looking for her?'

Anna thought for a moment. 'It was the day after my niece arrived, so that would have been Thursday, the ninth.'

'Twelve days ago,' Rinaldi said to herself. 'What did he look like?'

'Young, maybe late twenties. Dark-haired. Good-looking.'

'Was he in uniform?'

'No.'

Rinaldi took some more notes. 'Anything else you want to tell me?' she asked Anna and Mr Vickery. They both thought for a moment, then shook their heads.

Rinaldi and Roche stood.

'Let's go downstairs and see what Mrs Dovner can tell us about Eddie,' Rinaldi said to Roche, then slid her gaze to Anna. 'Then let's get over to Starbucks. I'm dying for a latte.'

As soon as Rinaldi, Roche and Mr Vickery were gone, Anna called Beth.

'Something wrong?' Anna asked.

'You could say that.' Beth sounded furious. 'I got a strange call this morning from Kristen Bailey, the office manager at Schutz Fine Kovner.'

Oh no...

'Are you there?' Beth said.

'I'm here.'

'She got a call yesterday from someone at Harbor Memorial Hospital in Ocean Springs, Florida. Someone named Anna Winthrop had come in claiming to be an attorney with the firm. She said she represented a...' Paper rustled. '...Mr and Mrs Cyrus Montgomery and had come to visit their daughter Heather on their behalf. Tell me that wasn't you.'

'You know it was,' Anna said in a gloomy voice.

'But *why*?'

'I'm sorry, I shouldn't have used the name of your firm.' *I should have made something up.*

'Kristen said the woman who called from Harbor Memorial said you gave Schutz Fine Kovner as the name of your firm but a different phone number. When she called it she got a woman claiming to be the office manager and confirming that you were with the firm and were visiting the hospital on behalf of your clients the Montgomerys. Later the woman at Harbor Memorial looked up the number for Schutz Fine Kovner herself. Of course it was different from the one you'd given her. She called it and spoke to Kristen, who of course said the Montgomerys weren't clients of the firm. The firm didn't have an attorney named Anna Winthrop, however they did until recently have one named *Beth* Winthrop. Kristen didn't know I had a sister named Anna and thought the woman was me, using a different first name for some reason.'

'Why would you do that?'

Beth laughed incredulously. 'Why would *you* do *that*? Are you aware what you did is illegal? What the blazes were you doing there?'

'I'm so very sorry.'

'You didn't answer my question. Why did you go to the hospital?'

'It's complicated.'

'I'm listening.'

'At Libby's art installation you told me you thought Heather was still alive. You were right. I did some more investigating and traced her to Harbor Memorial. I wanted to see what Renser had done to her.'

'Why?'

'I thought finding out more about him might

284

help me figure out what happened to Eva.'

'Not her again!'

'I haven't had a chance to tell you. She's dead. Murdered.'

'Murdered?'

'A week ago her body was fished out of the Hudson.'

'Oh my ... That's horrible,' Beth said in a low voice, 'but it still doesn't excuse your behavior. By the way, whose number did you give the woman at the hospital the first time?'

'It was Patti's cell,' Anna said in a tiny voice.

'You dragged Patti into this?' Beth said incredulously. 'You are unbelievable. You used me, put me in an embarrassing situation. I may want to go back to work for this firm some-day.'

'Why would you do that? You've got your shop now.'

'Who knows what will happen? The shop may not work out ... the economy will improve and the firm may need more attorneys again. I need to keep my options open. What must they think of me now?'

'That you have a nutty sister?' Anna said meekly.

'That is exactly what they're going to think, because that is exactly what I'm going to tell them!' Beth slammed down the phone.

Slowly Anna replaced the receiver. Beth was right; what Anna had done was wrong. She would apologize again. But this would blow over ... Beth would recover.

Eva would not.

Anna walked to the garage and found Allen in his office. He looked up and frowned. 'I thought you went home.'

'I did.'

'Why do you look like that? What's going on?'

'Can I talk to you a minute?'

'Sure,' he said, looking bewildered.

Anna sat in his guest chair. 'I've got bad news.' When he raised his brows inquisitively she said, as gently as possible, 'Nettie is dead.'

'Nettie?' His gaze wandered as he took this in.

'She was murdered.'

'How?'

'Her neck was broken. My landlord and I found her in her apartment.'

'Who did this?'

'It looks pretty certain it was her ex-boy-friend, Eddie.'

'What did you say?'

'I said it looks as if the killer is her ex-boy-friend, Eddie.'

'Anna,' he said, leaning toward her, enunciating very carefully, 'Eddie is dead.'

TWENTY

Anna stared at Allen. 'What did you say?'

'Eddie, Nettie's ex-boyfriend, is dead.'

Anna shook her head as if to clear it. 'No, he's not. Nettie has been hiding from him. He's been after her, watching her, stalking her. I saw him.'

'I don't know who you saw, but it wasn't Eddie.' He slowly shook his head from side to side. 'Poor Nettie. I had no idea she'd gotten this bad. She seemed a little off the last time I saw her. I wondered if she was still taking her pills – "vitamins," her doctor and I called them. Now I know she wasn't taking them.' He looked at Anna. 'Nettie was psychotic. She lived in a hallucinatory world. Eddie Pushkar died over a year ago.'

'How?'

'It ... wasn't clear. He fell down the stairs in the building where he and Nettie lived.'

'Why isn't that clear?'

'He ... may have been pushed.'

Anna stared. 'You mean by Nettie?'

'There was a history of violence there. Woman in the apartment across the hall heard them arguing in the middle of the night but she didn't hear what they were saying, didn't see anything.' He shrugged, shook his head as if to say *Who knows?*

Anna nodded. 'Nettie told me he was abusive.'

Allen gave a cynical laughed. *'He* was abusive? It was the other way around. She would hit him with things, throw things at him, claw at his face. Other tenants in their building were constantly complaining about the noise she made when she went off. Eddie ... he was a teddy bear.'

'Why did he stay with her?'

'Because he loved her.'

Anna sat very still. Everything had to be re-examined.

'If Eddie is dead,' she said, 'then who was after her? Who came looking for her?'

'No idea. Whoever it was, he may very well have killed her. But he wasn't Eddie.'

In her office Anna phoned Santos. She had told him about Nettie's murder. Now she told him what Allen had said.

'Then who was that guy?' Santos wondered aloud.

Anna went back in her mind to that morning. She and Patti had come downstairs and seen Mrs Dovner speaking to a man. Now Anna remembered that he had looked familiar...

She sat very still.

'Are you there?' Santos asked.

She hadn't recognized the man because he was out of context.

'I have to go.' She hung up, hurried home and banged on Mrs Dovner's door.

She heard the tapping of Mrs Dovner's cane, then the door was flung open.

'What is it now?' Mrs Dovner snapped.

'That morning Nettie's ex-boyfriend came looking for her,' Anna said, breathless, 'did he actually tell you his name?'

'No.'

'Then how did you know he was Eddie?'

Mrs Dovner scowled. 'Who else could he have been?'

'What did you say to him? I need to know exactly.'

Mrs Dovner didn't look happy about it but she searched her memory. 'I remember. I said I supposed he must be Eddie, that Nettie had told me all about him, said they'd broken up.'

'What did he say to that?'

'That yes, he was Eddie, and he wanted to see her, talk to her about getting back together.'

Anna processed this, eyes large.

'What? What's the matter?' Mrs Dovner said.

But Anna was already running up the stairs.

It was the Kirkmore doorman she had recognized that morning.

Nettie had been killed because of something she saw in the Kirkmore.

Anna considered calling Santos, who would alert the police, who would arrest the doorman;

but then Grigori, Yuri and Renser would be on the alert. She couldn't let that happen.

She had to get back into the Kirkmore. Specifically, she had to get on to the twentieth floor.

'They'll be upstairs for hours,' Michael told Irena gleefully as he slipped into the suite. This time he didn't bother kissing her at the door, instead leading her back to the maid's room and slamming the door.

He was rougher this time, grunting like an animal on top of her. She gazed blankly at the ceiling as her head banged the headboard. He was finished very quickly. He rolled off her and lay on his back beside her, his chest wet with sweat. 'I envy the guy who gets you,' he said, breathing hard.

She propped herself up on her elbow, traced her finger down the center of his hairy chest. 'What do you mean?'

His glance slid warily to her. 'Never mind.'

'No,' she said coaxingly, her hand traveling downward, taking hold of him, 'tell me.'

Instantly he was ready for her again. 'Here we go,' he said, rolling toward her.

With a giggle she bounded from the bed, grabbed his heap of clothing from the floor and ran naked down the hall.

'Hey, what the—?' came his voice as he charged after her. He laughed. 'What kind of game are you playing?'

She darted into the bedroom, shut the door

and locked it. She threw his clothes on the floor, then grabbed her robe and put it on.

He pounded on the door. 'OK, fun's over. If you don't want to do it again that's fine, but gimme back my clothes.'

'No.'

'*No?* What's going on?'

'You tell me,' she said.

'Tell you what?'

'What man will be lucky to have me?'

Silence. 'I can't talk about any of that.'

'Then Doctor Renser comes back and finds you. Or you can leave now naked.'

He banged again on the door, swore. 'OK. Renser's going to sell you.'

'Sell me to who?'

'The highest bidder.'

'My sister Dasha, is she alive?'

'Yes.'

'Where is she?'

'I don't know, I swear. Now will you give me my clothes back?'

'Yes,' she said, but she didn't pick up his clothes. Instead she picked up something she had left near the door—a plastic knife she had painstakingly sharpened to a long, thin, razor-sharp edge against the rough marble tiles of the bathroom. She readied herself ... opened the door. He was standing there, furious.

'Here,' she said and plunged the knife into the middle of his stomach.

He gasped, looked down in horror at the

blood already flowing from the wound. He dropped to his knees, fell on to his back. Then he lay there, staring at the ceiling, his breathing labored.

She moved to his side, gaze fixed on his face. *Don't die yet!*

She took hold of the knife handle and twisted it. He gasped, his body tensing.

'Where is Dasha?' she demanded.

When he did not reply she twisted the knife again, harder.

He cried out in agony. 'Another suite. They're taking her upstairs.'

'Where upstairs?'

'Twentieth floor.'

Bending over she grabbed his feet and began pulling him. He was a big man, heavy, and it was slow work. He was still alive, moaning, as she dragged him down the hallway to the kitchen and then into the maid's room. There she dropped him. He was dead now. With considerable effort she shoved his body under the bed, far enough so it could not be seen from the doorway.

In the kitchen she retrieved the pile of hand towels and bottle of Windex she'd placed in a cupboard. His body had left a smear of blood down the hallway. It was a laborious process but after ten minutes or so she had it all cleaned up. She was breathless. Running back to the kitchen, she put away the Windex and shoved the bloody hand towels to the back of a deep cabinet. Then she went to the bedroom and dressed.

She had noticed that the maids always came to clean between ten thirty and eleven. She checked a clock by the bed. It was ten fifty. She waited.

At ten fifty-eight she heard the snick of a key in the lock. She ran across the foyer and down the hall to the kitchen. Picking up a heavy over-size wooden candlestick she had carried in from the den, she positioned herself behind the open door and let out a moan.

'Hello?' came the maid's voice from the foyer. 'Are you OK?'

Irena moaned again.

'Where are you?'

Irena heard the maid moving from room to room looking for her. Then her footsteps sounded on the hallway leading to the kitchen. 'Where are you?' the maid called.

Silently Irena waited. The maid entered the kitchen, passed her and at that moment Irena brought the candlestick down with all her might on her head. She let out a grunt, blood flew and she went down.

She was even heavier than Michael, a giant immobile lump. Irena dragged her, too, into the maid's room. It takes a long time to remove clothing from an inert body but finally Irena had wrestled off the woman's white slip-on shoes and pale blue skirt and blouse. The woman was far too big to fit under the bed with

Michael, so Irena pushed her into the corner of the room, yanked the bedspread off the bed and draped it over her. Then she pushed a chair in front of her.

The shoes were slightly too big but would do. The blouse was huge on her but would be passable when tucked into the skirt. The problem was the skirt was so large that two of Irena could have fit in it. Without something to fasten it, it would fall right off. So carefully had the apartment been safeguarded against her escaping or attempting to hurt anyone or herself that there was not even a safety pin to be found. She screwed up her face, thinking. Then she had an idea.

A ring full of keys in the pocket of the skirt jangled as, holding up the skirt, she hurried to a desk in the library and found what she was looking for: a stapler. Apparently no one feared she would try to staple her way out of there. The skirt's waistband was too thick to staple but she was able to fasten the material snugly just below. She checked herself in the mirror. If anyone looked at her closely they would definitely notice something amiss, but who looked at maids closely? She tucked the blouse into the skirt.

Returning to the kitchen she retrieved the Windex and hand towels and cleaned up the smear of blood the maid's head had left. She stowed the bottle and towels. Then she ran to the foyer, took one last look around to make

294

sure nothing looked awry and wheeled the maid's supply cart ahead of her out of the suite.

She felt a thrill of fear as she moved down the silent corridor. A door opened and a well-dressed older woman emerged and saw Irena.

'Good morning,' Irena said in her best English and rolled the cart toward the service elevator.

TWENTY-ONE

Lucy, fiancée of Arnold, manager of Crazy Ice Cream, had once again proven useful, for a higher price. Anna entered the Kirkmore through the rear service entrance and turned right, heading for Carmela's supply closet.

She had borrowed a long black wig from Gloria. She patted it as she made her way down the service corridor to make sure it was secure. Grigori and Yuri were unlikely to recognize her if they saw her on the security camera. Even so, she walked quickly and with her head down.

Carmela was folding towels.

'We got a problem,' Anna said.

Carmela looked up, a question on her face. 'Who are you?'

'Janet, from the Kemp Agency.'

'You new?'

'Been here a week.'

Carmela shook her head as if to question her own sanity. 'What's the problem?'

'Mr Eckart can't get into his office.'

'Why not?'

'Can't find his key. Boy, is he mad!'

'Mad?' Carmela grabbed a key from the

board. 'Who's he mad at? *We* didn't forget his key.'

Anna rolled her eyes. 'You know how he gets.'

'Bring it right back,' Carmela said, handing her the key.

Anna took the stairs to the second floor and found Mr Eckart's office. Behind the frosted window it was dark. Making sure no one was coming she unlocked the door and slipped inside. Some of the light from the corridor penetrated the frosted glass and cast a pale glow over the room.

She looked first where most people in offices keep keys: in the top drawer. She found only pencils, pens and assorted papers. Then she opened the small left-hand drawer and peered down at a veritable mother lode of keys on a ring. Which one? She grabbed them all, stuffing them into a pocket of her uniform.

She opened the door a crack and, satisfied the corridor was clear, exited and relocked the door. Then she returned to Carmela and handed her the office key.

'He still mad?' Carmela asked with an irritated scowl.

'Not anymore,' Anna said brightly. 'Thanks.' She started to walk away.

'Wait a minute,' came Carmela's voice behind her.

Anna froze, turned.

'I didn't give you your cleaning assignments.'

Anna laughed. 'Yes, you did. Don't you remember? I told you your hair looked nice.'

Carmela shrugged. 'Where's your cart?'

'Around the corner.'

Carmela returned her attention to her towels and Anna hurried off. When she reached the service elevator two other maids were waiting with their carts. Anna made a show of searching in her cart for something, did some rearranging of supplies, anything to give the two maids time to get on the elevator without her. When the doors had closed she waited a moment and then pressed the call button. The elevator returned a few moments later, empty. She got on with her cart and pressed 3. When the doors opened she rolled off her cart, pushing it to one side. Then she got back on the elevator.

As soon as the door had closed she grabbed Mr Eckart's keys from her pocket and began trying them, one by one, in the lock beside the button for the twentieth floor. She began to sweat. What if the doors opened again and someone saw her? She worked faster, inserting key after key ... with no luck. Finally she was down to two. The one she picked up first was short and squat, different from the others. 'Now *you* look like an elevator key,' she muttered softly. 'Why didn't I see you earlier?' Frantically she inserted the key in the lock and pushed. It went in smoothly. 'Yes!' she said as she turned the lock and heard a click. She pressed 20. The button lit up and the elevator began to rise.

The first thing she noticed when the doors opened on the twentieth floor was an odd, not unpleasant antiseptic smell. She stepped off the elevator and the doors slid shut behind her. The corridor was dark except for dim shafts of moonlight coming from widely spaced sky-lights. She looked to her right. The corridor ended after a few feet. So she went left, passing doors with darkened frosted windows like Mr Eckart's. Eventually she came to a darkened reception area.

There was a door at the back of the reception area. Anna went through it and found herself in another corridor. Suddenly she grew still. From the far end of the corridor came the sound of a man's voice.

She moved toward the sound, keeping close to the right-hand wall. At the end of the corridor was a door, this one of solid wood. Ever so slowly she turned the knob and opened the door a crack. It was dark on the other side but she could hear the voice more clearly now. She passed through, closing the door silently behind her.

The hallway she now found herself in re-minded her of a clinic or hospital, its antiseptic white walls unadorned, with wooden handrails. Several windowed doors opened off this hall-way, all of them dark.

She tiptoed down the corridor. When she had gone halfway she heard the door she had come through opening. In a panic she tried the nearest door but it was locked. It was too late. The door swung slowly open.

It was a maid, a beautiful young woman with long blonde hair and frightened green eyes. When she saw Anna she drew in her breath sharply, then recovered and gave her a little smile. 'I clean too,' she said in a low voice.

She had a foreign accent. She watched Anna warily. Anna approached her, took in the terror in her eyes. She was no more a maid than Anna was. 'Who are you?' Anna whispered.

The woman did not reply.

'I'm not a maid either,' Anna said. 'I'm trying to find out what's going on here. Women are being brought here and disappearing. One of them has been murdered. The man behind it is named Renser. Dr Renser.'

The young woman nodded rapidly. 'Yes, Renser! I am one of these girls. He has my sister Dasha. She is on this floor.'

'My name is Anna.'

'Irena.'

'We have to hide,' Anna said, 'figure out what to do.'

Together they hurried to the end of the corridor and passed through another door into dim light.

They were at the corner of a vast operating room, a ghostly assortment of tables and equipment. The two women frowned. From far in the opposite corner came the lights and darks of a

TV on a stand.

They crept closer, the man's voice growing louder.

In front of the TV a man sat in a chair, watching. Suddenly he rose and turned to them. It was Yuri.

'Come on!' Anna breathed and she and Irena turned to run but he came after them, quickly catching up, and grabbed them both by the arms, holding them immobile. He was surprisingly strong. He looked at Anna's face, then at Irena's and did a double take. He yanked off Anna's wig and threw it aside. Then he nodded, admiration in his look.

'Don't leave yet.' He spoke like a host to a valued guest. 'You have not seen what you came to see.'

He dragged them to the TV.

'Now watch,' he said, stepping behind them and at the same time taking out a gun which he trained at their backs.

Anna saw now that below the TV a DVD player was running. On the TV screen was Eva. She lay face up on an operating table, eyes closed. On her head was an odd white-plastic headset extending from ear to ear, with a piece in the center that came down over her nose almost to the tip.

The man's voice spoke. Anna recognized it now. It was Dr Renser. 'As you can see,' he said, 'the patient is wearing the same headset she wore in Radiology while the CT scans were taken. The infamous transorbital lobotomy, such as the "ice pick" procedure performed by Walter Freeman, was a blind operation in that the surgeon did not know for certain if he had severed the nerves. He would use a rubber mallet to hammer the pick into the skull, just above the tear duct, and wiggle it around. Hardly scientific.'

Now a man's hand holding a long, needlelike instrument came into view.

'I don't want to watch this,' Anna said to Yuri.

'You will watch!' he shouted. Reluctantly Anna turned back toward the screen. Irena was watching, transfixed.

'Neurosurgery has come a very long way,' Dr Renser went on as he inserted the instrument into the corner of Eva's eye and carefully, slowly, fed it in. 'The software builds a computerized model of the patient's brain anatomy with the CT scans taken prior to the surgery. Thanks to an electromagnetic tracking system that links the surgical instruments to the computer, we are able to achieve microscopic precision.'

Behind Eva, a monitor came to life. Two fine lines intersecting at right angles were superimposed on a close-up view of wet pink brain tissue.

'As you can see,' Dr Renser went on, 'the instruments appear on the computer display screen as a set of crosshairs that move through the three-dimensional computerized model of the brain. This allows us to see the exact location of the instruments in direct relation to areas of the brain that cannot be seen through an endoscope. Highly accurate visual updates guide us at every step.'

On the screen, the instrument made a tiny cutting motion, separating brain matter.

'Ah,' Dr Renser said. 'Very good.' He gave a small chuckle. 'Of course, we do not achieve our amazing results with this technology alone. Also vitally important are my long career as a neurosurgeon and my intensive study of the brain over the past ten years, during which I perfected this process. Using what I have learned I am able to alter the subject so she becomes passive, obedient, always willing to please her owner.'

'I won't watch any more of this.' Anna walked over to the monitor and switched it off.

'You wanted to know what happened to Eva,' Yuri said. 'There it is.' With the gun he motioned for Anna to stand next to Irena again.

'She's not the first, is she?' Anna said. It was a statement, not a question.

'No. He made three other "perfect women" before Eva.'

'But in Eva's case,' Anna said, 'something went terribly wrong.'

'You mean that I killed her.'

'I mean something that happened even before you killed her.' Anna gave a pitying smile. 'You fell in love with her.'

TWENTY-TWO

Yuri backed up and leaned against a counter on which medical supplies had been laid out. He looked exhausted. 'I knew her in Ukraine. Not well. I admired her – how do you say – from afar. She was the most beautiful creature I had ever seen.'

'And you recruited her for Dr Renser?' Anna asked incredulously.

'No! Grigori did that. He saw her with me in a bar in Kiev. I had no idea he had taken her until she got off a plane at JFK with a group of other women. She saw me, pleaded with me to help her. And of course I tried...'

'Like the day I saw you in Grand Central Station?'

He gave one nod. 'So you knew what was really happening?'

'I didn't figure it out until today. You weren't chasing after Eva who was escaping. *You and Eva were escaping together.*'

'How did you know?'

'I realized that two things I had seen were not at all what I thought. When I first saw Eva in the pickup truck, you took her face in your

304

hand. I interpreted this as a rough gesture of warning, a way of saying "look at me." But it was actually a tender gesture. You weren't warning her, you were assuring her you would help her.'

Yuri nodded. 'I had found a way to leave this building unnoticed. The day you saw us, Eva and I went down into the subway at Times Square and took the shuttle to Grand Central Station. From there we would take a train somewhere, anywhere, just to get away.'

'That's where you and she were going when I saw you both in front of the Oyster Bar.'

'Yes. I did not want us to be seen together so I told her to walk slightly ahead. Then you stopped her.'

'I ruined your escape,' Anna said in a desolate tone. 'If it weren't for me, she would be alive today.'

But Yuri was shaking his head. 'Grigori would have caught up with us. I was fooling myself. As it turned out, he had seen us leave and followed us. When he appeared behind Eva and me in the tunnel, I had to pretend I was *going after* Eva rather than fleeing *with her*. My hope was that we would try again.'

'But Eva wanted to keep trying. When you and she struggled, your sleeve tore – not because you were pulling on her, but because she was pulling on you to come with her, to not give up. But you never had the chance.'

Tears welled in Yuri's eyes. 'One night when

I knew Dr Renser was out I went to the suite where he was keeping her. I knew immediately that he had performed his surgery on her, that I was too late. I had failed her.' His face contorted with the memory. 'She did not know me. I told her who I was, pleaded with her to recognize me. She stared into my face. Suddenly she looked very confused, as if she was trying to get *around* what he had done to her, to recapture what she had known ... But then it was gone and again she was like a zombie, created to please a man, any man. She put her arms around my neck and kissed me, rubbed herself against me. It was my Eva and yet it wasn't. It was obscene.'

Backing up against a counter, his gun aimed at them, he met Anna's gaze. 'I loved her so very much,' he said pleadingly. 'I could not bear the thought of her living that way, never knowing what had been done to her, being some rich man's toy.'

'So you killed her.'

'I once saw a film called *Cuckoo's Nest*. A man is given a lobotomy and his friend kills him because he knows the man would not want to live like that. That is what I did to Eva. It is what she would have wanted. I smothered her with a pillow, like in the movie, and then I ran out.'

'And Dr Renser returned and found her.'

He nodded. 'He still has no idea who killed her. He made me dump her body in the Hudson.' Now he was crying in full force. 'Please forgive me, Eva.'

He placed his gun on the counter, turned to Irena. 'You will find your sister there,' he said, pointing to a door across the room. Then in a sudden movement he grabbed a plastic bottle from the counter marked Chloramine-T – Cleaner & Disinfectant. Before Anna and Irena knew what was happening he unscrewed the top, brought the bottle to his lips and began taking great gulps.

Immediately he dropped the bottle and doubled over in agony. He let out a gasp, his eyes wide as if he were surprised he could feel so much pain. He fell to his knees, vomited forcefully, then collapsed completely and lay still. Stepping closer to him Anna saw froth coming from his mouth. His eyes stared blankly in a face that had begun to turn blue.

Anna took Yuri's gun from the counter and slid it into the waistband of her skirt. Then she whipped out her cell phone and called Santos. She got his voice mail. 'Kirkmore, twentieth floor,' she said. 'Bring help. Hurry.'

They ran to the door Yuri had indicated. Anna opened it a crack to make sure no one was around, then they passed through into a small hallway. Now they heard a man's voice – Dr Renser again – and followed it.

Suddenly they found themselves at the back of a small, luxuriously appointed auditorium. In the first few rows sat about a dozen men. Some wore suits, others blazers and polo shirts, one a white Arab headdress.

On the small stage stood Dr Renser in a dark suit. A screen was retracting into the ceiling. '...and so I think you gentlemen will agree that everything possible has been done to make our companions as pleasing to a man as any woman could possibly be.'

There were nods of assent in the audience.

'One announcement before we begin,' Dr Renser continued. 'Due to unforeseen circumstances Eva, the girl in the brochure you originally received, is no longer available.'

The men in the audience looked at one another in surprise.

'However,' Dr Renser said, 'we do have an equally lovely girl for you today. Before I bring her out I should mention that the procedure has not yet been performed on this subject. Being, after all, human, she caught the flu recently, and this delayed the process. Please bear this in mind when you view her. I will perform the procedure on her tomorrow and she will be ready to accompany her new owner home by tomorrow evening. And now I would like you to meet the lady herself.' He looked offstage. 'Dasha, will you come out, please?'

Beside Anna, Irena gasped. The two women watched as Grigori led a young woman on-stage. She was exquisitely beautiful, with straight silky blonde hair to her shoulders and large green eyes like Irena's. She wore a diaphanous scarlet gown and matching stiletto heels. Anna saw now that she was crying, her shoulders hunched slightly. Grigori tugged on her arm and she straightened. Dr Renser smiled. 'Crying, I assure you, gentlemen, is something you will never have to contend with.' Some of the men laughed. 'Dasha will be everything you want in a woman ... and nothing you don't. You will find her exact statistics in the brochures given to you at the beginning of this presentation. Are there any questions?' No one spoke. 'Good. Then let's start the bidding at fifty million.'

A hand went up. 'Fifty-five million.'

Another hand. 'Sixty.'

Anna watched, mesmerized.

Suddenly Irena grabbed the gun from Anna's skirt and, holding it straight ahead of her with two hands, strode down the aisle until she was a few yards from the stage. The men in the audience twisted in their seats to watch her, eyes wide. 'I have a bid!' she shouted to Dr Renser. As he opened his mouth in shocked protest she pulled the trigger. The gun exploded and he jerked back violently, blood blooming crimson on his white shirt, and collapsed. Irena moved to the right and trained the gun on Grigori, but he grabbed Dasha and shoved her in front of him as a shield. Frustrated, Irena moved from side to side, afraid to shoot.

Suddenly Dasha ground a red stiletto into Grigori's foot. He cried out in pain, momentarily releasing her. She hit the floor. Irena pulled the trigger, hitting Grigori's shoulder. Before he could recover she got off another shot, this time hitting him in the center of his chest. He fell backwards, arms out, and then lay still.

Dasha jumped off the stage and flew into Irena's arms. The sisters embraced tightly, crying. Meanwhile, the men had left their seats and were hurrying up the aisles toward the exits.

But before they could reach the doors they burst open. Out of the one nearest Anna came Santos, gun raised. From the other came Rinaldi, followed by Roche, also with guns drawn.

'Sorry, boys,' Rinaldi said. 'I'm the kind of girl you *don't* like.'

More police officers flooded into the room, hurrying down the aisles and handcuffing the men.

Across the auditorium Rinaldi threw Anna an admiring glance. 'Not bad, Winthrop. Not bad.'

TWENTY-THREE

It was three days later, Christmas Eve. Anna finished basting the turkey and closed the oven. 'Yum!'

Santos, relaxing on the couch, smiled. 'You need any help with that?'

She laughed. 'As if I could ever get you off that thing.'

She felt something brush against her leg. She bent down and picked up the new member of her family, home the previous day from the veterinarian. 'Hey, King,' she said in a high voice, 'you hungry again?'

She carried him past the table set for two to the living room, sat down on the sofa and placed him between her and Santos. King immediately lay down and rolled over.

'Aw...' Anna stroked his fluffy black belly. 'Is he a love bunny, or what?'

'I think I'm going to be sick.'

She gave him a play hit on the head. 'I don't care what you say. Fate sent this little guy to me for a reason. I'm going to give him all the love he needs and then some.'

'What did you call him? King?'

She smiled. 'Mm-hm. I finally decided on a name. This is Christmas ... and he brought lots of gifts, though they weren't frankincense and myrrh. So I figure he's one of the Three Kings.'

'You're lucky cats are allowed in this building.'

'Much to Mrs Dovner's displeasure,' Anna said with a laugh. 'She saw me come in with the carrier and had a fit. "I'd better not smell that animal in my apartment!"'

Still stroking King, she gazed at the cozily twinkling Christmas tree and her face grew sad.

'What is it?' he asked.

'You know. I'm thinking about poor Eva ... about the other three girls Renser performed his procedure on.' All three had been found, each with her respective owner – one in Las Vegas, one in Hollywood and one in New York. 'What kind of lives can these women have?'

He shrugged sadly. 'At least they won't be kept as slaves. And they have no memory of their lives before the surgery. That's a mercy.'

She nodded. 'That's what Grigori meant when he said to Yuri, "She won't be able to tell anyone." He meant Eva wouldn't know what had happened to her.'

'Dasha and Irena, on the other hand, know exactly what happened to them.'

Anna nodded eagerly. 'Yes, fill me in on everything. You've been so busy dealing with the case that this is the first time we've been able to talk.'

'The two sisters are telling their stories to the police. Their parents are already on their way from Ukraine.' He shook his head in wonder. 'That Irena's got guts. To get out of Renser's suite she killed a doorman and gave a maid a concussion.'

'What about all the other women?'

'The ones Grigori was holding prisoner in the Taylor Hotel are also talking to the police, and through these women we've learned about more girls Grigori has had working for him in Mexico. We're following up on those leads. All of these women are being treated as victims, not criminals.'

Santos continued, 'We've arrested Eckart, manager of the Kirkmore, who facilitated Renser's operation, and a doorman and a slew of maids and other staff at the Taylor and the Kirkmore who were complicit in what was going on.'

Anna said, 'One person who hasn't been caught is the woman who called herself Margo Rayburn.'

'True. We have no idea who she really is. The person who might have told us – Grigori – is dead.'

Anna gazed at the Christmas tree ... and was reminded of another Christmas tree much farther south.

'What about Heather Montgomery? Have you pieced together what happened to her?'

'Pretty much. Cyrus and Edwina have been

quite forthcoming. They're relieved it's all over.'

Santos went on, 'As we know, Renser treated Cyrus for Parkinson's. Cyrus told Renser about his daughter Heather who was out of control – taking drugs, sleeping around, defying her parents in every possible way. They were at the end of their rope. That's when Renser suggested a procedure he'd been perfecting over the ten years since he'd "retired." It would make Heather calm, manageable, happy ... yet not alter her personality. They jumped at the chance. So one night Renser arrived at the Montgomerys' house in Hoboken with an ambulance and two EMTs who restrained Heather while Renser sedated her. They took her to his rehab center in New Jersey, where he performed his procedure. But it went horribly wrong. The procedure was far from "per- fected."'

'I thought Renser's treatment had involved drugs,' Anna said. 'When I asked the nurse at Harbor Memorial what drug she had been given, he knew immediately that I was not who I said I was.'

Santos took over the stroking of King's belly. 'Heather was reduced to a vegetable, as you saw. This would have been a terrible embarrass- ment for Renser, who had huge plans for his surgery. He must keep Heather a secret at all costs. So he made a deal with Cyrus and Ed- wina. If they would tell the world Heather was dead, he would not only pay them an exorbitant amount of money but also pay for her to be institutionalized for the rest of her life.'

'Monsters,' Anna said. 'Letting him do that to their daughter.'

Santos tilted his head thoughtfully. 'They weren't the first people to resort to psycho-surgery to control "difficult" family members. I did some research. About fifty thousand loboto-mies were performed in the United States alone. Many well-meaning parents thought they were doing the right thing for their children.'

For several moments they stared at the tree, both stroking King's belly.

Santos put his face close to Anna's and spoke in a soft voice. 'I'm very proud of you.'

'For what?' she asked, surprised.

'For trying so hard to save Eva ... for having such a good heart. I want you to know that when you put yourself in danger to help people, I understand, but sometimes it scares me to death, makes me afraid I'll lose you.'

Anna placed her finger under a chain around Santos's neck and lifted out the medal his mother had given him on his first day at the police academy. Saint Michael, patron saint of police officers. She rubbed the smooth silver, let it drop. 'They say wives of police officers worry the same way.'

In response, Santos hopped off the sofa and picked up a present from under the tree. It was a small gold-wrapped box. 'Merry Christmas,

315

darling,' he said, sitting down again and handing it to her.

She stared at him solemnly, then, her hands shaking, unwrapped the box. Opening the lid she gasped at the flash of diamond and platinum against black velvet. 'Oh, Santos...'

'I love you, Anna. Will you marry me?'

'Of course,' she said, crying, and in the next instant their lips met in a long, lingering kiss.

Between them, momentarily forgotten, King purred happily away.

AUTHOR'S NOTE

One of the things I enjoy most about writing the Hidden Manhattan mysteries is sharing secret places in New York with you.

The Whispering Gallery outside the Oyster Bar in Grand Central Terminal is a real place. If you're in the area, be sure to try it out.

But Grand Central holds other secrets as well. Beneath the terminal lies a hidden network of storage areas, steam-pipe tunnels and underground tracks. There is also a train platform with a secret entrance and an elevator up to the Waldorf-Astoria Hotel directly above. Reportedly Franklin D. Roosevelt used this as a secret means of entering New York City, a way to get from his train to the hotel without being harassed by reporters. Sadly, it's not possible to view this secret passage as today the elevator door is welded shut. Perhaps someday it will be opened.

Another Grand Central secret is the Biltmore Room, located on the Grand Concourse across from Starbucks. During the golden age of train travel in the 1930s and '40s it was known as the Kissing Room, because it was here that the famous 20th Century Limited train arrived, and here that its passengers greeted loved ones with hugs and kisses. Often these passengers, many of them wealthy politicians and celebrities, would then climb the stairs to the equally famous Biltmore Hotel, which sadly no longer exists (on the site today is the Bank of America building).

Another of Grand Central's secrets is known as the annex. When the terminal opened in 1913, this 40,000-square-foot third-floor space facing Forty-Second Street was left vacant, but over the years it has been used for an amazing variety of purposes. In the 1930s it was used by department stores to display furniture. From 1939 to 1964 it was the home of CBS's studios. Episodes of 'What's My Line?' and Edward R. Murrow's 'See it Now' (including the one with Senator Joseph McCarthy) were broadcast from here.

But eventually CBS was driven out by the ever-growing train vibrations. In 1965 a former Hungarian freedom fighter named Geza Gazdag converted the studios into the Vanderbilt Athletic Club. A special feature was a 65-foot ski slope made of plastic brush. In 1970 Tennis International bought the club and gave it a stylish makeover, attracting mayors, New York luminaries and celebrities including Johnny Carson to play here.

In 1984 Donald Trump began leasing the annex and used it as a place to play tennis and also store his architectural models. Tennis greats such as Martina Navratilova and John McEnroe practiced here. But as the years passed the space grew shabby.

Now, however, Metro-North, the commuter rail service that runs to and from Grand Central, is spending $21 million to transform the space once again. The annex will be divided into two floors, with a city tennis club above and an employee facility below. As part of this dramatic makeover, immense rounded Beaux-Arts windows that look out on to 42nd Street will be cleared of obstruction for the first time in seventy years. Two disused elevators are being restored to use for tourists and tennis players. The complex is scheduled to open in April 2011.

Perhaps Grand Central's best-known feature is the beautiful mural of stars on the ceiling of the Main Concourse. What many people don't know about this mural is that its depictions of the signs of the zodiac are backwards. Some people have speculated that the artist, Paul César Helleu, simply made an error. The truth, however, is that he was working from a medieval manuscript showing the heavens as they would look from *outside* the celestial sphere, and that is why everything is turned around.

Here's one more secret about the ceiling. If you look hard you will find a small dark patch on the mural, above Michael Jordan's Steak House. It shows the color of the ceiling before it was restored, and was left as a reminder of how much work was done. Next time you find yourself in Grand Central, don't forget to look up!

If you have any Manhattan secrets you'd like to share, you can e-mail me at
evanmarshall@optonline.net.

To learn more about Hidden Manhattan, visit my website at
www.EvanMarshallMysteries. com.

Evan Marshall